# FOREST OF SECRETS

*Also by Fiona Buckley*

*The Ursula Blanchard mysteries*

THE ROBSART MYSTERY
THE DOUBLET AFFAIR
QUEEN'S RANSOM
TO RUIN A QUEEN
QUEEN OF AMBITION
A PAWN FOR THE QUEEN
THE FUGITIVE QUEEN
THE SIREN QUEEN
QUEEN WITHOUT A CROWN *
QUEEN'S BOUNTY *
A RESCUE FOR A QUEEN *
A TRAITOR'S TEARS *
A PERILOUS ALLIANCE *
THE HERETIC'S CREED *
A DEADLY BETROTHAL *
THE RELUCTANT ASSASSIN *
A WEB OF SILK *
THE SCENT OF DANGER *

* *available from Severn House*

# FOREST OF SECRETS

Fiona Buckley

SEVERN
HOUSE

First world edition published in Great Britain and the USA in 2021
by Severn House, an imprint of Canongate Books Ltd,
14 High Street, Edinburgh EH1 1TE.

Trade paperback edition first published in Great Britain and the USA in 2021
by Severn House, an imprint of Canongate Books Ltd.

severnhouse.com



*British Library Cataloguing-in-Publication Data*
A CIP catalogue record for this title is available from the British Library.

ISBN-13: 978-0-7278-5050-8 (cased)
ISBN-13: 978-1-78029-774-3 (trade paper)
ISBN-13: 978-1-4483-0512-4 (e-book)



*All Severn House titles are printed on acid-free paper.*

Typeset by Palimpsest Book Production Ltd.,
Falkirk, Stirlingshire, Scotland.
Printed and bound in Great Britain by
TJ Books Limited, Padstow, Cornwall.

To my dear friends Susan and Jean

# ONE
## One Thing After Another

The year was 1586, the date, the 22nd of May. We had been on the road for over three weeks, journeying from south Devon to my Surrey home of Hawkswood, and springtime had burgeoned while we travelled. We had had fair weather and dry roads, but we had all had enough of travelling: myself, my excellent manservant Roger Brockley, his wife Frances, who was my maid and still answered to her maiden name of Dale (which I used out of habit), and my gentlewoman companion Mildred Gresham.

In addition, there was Eddie Hale, the cheery young groom who was driving our little carriage, and the two new maidservants I had found during my time away: Bess Hethercott and Hannah Durley. I had been glad to find them because Hawkswood was in sore need of extra hands. We had brought my small carriage for the luggage and for Dale and now it also accommodated Bess and Hannah, neither of whom had ever ridden, even on someone's pillion. Though the carriage jolted so much when the road was rough that it was hardly more comfortable than a horse.

We were all glad when we came through the woods around Hawkswood, and saw its gate ahead of us and heard the dogs already barking a welcome. If the dogs had scented us, my bay gelding, Jaunty, had scented his home stable too. He pricked his ears and pulled a little, eager for his own familiar stall, a rub down and a bran mash. He broke into a trot I hadn't asked for, pulled away from the rest of the party and then without the slightest warning, squealed, plunged and reared up on his hindlegs.

He would have unseated me, except that my side saddle was very safe. It was made to the pattern that Queen Catherine de Medici of France had invented, and I had improved the design for myself, having my saddles made with high cantles to support my back and a roll of leather in front of my left knee, a safeguard against slipping forward. Jaunty came down again on to all fours but then started to buck, upsetting the other horses, who sidled and snorted. Even placid old Rusty in the shafts of the carriage, laid back his ears and balked.

I held on, pulling Jaunty's head up and talking to him, aware from the corner of my left eye, that Brockley had sprung from his horse, flung his reins to Mildred and plunged into the woods. As Jaunty finally quietened down, Brockley reappeared, dragging a terrified looking urchin with him.

'Brockley, what on earth . . .?'

'Madam, you may well ask. This *brat*' – here Brockley shook his captive savagely – 'has been fooling about with a bow and arrows! *This* bow!' With his spare hand he brandished a small bow at me and at the same moment I saw the little quiver on the boy's shoulder, with the tops of the arrows poking out of it. 'Meant to be toys but mighty dangerous toys!' Brockley thundered. 'And I know who you are, you stupid mumphead!' He shook his prisoner again, and the boy, who could only have been about nine, and looked faintly familiar, began to sob. 'Dear little Tommy Reed from Hawkswood village, that's who you are,' said Brockley, 'Marge Reed's lastborn; arrived after his father died and never had a man's hand to guide him. His tribe of brothers don't bother, well, that's what you'd expect from that family. What have you got to say for yourself, you murderous little wantwit?'

'They're only toys! I were aiming at a sparrow!' yelled Tommy, unconvincingly. 'Horse jumped forward of a sudden and got in the way.'

Brockley said: 'Huh!' and dragged Tommy towards me. He used the bow to point with. 'There's where the arrow hit and it was sharp. There's a wound on your Jaunty's haunch, madam. Get it seen to as soon as you're in. He's got metal tips on his dear little *toy* arrows. Been making use of the brother that works in the smithy, I dare say. I'll be talking to him as well. Meanwhile, I'll take this brat home.'

He pulled the quiver off Tommy's shoulder, thrust it and the little bow down into one of his saddlebags, tossed Tommy up on to his own mount's withers, and then mounted behind him. 'Where be you taking me?' Tommy wailed.

'Home,' said Brockley in a menacing voice. 'To the village, to see if your eldest brother is there. Best thing I can do, madam.' I nodded, technically giving him permission, and perfectly aware that he wasn't actually asking for it. Brockley always was a law unto himself. 'I'll hand you over to him,' said Brockley into Tommy's ear. 'No doubt he'll know what to do with you, once he understands it's our orders. Pity he didn't take you in hand much sooner. No use expecting Marge to do it.'

The threat of his eldest brother seemed to terrify Tommy even more than Brockley did. He burst into tearful protests, which Brockley ignored, as he put his big dark chestnut, Firefly, into a canter along a right-hand track that branched off just ahead. Firefly, like Jaunty, had sensed the nearness of his home stable and didn't want to be deflected from it, but Brockley, standing no nonsense, used his spurs and in a moment, he was out of sight, and Tommy's wails were receding into the distance.

Soberly, the rest of us went on. We found most of my household in the courtyard, full of alarm. Someone had apparently witnessed the drama from an upper window. My steward, grey-haired Adam Wilder, came anxiously to meet us, with my two cooks, John Hawthorn, as big and burly as ever, and his assistant Ben Flood, short and stocky and bald, just behind him. Phoebe, my head housemaid, who had run the house in my absence, was with them, her lined face full of concern, and behind her came her under-maids: Margery, Tessie and Netta. On their heels came aged Gladys Morgan, hobbling badly, leaning on a stick, mouth open in a smile full of brown teeth with gaps in them.

Gladys was gifted with potions and had twice escaped being executed for witchcraft. We had rescued her on both occasions and after the first time, she had attached herself determinedly to me. I had never invited her into my household but here she was and always would be. If she had been present when Brockley apprehended Tommy Reed, she would probably have cursed the lad. Gladys's curses were both lurid and famous.

Hard behind them all but now pushing to the fore came my elderly head groom, Arthur Watts, and his two assistants, Simon Alder and Joseph Henty.

'Madam, Phoebe says she saw Jaunty plunging – he never does that – what ailed him . . .?' Arthur gasped.

'A silly boy from the village with a bow and arrows ailed him,' I said, as Joseph helped me dismount. 'With a metal-tipped arrow, so Brockley said. He says there's a wound on Jaunty's haunch, the offside one, I think . . .' I walked round Jaunty to see for myself. 'Yes, there it is. It wants tending.'

'I'll see to it.' Arthur came beside me and looked keenly at the damage. 'It could be worse. It came in at a shallow angle. It's a long cut but not too deep. Done with an arrow, then, was it? Dear God! Even with a small bow you can kill a man if you have a sharp metal tip. No wonder Jaunty went wild. You leave him to me now, madam. Joseph, lead him inside and get some warm water and find my pot of salve.'

Jaunty was in safe hands. I didn't know what went into Arthur's salve for injured equines; I only knew that it smelt nasty and always worked and that he had got it originally from Gladys.

My son Harry, fourteen and leggy as a colt, now came running from the house, with his tutor, Peter Dickson, following after. Dickson was at least seventy and couldn't move fast. Harry bowed to me as a son should when greeting his mother, and then ran to hold me and kiss me in welcome, and I saw that his fingers had fresh ink stains on them. 'Have we interrupted a lesson?' I asked.

'A most important one. Double entry book-keeping,' said Dickson, and smiled. 'Always difficult for him, but he is learning, Mistress Stannard.'

The maids were emptying the carriage and taking the luggage indoors. Dickson, insistent on finishing his lesson, led Harry away and the rest of us trooped into the great hall. Adam Wilder talked to me as we went.

'You sent couriers ahead, madam, to say you were on your way home, and warn us of the new maidservants and we are well prepared for you all. I will have a sheep on the spit tonight. I'll instruct Hawthorn . . .'

His voice trailed away. We were now in the hall and the happy bustle of homecoming was all around me, but it suddenly struck me that it wasn't as happy as it ought to be. Phoebe, who had followed us in, still looked anxious, even though I was now safely down from Jaunty's saddle, while Wilder seemed as though his mind were half on something else. I shook myself. I was imagining things. I introduced Bess and Hannah to Phoebe who at once summoned Margery and told her to take them to the servants' quarters. Then, with more ceremony, I introduced Mildred to Phoebe and Wilder.

'I have had a room prepared for you, madam,' Wilder said to Mildred and to me: 'It is the one your ward Mistress Frost used to have, madam, a very pleasant room. I wish her great happiness now that she is married in Devonshire.'

'My thanks on her behalf, Wilder,' I said, and noticed that his eyes were not meeting mine. No, I *wasn't* imagining it. Something was amiss, but what? Meanwhile, Mildred, anxious to help, was offering to find her way upstairs and unpack for me while Dale was shaking a vehement head and saying that that was her task. 'Tired I might be, but I know my duty and I can't abide interference,' she said. Mildred looked quelled and I gave her a reassuring smile.

Of us all, poor Dale probably had the best right to be tired. She was no longer young and in my service she had endured gruelling journeys and frightening dangers, a state of affairs to which she was not at all suited. Dale was marked with a childhood bout of smallpox, the same disease that had killed my first husband, and when she was frightened or weary, they seemed to become more prominent, as did her round blue eyes. They were noticeable now. But she removed my riding boots for me and then departed determinedly to do the unpacking. I stayed where I was, not having the energy to change my dress just yet, and since Wilder seemed to be hovering, I asked him to bring some wine.

I had to ask twice, for it was as though he hadn't heard me the first time. He turned to me with a start. 'It's being made ready, madam,' he said, and if that wasn't a distracted tone of voice, I had never heard one. I stared after him in surprise as he hurried away. He returned a moment later with a tray of wine and small chicken pies, warm from the oven, and set them down on the big hall table. He still looked worried, for no apparent reason.

He left us again and Phoebe went with him and I heard them whispering about something just outside in the lobby. I half rose, meaning to go after them, but at that moment, the door to the courtyard opened and Brockley came in. I sat down again, raising my eyebrows at him in a questioning fashion.

He was carrying Tommy's bow and quiver. He put them on the table, pulled off his riding cloak, unbuckled the sword he always carried when we were travelling and threw them on to the table as well. I signalled to him to be seated. He did so, with a sigh. He too had had enough toil for the time being, I thought.

'You took Tommy Reed home?' I asked.

'Aye. I found that eldest brother of his there, bit of luck, that. He was furious when I told him about the so-called toy bow and arrows. As you see, I haven't given them back. And I told the brother, Abel, his name is, to see Tommy never gets his hands on another such toy, though he probably will. Most lads can make them. I could, at his age. In the village where I grew up, the boys were encouraged to make bows and arrows and encouraged to practise at the butts. Of course, we weren't supposed just to wander about, shooting at any old mark, though we did!'

Brockley suddenly grinned, reminiscently. 'I killed a spaniel once, by mistake, of course, but its owner half-killed *me*. I had a pretty good eye, and I was aiming at a tree stump, but the spaniel came out of nowhere and got in the way.'

He sounded as though he had softened towards young Tommy. 'I hope you weren't too hard on the boy,' I said.

'Not up to me. I told Abel Reed what had happened and he was angry, as he should be. I pushed Tommy at him and then left them. But as I rode off, I heard Tommy start to howl. If ever he does make another set of bow and arrows, I hope he'll be more careful with it. I went to the forge to have a few words with the Reed boy, Sim, that's an apprentice there, and I found him at work with the blacksmith, Rob Jackson.'

'Ah. Jackson,' I said with some relish. 'What did he have to say?' Jackson was a respectable craftsman with powerful muscles and a powerful voice to match.

'He clouted Sim on the ear and swore that if he ever caught him tipping toy arrows with iron again, Sim would be out of work and out of Hawkswood as well and begging his bread from door to door. Sim was down on the floor and sobbing, poor little brute. He's only sixteen. I don't think there'll be much more trouble from that quarter.'

'I'm sorry,' I said. 'For both Tommy and Sim. I have never allowed Harry to be beaten, as you know.'

'Harry has sense,' said Brockley. 'He doesn't need beating. Where is he now?'

'Dickson has marched him off, back to a lesson on double entry book-keeping. Brockley, what is going on? Have you noticed it? Everyone looks worried and Wilder has something on his mind, I know he has. What's wrong?'

'I've only just arrived,' Brockley said. 'I haven't had time to notice anything.' I nodded to Mildred to pour wine for him and he accepted it gratefully. 'The best thing to do,' he said, 'is ask Wilder what's happening, if anything. Here he is! Wilder . . .'

Wilder had returned, this time looking resolute. 'Madam, I know you have travelled far, and you told us in your letters that you had a dangerous time in Devonshire. And here you are, just back, literally just off your horses, and after all that to-do because of that boy with his bow, but we have to tell you . . .'

He seemed to hesitate on some kind of brink and I encouraged him, impatiently.

'Tell me what? Come along, Wilder, I've already realized that something's amiss here. Is there smallpox in the village? Have the stud stables burned down?' To add to Harry's future inheritance I had established a stud of the fast trotting horses that were now so popular. The premises adjoined Hawkswood land half a mile away. 'Out with it!'

'Well, madam, the truth is, you have a guest. She is quite determined to speak with you. She's been here two days. She says she has heard of Mistress Ursula Stannard, who solves mysteries and has the ear of the queen and her council, and she hopes you can help her.'

I felt myself sag against the cushions on the settle where I had been trying to relax. 'Wilder, I have only just returned from a long journey, and in Devon, I did indeed meet danger. I came near to getting myself killed. And now, before I have even spent one night at home . . .! Who is this woman and where is she?'

'I knew you wouldn't be pleased, madam. None of us are! Coming out of nowhere, wanting you to rush off somewhere to a place none of us have ever heard of, and all over nothing as far as I could make out . . .'

'Never mind all that, Wilder. *Where is she?* And where is she from?'

'Just now, she's in the little parlour. She came alone, on a mule, with clothes and things in bulging saddlebags and a shoulder pack and she had a little foal on a long leading rein, trotting alongside. A very little foal, madam.' Wilder looked really unhappy. 'Madam, it suckles from the mule! I never heard of such a thing but it seems the mule's its mother!'

'No, Wilder, that can't be right,' I protested.

'I'm afraid it is, madam,' said Wilder in a hopeless tone of voice. 'She comes from the New Forest, she told us, from somewhere called Chenston. I've never heard of it but she said it was near Minstead. I've never heard of that, either. I told her you were not here, but Margery came to me just at that moment to ask something about the preparations for your return, and this woman at once said that if you were expected soon, she would wait. She said she would find lodgings in the village, but that seemed inhospitable, so we found her a space in our quarters. She has passed the time in doing some embroidery she's got with her, and playing board games with herself. We lent her your set of draughts, madam. We offered her something to read but it seems she can't read or write, beyond signing her name. But half the time she just sits and stares out of a window as if hoping to see you return.'

'I've just spoken to her.' Dale, carrying a shawl of mine over her arm, had followed Wilder into the hall. 'I was bringing you this shawl because it's cold for May, and the door of the little parlour was half open. I caught sight of her and I went in and asked her who she was. She said she had come to see you. I thought it was too much to ask you, ma'am, to attend to her just now, and I said so, perhaps a bit sharply, only then I was sorry because I think she's frightened. I could feel it.'

Now and then, Dale could be very percipient. If she said that my unwanted guest was frightened, then she was very likely right.

'I agree with Dale,' said Wilder. 'She is nervous and she is certainly determined on seeing you, madam.'

'What is her name?' I asked. 'And what is her trouble?'

'She speaks of what she calls strange goings on in her village. She says she has tried to talk to the vicar there, but he tells her she is talking nonsense. Also, she has been threatened, on account of the foal, that should never have been born. Then she thought of you. She says that she thinks these Goings On, whatever they are, could have something to do with Mary Stuart. I asked her if really, she'd just come here to get away from the threats, but she said no, that she has grown children she could go to if it were only that.'

'I see,' I said untruthfully. Wilder's account made little sense to me. 'And what is this woman's name?'

'Etheldreda Hope, madam. Will you see her?'

I groaned inwardly. Years ago, when I was on a journey to East Anglia, a flight of wild geese had passed overhead. The friend who was riding beside me said then that I had a wildness in me; that I followed adventure, as a wild goose follows the call of its kind. There had been some truth in that. But not now. I had outgrown my youthful wildness long ago. Weary after my latest adventure and thankful to have come through it safely, I wanted only to rest.

'I will see her now,' I said.

# TWO

## A Mule Can't Breed

I had no choice but to see her. She was waiting in my parlour and she had been here for two days. She was a guest and I was her hostess whether I liked it or not, and however muddled her account of herself seemed to be, she might well be in genuine trouble of some kind and not just that. If the trouble concerned Mary Stuart then I could not possibly ignore it.

And I was as tired as Dale was, not just because of the three weeks on the road from Devonshire, where I had indeed been in grave peril but also because I was weary of having my peaceful domestic life continually interrupted and because I was very tired indeed of the name Mary Stuart.

Years ago, when I was young, newly widowed by the death of my first husband, Gerald Blanchard, I had little money, but useful connections. I was able to find employment as a lady-in-waiting to the young Queen Elizabeth. But my pay was modest and I still had to arrange a nurse and accommodation for my small daughter Meg. I welcomed any chance to earn a little extra and I undertook a secret mission, for which I was paid. Since then, I had been constantly employed in secret missions. The queen's principal advisers, her Lord High Treasurer Sir William Cecil, now Lord Burghley, and her Secretary of State, Sir Francis Walsingham, would call on me whenever there was something to be done that they thought I would do better than one of their male agents.

Once my circumstances had improved, I tried to put an end to this but when I learned that my hitherto unknown father was King Henry the Eighth himself, and that I was therefore a half-sister to the queen, my chances of breaking away were at an end. Elizabeth already knew that I was her half-sister and I still at times served as one of her ladies. Once I too knew of our relationship, we drew close and a bond was formed. From then on, I well understood that any mission I was asked to undertake was for her, even though my orders came from Cecil or Walsingham. I could not refuse them.

Nearly all those missions had in some way involved Mary Stuart, the exiled queen of Scotland, thrown out of her realm because she was suspected of having a hand in the murder of her consort and now a prisoner-cum-guest of Her Majesty Queen Elizabeth. She was known to be trying to plot against Elizabeth, with a view to seizing the English throne. She had been at it for years. I was weary to death of the sound of her name.

But she was a danger to my country and to the queen my sister and so, like it or not (and I didn't like it at all), I must face this exasperating stranger, this oddly named Etheldreda Hope. With the dust of the journey from Devon still upon me, I got to my feet. 'In the little parlour, you say?' I said.

She stood up as I came in. The little parlour was a pleasant, snug room, though small. I had a bigger parlour, known as the East Room because it got the morning sun, but I used that one for gatherings of several people and sometimes for doing the household accounts, since the light in there was so good. For relaxation, though, I preferred the little parlour and the light there was quite good enough to show my visitor clearly, a middle-aged woman in a dull brown gown, with a small ruff, no farthingale and a respectable white coif over her hair. Her eyes were pale, with an intent gaze.

She curtsied to me as Wilder announced my name and repeated hers to me. I said: 'Please be seated,' and dismissed Wilder. We both sat down. Through all these preliminaries, those intent eyes had been fixed on me, their expression both searching and wary. She was nervous of me but also assessing me.

I said: 'I believe you seek my help. In what way?'

She cleared her throat. 'I got to ask your forgiveness, disturbing you when you're just home after a long journey.' She had a country accent. 'I've heared of you, madam, heared of things you've done, mysteries you've searched out, so I thought maybe, just maybe you'd help. It's only about four weeks or thereabout until Midsummer.'

I jumped. I think my body actually jerked. It was her tone of voice. She had pronounced the word *Midsummer* as though it were Christmas or Easter. 'Midsummer?' I said.

'You're surprised,' said Mistress Hope. 'In Chenston, Midsummer is special. There's old traditions in the village. Everyone takes them for granted. Deep in the New Forest, Chenston is. Every midsummer, Chenston folk hold a midnight gathering in a clearing nearby. Have done for centuries. Our previous vicar used to preach against it, but the present one seems not to mind overmuch. Even though, this last two or three years or so, things have changed, got more serious. There've been extra meetings at other times, like Lammas . . .'

'August the First?' I said.

'Yes, that's Lammas. The Lammas feast goes back to the days of King William Rufus. It's said he was a sacrifice to the ancient gods, and didn't die by accident at all. He died on the second of August, not the first but the story goes that he was feared to go out hunting on the first. Whole village knows the tale. It used to be just a tale. Only now . . .'

I nodded. I was well acquainted with the legend about William Rufus, otherwise William the Second. I had a second house, in Sussex, called Withysham. The queen gave it to me as a reward for my services, and chose it because it was actually linked to my family. Until my father King Henry destroyed the monasteries, it had been a house of nuns and girls from my family, the Faldenes, who lived quite near – in fact where my Uncle Herbert and Aunt Tabitha lived now – had often joined the community there. One of them had started a chronicle, which had been kept up by her successors. I knew, therefore, that back in Rufus' time, a Faldene girl had married one of his men and gone to live with him on a property in the New Forest, where her husband had witnessed the death of the king. When the legend sprang up round that death, the chronicle recorded that too. A later part of the chronicle said that a descendant of the New Forest branch had married back into the Faldene family, the line that led to me, so that I was probably descended from both lines.

Even the name Chenston gave me a curious feeling. The place that the original Faldene girl had gone to had been called Chenna's Tun. Chenna's Tun . . . It rang in my head. Chenns-tun . . . Chenston. Could it be? Had the original name been weathered and worn down and changed from the one to the other? At any rate, the name of Chenston echoed in my mind, insisting that I attend to it. Suddenly, my uninvited guest was less of a nuisance. I wanted to know more.

'Well, and now?' I enquired, since she seemed to have come to a stop.

'This year,' said Etheldreda, 'there's been a feast at Walpurgis as well. May Eve, I mean. More feasts every year. I've never been to one of these forest feasts. I'm not Chenston born. I come there when I married. My parents had a smallholding near Winchester, just about made a living for themselves and half a dozen of us, growing cabbages and onions and keeping goats and chickens, selling eggs and cheese and a few chicks and goat kids as well, now and then. I were the oldest, used to help at the market stall we had in Winchester, caught the eye of a man from Chenston when he were selling hens and piglets there. He brought me to Chenston but they Chenston folk; you need to be born there to belong. My Sylvester weren't born there either; he come from near Salisbury, inherited the tenancy in Chenston when an uncle of his died, moved in when he were a man grown. I've been there twenty-five years and Sylvester a couple of years more. We had four childer, all grown and married and gone away now. But all the time, both of us, we'd still been the strangers from Winchester and Salisbury. Year and a half back, Sylvester died. Left me a home and our smallholding so I'm well off enough with my fat old sow and my hens and a few vegetables, and I get some help from Nick White as has the place next to me . . . my back hurts me if I stoop too much and I get tired but I need the money and I don't want to live with any of my childer; I visit them now and then but not for too long for they either haven't room enough or I don't get on that well with their wives or husbands though I'd still have gone to one of them and not to here if it hadn't been for these goings on . . .'

She was rambling. I interrupted. 'Please tell me, just what brought you here.'

'My Sylvester didn't like what he called Goings On,' said Etheldreda, 'so he never went to any of those forest gatherings I've just told about. Said they were witchcraft. Well, I don't think that; I think it was all customs like the maypole at Minstead – that's an estate not far from Chenston – and the hobby horse they have there . . .'

'Please keep to the point!' The woman was still rambling and my spark of enthusiasm was being damped. She was going round and round the heart of her tale like a sheepdog circling a flock, never getting close.

She looked upset by my interruption. 'I'm telling you, aren't I? You put me off, keeping on breaking in, it gets me all muddled. I'm trying to say, I always reckoned they were just customs, harmless enough, like the maypole and that. But now they're held oftener and Nick says he thinks there's some sort of point to them only they've not got to the point yet.'

She paused. To encourage her, I said: 'Yes?' I longed to say *What sort of point?* at the top of my voice but I knew that if I did, she would get flustered and ramble more than ever.

'It's what Nick says,' she said. 'Nick, he's kind to me, we're friends, and he does *go to the Wood*, as we call it. Most of the village does. Nick's told me the way things have changed in the last two–three years. First it was extra meetings being called: suddenly, one Midsummer, folk were told, come back at Lammas, and now it's Walpurgis too, like I said, and Halloween as well! Then the leader – only they don't know who he is as they're all masked and cloaked – started invoking some old woodland god, Herne the Hunter he calls him, according to Nick, and that's not right for Christian folk. And the latest is that whoever he is, he's been calling on this old Herne to . . . well . . . I hardly like to say . . .'

'But you came here to say it.' With great difficulty I kept my tone quiet and kind, though by now I was repressing a powerful urge to take her by the shoulders and shake her. 'Please, Mistress Hope, will you say plainly what has brought you here? I've never heard of this Herne.'

Etheldreda said: 'He's got antlers.'

Again there was a jerk in my mind. The aunt and uncle who had brought me up had let me share my cousins' tutor and he had been a highly educated man who had told us a great deal about ancient people and ancient beliefs. Uncle Herbert and Aunt Tabitha would have fainted in horror if they had ever heard him expounding as he sometimes did, on what they would have called pagan lore. In fact, they did eventually get rid of him because they had found out about some of it.

By then, however, the tutor had told us about the horned god of the greenwood, though not by the name of Herne. According to my cousins' tutor, the Greeks called him Pan and the Celtic people who lived in England before the Romans came called him Cernunnos. The tutor told us that the Green Knight who featured in the tales of King Arthur was a memory of him. He said too that he knew of inns called the Green Man, and that these were another lingering trace of Cernunnos.

'What is it,' I asked, 'that the unknown leader of these midnight rites has asked this Herne to do?'

'He has asked him,' said Mistress Hope, coming out with it at last, 'to bring about the death of an evil queen, to save an honest queen.'

There was a silence. Then I said: 'What is the name of the queen he calls evil?'

'He never says, according to Nick.'

So Mary Stuart had not been named, either as an evil monarch or a true one.

'Doesn't anyone *know* who this leader is? In a small place like Chenston – I suppose it's small – can people really not recognize someone they must know well, even in disguise? Not recognize his voice, his walk . . .'

'They mostly think it's the innkeeper, Felix Armer. But if anyone asks him, he laughs and won't say. Says, if it is him, he'd be sworn never to admit it. But some folk' – she dropped her voice, as though she feared that spies might be outside the door with their ears pressed to it – 'think the evil queen is this Mary Stuart that's meant, the queen of Scotland as was, that there's always such a fuss about. Only others, Nick says, are whispering that perhaps all this is in support of Mary Stuart and that it's, well . . .'

'Our own Queen Elizabeth that is meant,' I finished for her. 'I fancy that could be called treason. But . . . does this man Nick say that any actual plots are being laid?'

'He's not said so.'

'It's nasty,' I said. 'Very nasty. But . . . if it's only a matter of praying to a god that doesn't exist, and nothing more, then . . .'

'I don't *know*. And I can't go asking questions. The villagers don't like me. Oh, maybe that's partly because Sylvester always said we were a bit above the village folk; got a bigger house, you see. He liked us to keep ourselves to ourselves. But lately, something's happened . . . they've been calling me a witch. I've got scared. That's most of why I'm here. I'm used to travelling, go off now and then to visit my childer. Seeing what's just happened, that's started this whispering about me, I thought I'd best go travelling again for a while.'

'What do you mean? What's just happened?'

'My mule dropped a foal, that's what's happened. I can't understand it. Mules aren't supposed to have foals. They can mate but they can't breed. Well, my mule's a female and she must have mated; one of the half-wild forest stallions, likely enough. A month ago, in April, she dropped a foal and that's when the murmuring started and it's got worse and they're saying in the village that I must have bewitched her.'

'But mules *can't* breed! You've just said so.'

'Mine has,' said Etheldreda glumly.

'And you brought the foal here with you?'

'Wouldn't have been safe to leave her behind. She's a pretty thing, too, a proper little filly, a horse filly; no sign of donkey about her, sorrel with a little white on her, like ponds and trails of white paint, not quite skewbald but almost. But there's some in the village called her a devil's spawn. Twice Nick's chased off boys throwing stones at her. That nasty Jacky Dunning, only thirteen years old, he was in the lead both times, even older boys follow him, even the Orchard boys and they're nigh grown up.'

She spoke as though I must be acquainted with Jacky Dunning and the Orchard boys, though to me they were only names.

'There'd be folk staring at her over the field gate, too. Vicar in his pulpit one Sunday said she was an act of God; that kept things quiet awhile. But like I said, the villagers don't like me and now there's this. I've had children calling *witch* after me in the street, women making the sign against the evil eye. I've been getting more and more scared. It's made me think: I got to get away. I got to ask for help. Then I thought of you and all I'd heard of you, Mistress Stannard.'

Her pale eyes were more than intent by now; they were pleading. 'I can't explain right. There's me being called a witch, and there's what goes on in the Wood. They're different things. But I keep feeling as if they're mixed up together. And with what Nick's told me about the Wood, I can smell something wrong.'

We were silent for a moment. Her narrative seemed confused, I thought. Like Etheldreda, I failed to see any link between remarks made about evil queens while ancient forest rites were taking place, and the birth of the filly with the improbable pedigree. But that phrase *I can smell something wrong* had caught my attention. I knew that feeling.

Cautiously, I said: 'You have not come here simply because you are angry with those who call you a witch? You have not just come here to make trouble for them?'

Etheldreda actually snorted, aloud. 'I haven't come for spite if that's what you mean. I'm frightened, that's all about it, and then there's what's going on in the Wood. I tell you, there's *something wrong*.'

I said: 'What do you want me to do?'

'I beg you,' said my unwanted guest, 'to find out what's really going on in the Wood, find out if there *is* something afoot that's dangerous, about queens and such. That's not for simple folk like us to meddle in. I tried to talk to our vicar but he don't like me any more than the rest of them. He were all right about my filly but when it comes to feasts in the forest and evil queens, well, he just laughed and pooh-poohed me and said he don't approve of Goings On – he said that in a special voice; you'd know what I mean – but the village has its old customs, he said, and if they want to hold silly gatherings in the forest in the middle of the night, well, he just hopes they won't catch cold, for it's only play, like the May Day games at Minstead. He thinks I'm just a daft woman. He shooed me away. Oh, he has preached a sermon or two about how wrong it is to pray to any god but our own, but I doubt that made any difference. I thought, after Walpurgis that's just gone by, that it had got folk kind of excited. That's when Jacky Dunning and his nasty friends started throwing stones and the whispers began about me. Poor little filly,' said Etheldreda indignantly. 'How she come to be born of my mule, only God knows, but she's a proper little horse and pretty as they come and I want to keep her safe. Yes, and get the price of her one day when she's grown. A windfall from heaven, I call her. Windfall is her name. Mistress Stannard, will you help?'

'I think,' I said, when I had sent Mildred to keep Etheldreda company while I talked with the Brockleys, 'that I am being called upon as much to protect a filly and clear Etheldreda's name of witchcraft, as I am to enquire into who is apparently praying to a pagan deity to injure some unknown queen. Let's hope the proposed victim is Mary Stuart. Either way, I suppose someone ought to find out whether they actually intend to do anything about it. I can't understand this business of the foal being born to a mule. That's impossible!'

'No, it can happen,' Brockley said unexpectedly. 'When I was a soldier in King Henry's army, long ago, one of my comrades was a farmer's son, from Lincolnshire. He told me there was a Barbary stallion on a place next to his father's farm, that was a demon for getting out of his field and boarding other people's mares, not that most of their owners minded. They got a free service and very likely a valuable half-Barbary foal. Well, his dad had a mule and he reckoned the Barbary got at her too and lo and behold, she dropped a foal herself. That was a pure horse filly, too. My friend said she grew up with a Barbary shaped head and a short Barbary back. She was a good ride, and she had foals of her own, all pure horse, seemingly, no trace of donkey anywhere. I don't like the sound of this place Chenston,' he added.

That sounded like a non sequitur but was not. I knew

Brockley. I knew every expression in his steady blue-grey eyes; when he frowned, I could read every furrow in his high, gold-freckled forehead, and when he spoke, I could interpret every tone of his voice.

'You think I ought to go there,' I said crossly. 'You don't like the sound of Chenston, so it ought to be investigated. That's it, isn't it? It's been one thing after another. Urchins with bows and arrows and now this. I have no peace.'

'A night's sleep will revive us all,' said Brockley. 'You can decide then, madam. If you haven't already decided, that is.'

# THREE

## A Thorn in the Finger

I hadn't made my mind up at all; far from it. Tired though I was, I slept poorly that night, as I tried to think things through.

For a start, even if this place Chenston was the same as the place where two of my ancestors had once lived, all that was far in the past, and had nothing to do with Etheldreda's story, which to me sounded absurd. What after all did it add up to? Here was a remote village which preserved a memory of ancient rituals on certain dates – dates traditionally said to be those when covens of witches met. It seemed as if someone was coaxing the villagers of Chenston, who already habitually kept one of these ancient rituals, into reviving the others. It also seemed to me, that if so, the said villagers hadn't much right to throw accusations of witchcraft at a respectable woman who didn't attend their carryings on.

But what did those carryings on actually amount to? The leader, whoever he was, apparently made speeches, and there was probably a bonfire. There would *surely* be a bonfire. It would be cold in the forest at night. Maybe they danced round it. The current leader, by the sound of him, enjoyed making his speeches sound important by talking about evil queens, whoever they might be, and he probably enjoyed commanding his flock. Very likely, that was all there was to it. Only, was there, could there be, something genuinely treasonable at work? Could these feasts be a cloak for genuine conspiracies but if so, how? What kind of conspiracies? In whose favour?

I was being invited to go and find out but did I want to? No, I did not. I wanted to stay at home. Etheldreda Hope's tale would only lead me to a mare's nest. Or a mule's nest, said my mind, beginning to sink towards sleep.

Only, what if it proved to be a hornets' nest instead? This

depressing idea woke me up again. What if I refused to enquire into it and then found that I had made a mistake? I needed advice as much as Etheldreda did!

But she wanted more than just advice. She wanted me to go to the New Forest and probe into the matter of the evil queen. Surely, surely, all that was nothing but hot air, some man or other making himself important. *Oh, for the love of heaven, I'm going round in circles . . .*

Sleep overcame me at last, but when I woke I found that I had decided what to do. Immediately after breakfast I wrote a letter to Sir Francis Walsingham. I then told Brockley to fetch Laurence Miller, the chief groom in my stud of trotters.

Miller was already on hand in the home stable yard, as he was expecting my summons. He would want to give me an account of how the stud had fared in my absence, but not just that. For Miller was something more than a groom. Because I was the queen's sister, Sir William Cecil and Sir Francis Walsingham insisted on being kept informed of events in my household. At one time, their spy (they called him my guardian) had been the vicar in St Mary's church in Hawkswood village. When he retired, they planted Laurence Miller on me. I endured it because he was actually an excellent head groom and because I knew at heart that he was there for my protection. In the course of my unlikely career, I had made enemies, and anyway, the kinsfolk of a queen are always vulnerable.

I needed to see him now and not only to hear his report on the stud and to tell him what had passed in Devon. I had sent a report to Walsingham from Devon, but I knew that Laurence would want to hear the tale from me. I also needed his help in getting my letter to Walsingham. Elizabeth's court moved often, back and forth from one Thames-side palace to another and generally, her councillors went with it. The report I despatched from Devon might well have had to chase Sir Francis along the Thames from Greenwich to Windsor. I wanted the letter I had just written to go straight to the right place and Miller would know where that was.

Laurence Miller was a tall, unsmiling, taciturn man, with whom I never felt really comfortable, even though his good manners never faltered. He presented the report on the stud in a succinct fashion and I gave him mine on the events in Devon in a similar way. Then, before I could say anything more, he said: 'I hear that you have a guest, who wants to ask something of you. Mistress Etheldreda Hope, I believe. What is her purpose?'

He was bound to know about Etheldreda's arrival of course. I explained and then, once more stepping in ahead of me, he said: 'Will you wish to send word of all this to Walsingham?'

'Yes,' I told him. 'Where is the court at present?'

'Richmond, I think. Shall I be your messenger? I can leave at once. I'll take one of my light training carts and give one of our young teams a good run.' He smiled, which made him look friendly.

'I have a letter ready,' I said. 'If possible please wait for a reply.'

Miller was off within the hour. Nothing could have been done with more despatch. Relieved, I set about the other tasks that awaited the lady of the manor after her long absence. Adam Wilder would want to tell me about anything of note that had happened in the house; I must also talk to Peter Dickson about Harry's studies. I must see to these things.

I learned that the house had run smoothly under Phoebe, though there was serious need for extra help and the arrival of Hannah and Bess was most welcome. Harry had been diligent and after a lengthy tussle seemed to have grasped the principles of double entry book-keeping at last. Mildred sat with me, learning the ways of Hawkswood, and I tried to set her a good example by listening attentively to everything, which was difficult, as half my mind was on Miller's errand. I was wondering how many days would pass before he would return.

To my surprise, he came back that same evening, just as dusk was falling, arriving in the stable yard with a clatter of hooves and a creaking of wheels. I hurried out to meet him. He had driven back in evident haste, for the matched pair of young trotters were sweating and excited, stamping and tossing their heads. We left my grooms to unharness them and rub them down, while I took Miller indoors.

'Did Sir Francis receive my letter?'

'He did, and I have the reply you wanted, madam,' said Miller, and handed it to me.

Standing there by the hall fire, I broke the seal at once. Walsingham thanked me for my communication and wished me to attend on him the following Wednesday, the 28th of May, at two of the clock. The timing was considerate; I could travel there in the morning and return home by evening, as Laurence had just done. But I wasn't as relieved as I had hoped to be. I had written to Walsingham seeking his advice but I had really hoped he would dismiss Etheldreda's story and tell me to pay no heed to it. Instead, he wished to discuss it in person and that was ominous.

I then found myself embroiled in an exasperating argument with Brockley and Dale, about who was to go with me and what we were to ride.

'A lady can't go unattended to the court, ma'am,' Dale insisted. 'I ought to come as well, and Brockley too. I don't mind. I've got an ambler now.'

Dale was a poor horsewoman, but in Devon she had for a while been lent an ambling mare. Because the easy ambling pace was so much smoother than the ordinary trot, she had managed quite well. In one of the letters I had sent ahead of us, I had given instructions that Arthur Watts was to find an ambler for her, and so he had. That very morning, Dale had been trying out a blue roan ambling mare, appropriately called Blue Gentle.

However, I wasn't to be allowed to ride Jaunty. 'That wound on his haunch is healing,' Arthur said, leading him out into the courtyard so that I could inspect the damage for myself. 'But he needs a rest after all that travelling, and if he doesn't get one, that cut could open again.'

Brockley had joined us, and agreed. 'All our horses need a good rest after all the travelling we did. I've turned Rusty out to grass; if we need to use the carriage again we can put Bronze in the shafts. And Jaunty shouldn't be ridden until he's fully healed.'

'Brockley, I wish you wouldn't try to give me orders. Jaunty is my horse, after all.'

'Madam, where the wellbeing of a horse is concerned, I will give orders to the Emperor of Cathay, or to the queen herself,' said Brockley.

He would, too; I knew it, and so did Arthur Watts, who was laughing. 'Then I'll take Laurence Miller as my male escort,' I said, 'and I'll use the carriage – as it adapts for two horses, we can give another pair of his youngsters a training run.'

'And you'll take Fran with you, madam?' Brockley said. 'And what of Mistress Hope? Shouldn't she go too?'

'Must I?' Etheldreda had come out of the house to join us. I had last seen her in the small parlour, doing her embroidery, and she was still clutching it. 'Madam, I wouldn't feel right, going to a place like the royal court . . .'

'No, you need not come. I'll do the explaining,' I said hastily. I could all too clearly visualize an encounter between Etheldreda and Walsingham. Tall, dark of hair and eyes and so dark of skin that Elizabeth called him her Old Moor, always clad in black clothes and surrounded by the aura of power, he would intimidate her and then Etheldreda's circuitous way of telling a story would probably become more circuitous than ever and irritate him, and then he would *really* terrify her. As for Dale, she was in need of at least a few days' rest.

'Brockley, I think you and Dale can both stay behind this time,' I said. 'I'll take Hannah. I'm thinking of making her maid to Mildred and this way, I can introduce her to her new duties. She can start practising on me.'

Hannah, though no more than sixteen, was a most intelligent girl and Mildred needed a maid of her own. The girl who had attended my former ward Joyce, had left us just before we set out for Devon, so Joyce and I had shared Dale's services until Joyce married. Mildred and I had been sharing them since then but that would have to change.

'But I want to come!' Dale insisted, not liking to see anyone in her place, even for a day. 'Now that I have Blue Gentle . . .'

At this point Wilder came out of the house as well and joined in the argument. 'Madam, if you are thinking to train Hannah Durley as maid for Mistress Gresham, then we must find another maid to replace Hannah, and indeed we could well do with two of *her*! Bess is willing but very young and Netta and Tessie are forever saying they can't come because one or other of their children has a cold or chicken pox or has fallen out of a tree; those two are hardly ever here . . .'

'I'm your personal maid, ma'am, and I can't abide the thought of you without me and behind those half-trained colts . . .'

'Jaunty's wound is improving but I insist that there's no question of putting a saddle on him yet . . .'

I put my hands over my ears and then shouted: 'I am travelling with Laurence Miller and Hannah Durley, in the carriage, behind two young trotters and that's final!'

I must have shouted very loudly, because after that, it was.

Walsingham had an office at Richmond just as he had in the other royal palaces. This one was essentially a room of charm, with linenfold panelling and casements with patterned leading. Most of its beauties, however, were concealed by piles of correspondence, ledgers, files, books and stationery, and the pins that fastened the several maps to the wall had done the beautiful panelling no favours. I left Hannah in our room and went alone to see Walsingham. As his chief clerk showed me in, he rose from behind his desk to greet me. Like Laurence, he was meticulous about his manners.

'So, Ursula, you have found another mystery. On the very day that you reached home after dealing with the last one, it seems. Well, seat yourself. You came in that little carriage of yours, did you not? I saw you arrive. That's a handsome pair of high-steppers that you had in the traces. You bred them yourself, I take it – I know from Miller that the stud is prospering. I suppose he is busy grooming them now, getting them ready for the journey home. It's fortunate that you live not too far away. How far is it? Sixteen, seventeen miles?'

'About that, Sir Francis.'

'Well, that concludes our pretty preliminaries. I have read your letter. Tell me, why have you not brought this woman, Etheldreda Hope, with you?'

It was no use prevaricating, not with Walsingham. 'She is a simple countrywoman; she can hardly read or write. When she tries to explain anything, she rambles, circles round the point. You would frighten her, Sir Francis, and then she would ramble more than ever. I decided to be her mouthpiece.'

'Hm. I know what you mean by rambling. You should hear how some of the prisoners I interrogate ramble – and stammer and gibber – before they confess. But I don't always set out to intimidate. I can be patient and kind towards honest men and women even if they do stammer. Ask my wife, and my daughter Frances.'

'I am sure of it,' I said politely, and wondered, not for the first time, just what Walsingham's home life was like. It was so very difficult to imagine that this saturnine man, who didn't hesitate to call upon executioner Richard Topcliffe in his terrifying quarters below the Tower of London, to ask whether the latest prisoner was ready for questioning, and if not, to listen unperturbed to the cries of a man on the rack, might under his own roof turn into an affectionate husband and father, making family jokes, playing at draughts or backgammon or admiring his daughter's skill with the lute . . . I could as easily imagine Beelzebub singing lullabies to a baby.

I said: 'I did think she would be nervous, and I can tell the tale just as well as she can, or better.'

'True. Your letter sets out her story very clearly. But it doesn't tell me what you think yourself.'

'I think – I hope – that all we have here is a village with a tradition of playing games in the forest at midsummer, born out of a legend about the death of William the Second, and a man who has somehow got control of these forest games and has built them up into something bigger, because it pleases him. He likes power, perhaps, and he likes arcane rites. That's what I think it amounts to, and it sounds – nasty and irreligious. But not treasonable. Only . . .'

'Quite,' said Walsingham. 'That's exactly how I read it. Nasty and irreligious and it certainly ought to be stamped out and the local vicar shouldn't let it continue. *Only* . . .'

'An evil queen,' I said reluctantly. 'Villagers muttering about Mary Stuart. This man apparently hasn't named the queen he means. I suspect that he's being careful. Whatever happens in the end . . .' I was being careful here myself, not wanting even to hint that Mary Stuart might one day prevail, but Walsingham was nodding. He knew what I meant.

'When the end of the conflict comes, he can always claim that the loser was the one he meant when he said *evil.* Are you acquainted with the phrase *hedging his bets*?'

'Yes. I think that is what he's doing. Only, what sort of bet? Is he up to something real, or not? It's like a tiny thorn in one's finger. One has to get it out.'

Walsingham was silent for a moment, apparently thinking. Then he said: 'There is something you didn't want to say aloud. But however unwilling you are to speak of it, the possibility is there that her majesty, our gracious queen and your beloved half-sister, could be murdered by Mary's crazed supporters, and the country laid open to a Spanish army come to install Mary on the throne of England. If that were to happen, we – you, me, Cecil and many others – would have to flee into exile to save our lives. You have good reason to pursue this mystery in Chenston, just in case it genuinely has some bearing on this matter.'

He had read my mind. I said nothing. I had no desire to pursue this mystery but I knew in my heart that I should.

'I think,' Sir Francis said, 'that I should tell you that I have decided, along with the queen and all her council – we have talked much on the subject – that the time has come to rid ourselves, once and for all, of the danger posed by Mary Stuart. I will not go into details for the fewer people who know those, the better, but I have designed a plan by which our sweet Mary may be led into, shall we say, unfortunate indiscretions. Then she can be lawfully removed. But the plan is not yet ripe, and meanwhile, if there are any unknown conspiracies in her favour, other than the ones I personally hope to encourage and then smash, then I want to know about them. I have no wish to be stabbed in the back by unexpected conspirators creeping out from the shadow of King William's great forest. Even the tiniest suggestion of such a thing does indeed feel like a thorn in the finger, as you so forcefully express it. You are in the best possible position for taking out the thorn. You have actually been invited to Chenston by this woman Etheldreda.'

He paused, sitting back in his chair. 'That's an interesting name. It's Saxon; used to be in fashion before the Conquest. It happens in some of these remote places. Memories of the distant past still linger. Babies are christened by ancient names and sometimes old traditions survive. I have a friend, a man I met at Cambridge, who is now vicar of a small parish in the Midlands. His flock have a centuries old custom of forming a candlelight procession every May Eve, and marching widdershins round the church. Even they don't know what it's for except that they think it's something to do with making sure the crops will grow. He can't stop them. He has given up trying. He just insists that afterwards, they come into the church to pray in a proper manner for successful crops.'

I found myself inclined to laugh but Walsingham's swarthy face remained sombre. He said: 'What I'm saying is that if the villagers of Chenston are indulging in absurd midnight antics in the forest on certain dates, that on its own is none of my business. It's up to their vicar. If he's willing to let them have their fun, that's that. What I am interested in, is any new threat to the safety of this realm, to the safety of our queen. In the last two years, fears for her safety have grown. Our English Catholics have been uneasy ever since Pope Pius's appalling Bull fifteen years ago, telling them that they court damnation if they obey our queen's laws. He virtually invited them to murder her! And lately – did you hear of it? – a leading Protestant in Holland has been assassinated. That was, well . . . an example, so to speak. A pattern that might be followed, as a woman follows a pattern when she makes a new gown or a mason follows a design for a new house.'

I nodded. The anxiety had been so great that Acts of Parliament had been passed to relieve it. The Act for the Surety of the Queen's Person had been the first one and then it was backed up by the Bond of Association, whose signatories were duty bound to hunt and kill anyone who conspired against her majesty. I knew all this; everyone did, for it had been cried in the streets of every town. It was meant to frighten off any would-be assassins.

Walsingham said: 'The Council has taken every precaution we can think of. But still, the fact remains that there are people who can be excited, led on, by dreams of glory and rich rewards or on the other hand by dreams of holy martyrdom, of dying for a cause. How many Acts of Parliament does it take to discourage them?'

I said: 'You really think that Mistress Hope's suspicions could be justified?'

'I do. In your letter you say that this woman Etheldreda Hope claims to feel as if she can smell something wrong. I know that feeling and it has a habit of being accurate.'

To my surprise, Walsingham then got up and walked round his desk to stand in front of me, looking down into my face, and in his dark eyes I saw something I had never seen in them before: concern.

'Ursula, I don't ask you to take risks. I am suggesting that you accept Mistress Hope's invitation because that way, the investigation can be discreet, and if it turns out that there's nothing suspicious in Chenston after all, well, no harm done. I have no wish to create a heavy-handed disturbance by sending soldiers in to turn a lonely village upside down and interrogate the vicar and the innkeeper or anyone else. It probably wouldn't work, either. I know well enough how country people think. It will be all wide-eyed innocence and oh yes, we hold feasts in memory of King William Rufus but where's the harm in that? Even our vicar, zur, he don't think there be any harm in it.'

For a moment, startlingly, he dropped into a rich country accent. Dropping it again, he said: 'They might even scratch their heads and chew straws and pretend not to understand London speech.'

This time I did laugh and Walsingham let himself smile. 'Nor can I very well arrest an entire village and clamp the whole lot of them into the Tower. There probably wouldn't be room! And all because of a vague whisper from a woman who's aggrieved because she's been called a witch. Caution would be better. Yes, try if you can find out the truth but avoid danger. The queen was horrified by the danger you experienced in Devonshire.'

He moved back to his seat at the desk. 'She would be anxious about this,' he said, 'and she has anxiety enough already. She well understands the reasons for the Act for the Surety of the Queen's Person, and the Bond of Association. She knows that this is for her a time of peril. She is brave, but her fears exhaust her. I only ask you to agree because in the end, her safety matters more than yours. Hers is the safety of this whole realm. However, I can give you a kind of protection. In fact, I have already arranged it. Sir Henry Compton is the lord of the manor at Minstead, an estate close to Chenston. Chenston isn't part of it – it's one of those remote villages that you find here and there, not attached to any greater estate, and it's a mystery how they ever came into being. Chenston actually belongs to the Earl of Leicester – he's the Keeper of the New Forest and at some time in the past Chenston apparently became one of the Keeper's perquisites. But although Dudley attends to such matters as arguments over grazing rights, and making sure that there are always deer there for the queen to hunt, he doesn't concern himself much with the quaint customs of the villagers, though his rent collectors go round every quarter day: that certainly.' Walsingham emitted a small sniff, which might or might not have been a criticism of Sir Robert Dudley.

He added: 'Minstead is near to Chenston anyway and Sir Henry was here at court when Miller brought me your letter. I have already ordered him to pack himself up and go to Minstead, where he is to prepare to receive you and your usual companions as his guests. Such gentlemen as Sir Henry frequently have guests to visit them; it will give you a kind of excuse for being in the district. Sir Henry was annoyed, but he will obey my orders.'

Walsingham looked as though he had rather enjoyed Compton's annoyance. 'Minstead isn't his principal home,' he said. 'Compton has a fine estate in Warwickshire and he doesn't like Minstead, thinks it small and dull. But he has a house there, mostly in the care of a steward. I made it clear to him that for once, he must be in residence. I told him that there are suspicions of conspiracy being fomented in Chenston. I didn't mention forest feasts. You can do that yourself, if you wish; I fancy he must have heard of them. I have ordered him to give you any help you require but not to interfere with you.

He pooh-poohed the idea that any plots could be brewing in Chenston. He even pooh-poohed *me*.' I began to like the sound of Sir Henry Compton. 'I just hope that all you will find is village superstition and tattle.'

I said: 'I can't imagine what sort of plots anyone *could* be hatching, there in a tiny forest village. They can hardly be raising an army!'

'They could be raising money. Or they could be dreaming of the kind of plot that only needs two or three gallant perpetrators. The sort that means three apparently noble ladies talking their way into Mary's presence and three apparently noble ladies leaving again, only one of them is Mary in disguise and one self-sacrificing lady – or man in women's clothing – is left behind to take the consequences. Or somehow getting into Elizabeth's presence as she takes the air, and using a bow or a firearm, or getting near to her and using a knife. The terrifying thing is that such plots might, just might, succeed. The snake may slither where the lion cannot enter. Go, Ursula, and find out if there are snakes in Chenston. For myself, I pray that this Chenston business comes to nothing.'

'How did Sir Henry explain his sudden departure to the queen?' I asked.

'I explained it for him. I told her that I had reason to want a reliable man of substance to be in the area. She agreed without asking for details. She rarely does ask for details when it comes to her safety. She would rather not know. She really is afraid, Ursula.'

'I know how she feels,' I said.

# FOUR

## A Toy Bow and Two Rabbits

I had come across Sir Henry Compton at court, naturally enough, but that isn't to say that I had really met him. We had exchanged a few sociable words now and then, when I found myself standing next to him in the crowd waiting in the anteroom for the queen to appear; another time sitting next to him at a tennis match; once at a reception for some foreign dignitary.

I actually knew little about him. I had heard that he had Catholic connections but he seemed to be in good odour with the queen and her councillors. He was probably one of the many who did have Catholic leanings, but appreciated the prosperous rule that Elizabeth had given to her people and had more sense than to let Pope Pius sway him. He was a qualified lawyer and liked to wear lawyerly dress; no ruff, but wide white bands and a black sleeveless gown. He was neither handsome nor ugly, a little full in the face, his nose just a little long. His eyes were dark and lit up when he smiled. He was currently a widower though he had been married twice. He was in his forties. That was all.

Except, apparently, that he didn't like Minstead.

The distance, as far as I could work it out from looking at the maps my husband had left, was about seventy miles if one was a crow in flight but probably nearer to a hundred miles for us, for I knew the tracks wouldn't run straight. It had taken Etheldreda eight days to reach us, because she didn't want to hurry the foal that was still so very young. Our return journey took much the same time. It included a Sunday, on which we didn't travel far. The little carriage for the luggage and for Hannah who was now Mildred's maid slowed us down more than Windfall, for the foal seemed to grow bigger and stronger with every day that passed, and pranced merrily alongside us all the way.

There was an amusing incident one evening, when we had stopped at an inn and after supper, when dusk was just beginning, Brockley looked out of the window and saw some rabbits playing on a grassy bank just outside. He murmured something and left us, to reappear half an hour later, when it was almost dark, carrying two dead rabbits which he presented to the landlord. Who was pleased enough by the prospect of free rabbit pie to reduce our bill.

I said to Brockley: 'But how did you . . .?' and Brockley said: 'When I was packing, I found Tommy Reed's bow and quiver lying about among my things. I thought then, well, I might get a chance for some sport and besides, I wouldn't want young Harry to get hold of them. It's time he learned archery and I was going to mention it to you, madam. But he must learn it properly, under supervision and with a man-sized bow. He's big enough now. So I brought Tommy Reed's dangerous toy with me. And I had my sport, as you see. I knew that Tommy's toy wasn't as much of a toy as all that.'

Afterwards, I said to Dale: 'Did you know that Roger had brought Tommy Reed's toy bow and arrow along?'

'Oh yes, ma'am,' said Dale. 'He told me he'd like to see how much use it really was.' She smiled. 'There's a boy hidden inside Roger, ma'am, for all he's nearly sixty-six. I know him so well, you see.'

There was just a small gleam of triumph in her eyes as she said the last sentence. Years before, there had been a time when Brockley and I nearly became lovers. It didn't happen and it never would, but there was still a silent bond between him and me, and Dale knew it. She also knew quite well that I was no threat to her, but nevertheless, she was jealous and now her eyes were saying to me: *I know him better than you do. I am his wife.*

I said: 'Well, he's a very good shot. Two rabbits, and in twilight!' and then we said no more.

We reached Minstead towards evening on Monday the ninth of June.

* * *

'Does Sir Henry Compton really not like this house? I can't understand that,' said Mildred as our little party drew to a halt at the gate of the Minstead manor house. 'Why, it's such a pretty place! I would like a house like that one day, though smaller, of course. I wouldn't be at ease in a place that size.'

I gave her a sharp glance. She had come with me from Devon because she was not happy at home with her puritanical parents, especially after she had refused to marry the man they had found for her. It was now my duty to find a husband for her, and if Etheldreda Hope hadn't intervened, I would have already been wondering who among my quite wide acquaintance in the county of Surrey might be suitable.

Back in Devon she had made it very clear what kind of life and what kind of man she *didn't* want, but never said much about the kind of life and man she'd prefer instead. She had fallen in love once, with a quite unsuitable young man, an affair that had ended disastrously. It hadn't told me much except that I knew she was capable of going suddenly head over heels, without warning. I would have to be on my guard about that.

My task would not be easy, for Mildred had no dowry and though not plain, had unremarkable features. Her blue-green eyes, which had a sparkle, and the curl in her light brown hair were her best features. She knew all that she should about the home and the kitchen; her parents had made certain of that. She also had courage and resolution and, I thought, a capacity for deep loving, but that isn't something that shows on the surface. Prospective suitors would have to take the trouble to get to know her before they could perceive that. I had a delicate task ahead. At the moment, she was sitting on the back of her horse, Grey Cob (her parents hadn't approved of fancy names for horses), and looking with great admiration at Sir Henry Compton's despised New Forest home, and she was demonstrating that at least she had good taste, for she was right; it was a pretty place.

It sat on top of a gentle rise. It was half-timbered, the lower storey made of brick, in comfortable earthen colours; the timbers above left their natural brown, not painted black as some people liked them, and the walls between the timbers were stained a dusty pink. The roof was thatched and the thatch swooped between the upper windows, like protective eyebrows. The windows were casements, with patterned leading. I liked it too.

'Well,' I said, 'here is where for the moment, we part, is it not, Mistress Hope? But we'll come to see you in Chenston, very soon.'

Just how we were to go about making enquiries in Chenston had been a regular subject of conversation, not to say argument, throughout our journey from Hawkswood. Rational discussion with Etheldreda was never easy for she really was a muddlehead and it was hard to keep her to the point, but we had finally settled that there could be no question of Etheldreda pretending not to know us. We had to have some reason for going into Chenston and, as Dale pungently put it, *trying to smell out anything odd.* I needed to talk to people there, see what emerged. Later, Brockley intended to spy on their Midsummer meeting in the forest.

I also thought that I ought to talk to the vicar who had so casually dismissed Etheldreda's fears. Perhaps he might take me and Brockley more seriously. I didn't think he would have been so dismissive of Etheldreda if he had known anything to the point, but she might have worried him more than he wanted to admit to her; and since then, he might have made some enquiries and perhaps found out something useful. He might even have done our work for us, I thought hopefully.

However, we must begin by assuming that he had not, and we needed an excuse to make visits to Chenston. Etheldreda would provide that excuse. We had agreed to say that we were strangers who had met her on the road and made friends.

So now, getting into practice, so to speak, we said: 'Keep safe on the very last part of your ride, Mistress Hope,' and, 'We'll call on you in Chenston soon; we would like to keep in touch,' and 'Very likely, we'll exercise our horses in that direction within a day or two.'

Etheldreda looked flustered but as though she were reciting words she had learned by heart, she thanked us for our company, said she had much enjoyed it and that she hoped to see us again soon. Her shoulder pack was in the little carriage and Hannah climbed out to hand it up to her. She shrugged herself into its straps and said: 'Till tomorrow, or maybe the next day; yes, let's say the next day,' and nudged her mule away from us, the foal capering a little on the end of its long leading rein. The rest of us turned towards the open gate to the manor house grounds.

We were a small party, for I didn't want to inflict too many guests on Sir Henry. After all, he hadn't invited us; he was just obeying orders. Now that Etheldreda had left us, there was just myself, Mildred, the Brockleys, Hannah and Eddie Hale, who was there to help Brockley with the horses and drive the little carriage. To look really convincing as guests of Sir Henry, we needed to make a show but this wasn't difficult. The carriage was smartly painted and we all had good horses. Even Bronze, the steady all-round bay gelding who had replaced Rusty in the shafts, had a dish-faced Barbary head and a Barbary tail carriage. As guests of Sir Henry Compton, we looked likely enough.

There was a lodge and the keeper had already seen us and was coming to ask if we wished to enter. I introduced us and yes, he said, we were expected, and his boy would run ahead and announce us. A few minutes later we were drawing up in front of the house and two grooms had come briskly through an archway on the right to meet us.

In moments, the baggage was unloaded and our horses and carriage were being taken off through the arch which presumably led to the stable yard. Eddie went with them. He could be trusted to see that the horses were properly cared for. Brockley was fussy about that, but he knew that I preferred him to come inside with me and Dale. A plump, businesslike man with a chain of office over his black doublet had come out of the front door to welcome us, announcing himself as Hayward, the butler. We followed him up a short flight of steps and into Sir Henry Compton's house.

I had expected the house to have a great hall and so it had, and we were shown straight into it. It was a welcoming place. The day was chilly for summer and there was a fire in the wide stone fireplace. There were tapestries on the panelled walls, rushes mingled with rosemary on the flagstoned floor, a long walnut table, settles and chairs to match and a scatter of bright cushions. Sir Henry was there and had apparently been reading by a window; I could see a book laid aside on the window seat and a branched candlestick nearby, for the weather was not only chilly but dull. The warm spell in which we had ridden from Devon was over.

Our host came across the hall to meet us, looking just as I remembered him at court, in a long dark gown, with white bands at his throat. 'So here you are, Mistress Stannard. And your usual companions.' He gave the Brockleys a nod. 'And this is . . .?'

I introduced Mildred and Hannah. Hannah was at once led away by Hayward, while Mildred, Brockley and Dale remained with me. Sir Henry eyed the Brockleys thoughtfully, but he knew well enough that I treated them as friends rather than servants; that was recognized at court. *Mistress Stannard has her eccentricities, you know.*

We were invited to take off our cloaks and hats and find seats in the warm. Maidservants came to take the discarded outdoor clothes away. Hayward disappeared for a while and came back bearing a laden silver tray which he carried with a great air, on an upturned palm. We partook of wine and meat patties and biscuits with goats' cheese on top. Sir Henry made polite enquiries about our journey. After that, quite abruptly, he came to the point.

'I know why you are here, Mistress Stannard. Sir Francis Walsingham has given his orders and I am obeying them, as is my duty, but I find them very puzzling. I understand that because of something you have been told by a woman from Chenston, you and also Sir Francis Walsingham think that some kind of plot in favour of Mary Stuart may be hatching in that village. Sir Francis asks me not to harass you with questions but to give you any assistance that you need.'

It was difficult to find a suitable reply to this. I did my best. 'I am sorry if all this seems puzzling and very sorry if it's inconveniencing you. But Sir Francis does have his reasons for sending me here. I may be about to go nosing into a mare's nest and will find nothing. Only, if I find a hornets' nest instead, then I may well need help. Please may I rely on it?'

'I bow to Sir Francis' judgement. But that doesn't prevent me,' said Sir Henry, 'from making judgements of my own. I obey his orders, but maintain my own opinions.' He held my gaze, rebukingly. 'I know your reputation, of course, Mistress Stannard. But I have to say that I feel that Sir Francis, if he needed to make enquiries hereabouts, would have done better to send a man. The work that you do, mistress, is better carried out by proper agents, who can travel alone, and can disguise themselves if necessary, as pedlars or charcoal-burners or grooms; or even *be* pedlars or charcoal-burners or grooms, who also carry out secret tasks. Women are not fit for such things.'

That put me into my place, I thought. On a scale of importance and competence, well below pedlars, charcoal-burners or grooms. I smiled as sweetly as possible in the circumstances and said: 'Chance led me into my curious way of life, Sir Henry. Anyway here I am and we must all make the best of it, must we not?'

'Do you, in fact, require any help from me, Mistress Stannard?'

'For the moment, only your hospitality. It is natural for you to entertain visitors. No one will puzzle over my presence and therefore I hope no one will suspect that I am anything more than a guest from court.'

Our rooms had presumably been arranged according to more instructions from Walsingham. Mildred and I were to share one, and also to share the big four-poster bed there, while a truckle bed had been provided for Hannah. The Brockleys were in a small room a little distance away. We found Hannah in our bedchamber, where she had been unpacking not only for Mildred but also for me, at which Dale pulled a disapproving face.

'Have I done something wrong?' Hannah asked anxiously as the Brockleys disappeared to attend to their own unpacking.

'Dale is very attached to me,' I said diplomatically.

'I just wanted to spare her trouble,' said Hannah dejectedly. Her pleasant blue eyes were full of anxiety to please.

'Best not,' I said, but I smiled as I spoke, and Hannah,

relieved, smiled back. Whereupon, to my alarm, Mildred said: 'I'm sorry for Sir Henry. I think he's lonely.'

'See here, Mildred,' I said. 'Don't go falling in love with Sir Henry Compton. He's in his forties, a widower twice over. He has a son in his early twenties, and also some daughters, probably living at his Warwickshire home, unless they've been sent to other noble houses where there are ladies to teach them refinement. At any rate, he is in a position to have all the company he wants, if he wants it.'

'I only meant . . .'

'Please don't!' I said.

The next day we decided to let Etheldreda settle into her home undisturbed while we began by learning about Minstead. Once again, the sky was heavily overcast, but it was dry to begin with. Like most country villages, the place had fields round it and beyond those, as we had already seen when we were riding in, there was some open heathland. We had seen ponies and small cattle grazing there. Mildred had been surprised because to her, the word *forest* meant woodland, but I explained to her that it actually meant a wild area that was kept for hunting. The New Forest had plenty of dense woodland, but it had open heaths as well.

The village itself had one main street and a narrow back lane. At one end of the street there was a church, dedicated to All Saints. During supper the previous evening, Sir Henry had mentioned it and told us that the vicar's name was Julian Robyns and that he was a scholarly man with a love of Latin and Greek, and a good preacher but troubled at the moment with indifferent health.

'Though he cares for his flock conscientiously when he's well enough,' Sir Henry said. 'He's suffering just now from a recurrent fever. The physician who comes from Lyndhurst – that's the town a little over two miles to the south of here – says that it will die out in time. Robyns visits the sick – he may have caught the fever that way – and he will get up in the night to give the last rites to the dying; and babies are baptized promptly.'

'What happens when he isn't well enough?' asked Brockley in his blunt way.

'Oh, we send for someone from Lyndhurst or maybe for Atbrigge, the Chenston man,' said Sir Henry. 'Chenston has its own church and vicar, small though it is. The vicar's name is Daniel Atbrigge. His church is tiny – St Michael's it's called – but there's just about room for all the villagers at one time.'

In the morning, we walked into the village of Minstead. We stepped into the little church, admiring its proportions and Brockley tut-tutted over a black gown which someone had left tossed over one of the benches. There was no one about to give it to, so Brockley picked it up, folded it neatly and placed it on the bench to be collected by its owner, most probably the vicar.

We went out again and strolled along the main street. There were cottages on either side and we also passed a smithy and a pottery. The smith was shoeing a horse while its owner lounged at the entrance, and the pottery door was open; we could see the potter at work on his wheel. A number of women were sitting in their doorways, so as to sew by daylight and nearly everyone we passed gave us a greeting. At the far end of the street, there was a well. As far as we could see, most of the buildings were in good repair and there was a general air of prosperity.

At that point, however, the overcast sky darkened still more and it began to rain. We returned damply to the manor house and resigned ourselves to a day indoors.

We found Sir Henry, who didn't seem to be at all lonely, in close conference with the butler Hayward, his personal man Rob Munn, whom we had met at supper the previous evening, and a thickset, tanned individual with dark hair going grey, who was briefly introduced to us as a combined steward and bailiff, Stephen Fellowes. He exuded efficiency, which no doubt explained why the village looked so well ordered, despite its absentee landlord.

For the rest of the day, which continued wet, we amused ourselves as best we could. Brockley joined Eddie at the stables, while Hannah and Dale brushed and pressed our riding clothes. Hayward showed Mildred and me to a parlour which he said Sir Henry had dedicated to our use while we were with him.

'We call it the West Parlour,' he said. 'The South Parlour is larger and Sir Henry prefers it as it adjoins his study.'

Mildred and I were happy with the West Parlour. We sat under the window and got on with embroidering a matched pair of cushion covers that we had brought with us. Unasked, a maid brought us candles to improve the light on such an overcast day.

In due course we were called to the hall to dine, and afterwards, our host played chess with Munn and I noticed that Munn didn't seem afraid to win, and that Sir Henry only laughed and congratulated him, which improved my estimate of Sir Henry. Mildred and I played cards and eventually there was supper, during which Sir Henry told us something about the track to Chenston.

'I wouldn't like you to get lost, since I suppose you'll want to go there. There's only one real track, though here and there you'll see a few thin paths, deer trails, leading off into the woods. The track's not straight – it used to serve a hamlet between here and Chenston. Another tiny place, so I believe. Grew up round a harbourer's cottage – his sons built homes there and their sons after. Edham it was called – the original harbourer was named Edward or something like that, I fancy. It's said that eventually an outbreak of plague killed nearly everyone in it and the rest packed up and fled. Now there's just a clearing with overgrown humps and some odd bits of stone wall still surviving. But the track still goes round by it and it makes the ride longer. Two miles in a straight line, but nearer three, the way the path meanders.'

When we retired to bed, I lay awake for some time, listening to the insistent rain as it blew against the casement, and wondering if we would be able to get to Chenston in the morning. But I slept at last and woke to sunshine and a brisk, drying breeze. Our plans could begin.

# FIVE

## Reconnoitre

I wasn't sure about leaving Hannah, who was still very young, alone in a strange place while we went reconnoitring in Chenston the next day and as she couldn't ride, I offered her the chance to come along on Brockley's pillion. We had tossed a couple of pillion saddles in with our baggage.

Hannah, however, declined. She was new to the business of being a lady's maid and she was very earnest about it. She said she was happy to stay behind and go through Mildred's clothes all over again. There were some mud stains that hadn't yielded to the clothes brush, she said. 'I'll ask in the kitchen if I can have some warm water and a sponge and a basin. And I would like to freshen up her spare ruff. That's something I need to practise.'

'All right. If anything worries you, go and talk to Eddie,' I said. 'He's going to spend the morning cleaning out the carriage. You know him, after all.'

With that settled, we could start out: the Brockleys, Mildred and me.

I had not visited the New Forest before. However, after supper the previous evening, just before we retired, Sir Henry had talked a little about the surrounding woodlands.

'The woods to the west of here, beyond the heath, belong to me and I see that they're managed properly. I have a good forester. But he doesn't touch the forest to the north-east of here. Some of it is mine and some is crown land but it has never been interfered with and never will be, to my mind. It's too wild and ancient.'

The track to Chenston led through that wild and ancient forest, and we saw what he meant.

The track itself was fairly wide, but even so, much of it was overhung by the trees on either side and despite yesterday's rain, it was not too muddy. But this forest was dense. In managed forests, the ranks are thinned. Aged trees are chopped down and others cut for timber; glades are kept open. But here, on both sides, we looked into green depths where huge oaks stood, whose memories, if trees had memories, went back for centuries.

Some of the oaks had girths immense enough to hold doorways and they cast a shade so deep that further in, the green depths faded into darkness. Many were wrapped in ivy, here and there stretching its tendrils from tree to tree. The trees seemed to press upon us, even though the morning was bright and sparkling, a proper summer morning this time, and the forest rang with birdsong: blackbird, song thrush, chaffinch, robin, dove and cuckoo. Their voices echoed from place to place.

Dale and Mildred both sensed the atmosphere, just as I did, and kept turning uneasy heads to look from side to side. Mildred remarked fearfully: 'There might be anything in those woods. Wolves, even!' and Dale let out a frightened squeak.

'There are no wolves in England now,' Brockley told them.

'There might be wild boar,' I said. 'But I doubt if they'd come near tracks or villages. I expect Sir Henry hunts them.'

'He keeps pigs,' said Brockley. 'One of the grooms told me. In autumn, I expect the pigs are turned into the woods to forage for acorns. I wonder if they ever breed with the wild boar.'

This interesting topic at least detached our minds from foolish fears and we argued about it in amiable fashion while the track, which meandered somewhat, led us north-west and into a place where the trees briefly gave way to a single open patch with gorse and bracken and grassy humps and a few young saplings. This was plainly the abandoned hamlet of Edham, for there were bits of tumbled masonry still visible, and the humps and bumps were probably places where grass and weeds had overgrown the rest. The path continued on the further side, veering eastward, and the forest once more closed in. It was another ten minutes or so before we arrived at Chenston.

It was very different from Minstead. It lay in a slight dip, which meant that as we came into it, we saw it more or less from above. Unlike Minstead, it had no heathland around it. Instead, most of the cottages had smallholdings behind them, and a few fields – hay or corn or grazing for animals – though none of these were big. There were no seven-acre meadows here, and the trees crowded to the very edges of these cultivated patches. 'The forest looks as though it was annoyed at having Chenston hacked out of it and wants to get its own back,' Brockley remarked.

'Oh, Roger, *please*!' implored Dale.

Such flights of fancy didn't appeal to me either. 'Well, there *are* people making a living here,' I said. 'Come on.'

As we rode in, we passed a well and then we saw the minuscule church that Sir Henry had told us about. There was a two-storey tiled house next to it, presumably the vicar's residence. The little church had a small churchyard and an arched gateway very close to the south door. After that came the cottages, only about two dozen of them, but they were strung out, for they all had wide gardens round them. They were mostly small, with thatch sweeping nearly to the ground, and I saw a few dormer windows poking out. The main and apparently the only street in Chenston was a quarter of a mile long at least.

As in Minstead, there were a few women spinning or sewing in their doorways, to make use of the daylight. The women all looked alike, I thought; the same round faces, the same round blue eyes and the same tow-coloured hair drifting out of the white coifs. The round eyes stared but whereas in Minstead, the women had called greetings, here in Chenston, they were silent. My spine prickled. The only men we could see were distant figures at work on the holdings.

At the far end, on our right, there were two larger dwellings, side by side. These too were thatched but they had proper upper storeys and their dormer windows jutted from the thatch above. The track here widened to accommodate a second well, and on the left was an alehouse, which must be the inn whose keeper Etheldreda had mentioned. Its sign was a weathered picture of a man with a crown on his head and an arrow in his chest.

The two large houses had long holdings behind them, with vegetables and fruit trees, and they also had adjacent paddocks. A bay cob was grazing in one of them, and in the other, we could see Etheldreda's mule. We knew it was her mule because the sorrel foal with the white splashes was there as well. Between the houses was a gate that gave access to both paddocks.

'That last house must be Mistress Hope's,' said Brockley. 'If the field the mule and foal are in belongs to her and I think it does. I suppose the other paddock belongs to that Nick White she's told you about. I don't think either of them are home. There's no smoke coming from their chimneys and' – he stood up in his stirrups to peer better – 'I can't even see anyone out on their holdings. There are some sheds. They could be in there.' He turned towards the inn. 'What do they call that place, I wonder?'

'Etheldreda told me it's called the William Rufus,' I said.

I was looking about me. Brockley was right. The lack of chimney smoke did suggest that no one was at home in either of those big houses and there weren't any signs of Etheldreda or anyone who might be Nick White out on the land. I didn't want to go prowling about on their property and peering into their sheds. Dale said what I was thinking. 'Ma'am, where do we go to now?'

Where indeed, and what, actually, were we here for? To enquire into the matter of mysterious rites in the forest, to see if they concealed any plots on behalf of Mary Stuart and also to find out if the village housed any such conspirators. We couldn't do much about either unless we could first find Etheldreda and talk to her seriously about possible suspects or any other indications; nor could we just stand about, looking noticeable.

But we were beside an inn and who needs an excuse to call at an inn? Also, the landlords of even the most modest alehouses heard every kind of gossip. Besides, this one actually was a suspect, since the villagers thought he was the leader of whatever it was that was going on in the forest. Here was a starting point, and the day was growing warm. The door of the inn was invitingly open and there was a fence where we could tether the horses.

'Let's buy something to drink,' I said.

There was also a trough. We watered the horses, eased their girths and ran their stirrups up, secured them to the fence and stepped through the doorway of the inn.

The place was empty, though there was fresh sawdust on the cobbled floor and the benches and wooden tables were damp, as though they had just been swabbed. There was a smell of baking bread. Then a streak of light and a rumbling noise led us to a side entrance and outside we found ourselves in a fenced yard where a big dark man with his sleeves rolled up and his shirt wide open to reveal astonishingly hairy forearms and an equally hairy chest was rolling barrels into a chute that presumably led into a cellar.

Another man, just as brawny but flaxen-haired and more discreetly clad, was sliding barrels off a low cart with its shafts in the air. The hefty horse which had presumably pulled the cart was tethered to the door of a stable, while an equally hefty woman, with fat flaxen braids flying free of an untidy coif, was washing its fetlocks.

Brockley cleared his throat and the man with the hirsute chest shoved a barrel down the chute and turned to us. 'Hah! Customers. You're early. Go you inside and I'll come directly. Friends of Etheldreda's, b'ain't you? She said you'd be coming. She described you.' He straightened up, brushing his palms together and looked at me. 'You'd be Mistress Stannard? Etheldreda told me your name.'

'Etheldreda! What sort of a name is that?' enquired the flaxen one.

'Oh, shut your mouth, Hal,' said the hirsute one. To us, he said: 'He's my cousin, I'm paying him for the moment to fetch supplies from Winchester way because the fellow that used to do our brewing has just died. My wife's taking that over but she ain't got into her stride yet. Hal don't know Chenston well. We use a lot of old names, Hal, from the days afore the Conker.'

'Conqueror, Felix,' said his cousin, grinning, and quite unimpressed by the rebuke.

'Does it matter?'

'Maybe not. Are you still holding your Goings On in the Wood? Who'll be the lucky lass this Midsummer?'

'*Will* you hold your tongue, damn you!' shouted Armer. Then, more quietly, he remarked: 'Story goes that after the Conker killed so many good English men at that battle, Hastings, wasn't it, there were a whole lot of widows left, all called Etheldreda or Edith or Winfrith or the like and the Conker made them marry his Norman men, and like enough, them Normans wanted their wenches called Matilda or Cecile. But there's places, pockets, remote like this, where any Normans that took over, well, we tamed 'un, and kept on calling wenches Etheldreda or whatever if we felt like it. This here's a place like that. My wife there, washing Hefty's feet, is called Winfred. Chenston's a world of its own.' He turned to us. 'You coming inside? I got ale and cider, well chilled. Cellar's cold as winter. One of our wenches'll be there to serve and we'll be in directly; we've only four more barrels to manage.'

We went inside and found that a tow-headed girl had appeared and was setting tankards out on a counter. She asked us what we wished to drink and after ordering, we settled ourselves on benches. The wench brought our drinks, pulled tables towards us to put them on and went off into some inner room. We then wondered what to do next.

'We're supposed to be reconnoitring,' I said. 'It sounds as if Etheldreda has told the innkeeper something about us, but if so, what? Has she said that we're here to nose into whatever happens at Midsummer and all the rest of it? And is this man, the landlord here, the master of the Midsummer ceremonies or not? And how do we start him talking?'

We didn't have to. At that moment, he came in, alone, and came straight over to us. Uninvited, he sat down, folded big hairy forearms on the table and without any preamble, said: 'I'm Felix Armer. Etheldreda's brought you here to find out what goes on in the forest at certain dates because people in high places are wondering what's meant by an evil queen.'

'Yes,' I said. 'How do you know?' Was it really going to be as easy as this?

No, it wasn't.

'Etheldreda went off because she was scared of the way folk were getting upset about her mule breeding and saying she'd bewitched it. Just afore she went off, she had a squabble with a couple of women at the well out there. They made the sign of the evil eye when she came past. She told 'em she knew about the talk of evil queens and maybe she'd get someone to come and find out what that meant. That made 'em back off but they didn't look happy. Then she goes away and now she's come back and what happens next? You come riding in. Everyone'll be thinking that you're who she fetched.'

So much for our clever pretence about being chance-met fellow travellers on the way here.

'If you're what she meant by that and I reckon the village will think so, well, I'll tell you now,' said Armer, 'there's some say that I should know who's meant by the words *evil queen*, that mine is the voice that intones prayers to whatever gods may rule the forest and the sky above, asking them to remove this evil queen. Perhaps it is. Or perhaps it isn't. But if it is,' he said, taking on a low-pitched and significant tone, 'the secret's not for sharing.' He grinned, but his dark gaze had no humour in it as it moved from one face to another, studying all four of us. Then altering his tone all in a moment, to something light or perhaps sardonic, he said: 'Is there anything else I can help you with?'

I sipped my cider and thought. Then the obvious answer came to me and I said: 'I don't think you can help us at present, Master Armer. However, we mean to call on the vicar while we're here. His name is Atbrigge, I believe.'

'Him? Dan Atbrigge? He won't help you much. He gave us a sermon one Sunday, all about what he called three wise monkeys. We should hear no evil, speak no evil, see no evil. You won't find much help there, I'm thinking.'

'Thank you,' I said politely and Brockley enquired: 'Do you offer any food? We might be hungry, come midday.'

'This here's an inn. Acourse we offer food. Some of the men come here for their noon piece. Our two wenches are making the bread now. There's cheese, a ham only cut yesterday, mutton ready for the spit or stew out of the stockpot; got bacon in and onions and cabbage.

'We shall be back,' I said, smiling.

# SIX

## The Vicar of Chenston

We rode slowly back through the village towards the church and vicarage. There was still no sign of life as far as Etheldreda Hope or her neighbour Nick White were concerned. The women working in their doorways were still there, taking the same silent interest in us. I tried calling a greeting or two but received no reply. Yet I knew, uneasily, that the round, unsmiling eyes were staring after our retreating backs.

'What's wrong with these people?' said Mildred. 'Oh, I suppose it's because Etheldreda told those two women she was going to bring someone to poke into things. They've decided that it's us, so they stare but they don't smile or call good day.'

'I think we've been labelled Friends of the Witch,' observed Brockley.

'Then let's turn ourselves into Friends of the Vicar,' I said briskly.

The vicarage was a sizeable half-timbered house, bigger than Etheldreda's, its walls partly covered with ivy. We tethered our horses to the fence and went into the front garden. It was laid out as a knot garden, full of bright patterns made of pansies, pinks, cornflowers and marigolds, edged with lavender. Daniel Atbrigge evidently had an eye for design. He must have seen us approach, because he opened the door before we reached it and stood in the doorway as we made our way towards him. He spoke first.

'You will be Mrs Hope's friends.' He used the modern custom of calling married women by the shortened form of Mistress. 'I have been expecting you. Do please come inside.'

He led the way into a miniature great hall, panelled, with doors on either side and a staircase going up at the far end.

The hall, if one could really call it that, seemed clean but unused and had no decorations on its walls. However, our host led us on through another door, half hidden under the slope of the stairs, and then into a parlour. This was a much brighter room, panelled in a lighter wood than the hall, and with diamond-paned windows lit by the sun.

Here, there was a fair amount of comfort, a padded window seat, some wooden chairs with arms and cushions, a settle, two small tables. Though there were still no wall hangings and no cushions on the settle. Our host invited us all to be seated and took one of the wooden chairs for himself. Mildred and I took the window seat while the Brockleys took the settle. 'I am Dr Daniel Atbrigge, at your service,' the vicar said. 'Though I like to be addressed as just Mr Atbrigge. Now, may I know your names?'

I performed the necessary introductions and told him that we were staying with Sir Henry Compton. As I did so, I was taking a good look at Atbrigge. He was slightly built, of medium height and I estimated in the mid-thirties. His thick brown hair, which he wore long and tied at the nape of his neck, had no trace yet of grey. He wore a long black gown, as a man of the cloth usually would. The most striking thing about him was his face. He wasn't exactly handsome but his features were arresting and not without attraction.

His was a thin face, with prominent cheekbones and skin that seemed to be stretched tightly between them and his small, inexpressive mouth. His eyes caught one's attention at once. They were dark grey, deep set, bright and round, with a keen gaze that I found almost disconcerting. It wasn't a comfortable face, I thought – and then, just as I was explaining who Mildred was, he smiled, and his face was transformed on the instant as though the sun had come out from behind a cloud. He exuded goodwill.

'I have to say what a pleasure it is to be entertaining new guests. In this isolated place one sees so few strangers, and I rarely have the chance to welcome ladies of such charm.' He looked about him as though searching for something he had mislaid. 'I have a housekeeper, Joan, who comes in every day. I think she must be making a welcome tray ready for you;

she saw you before I did. In fact, she called to me to open the door. But where she can have got to . . . ah!'

The door opened to admit a short, fat being with a round red face and small, fat hands, which were clasping, respectively, a jug that presumably contained something to drink, and a dish of pie slices. 'This here's all I can do at short notice. Vicar, you get out the cups. I'll put this here jug of cider down on the table.' As she spoke, she was pulling one of the tables near to the vicar, and using her elbow to push the other towards the window seat. 'And this dish of pie can go here. It's rabbit pie; all I had on hand; I've not got going with the day's cooking yet, though there's new bread if wanted. I brought that with me, same as usual. It's barley bread, nice and filling, and there's honey . . .'

'That will do, Joan,' said Dr Atbrigge, though he seemed to be repressing laughter and he had already left his seat and was stooping to get something out of the cupboard. He stood up again with his hands full of pewter tankards. 'We'll serve ourselves.'

Joan retreated, and Atbrigge put the tankards down and began to fill them with cider. 'She's a good soul,' he said. 'Married to Will Orchard, halfway along the street, on the opposite side. Got a family of youngsters to feed but Orchard just isn't a good husbandman, or else he's had bad luck. A fox got half his chickens one night last January and if you ask me, he's slack about sowing his vegetables and his barley patch, so his crops don't get to grow in their proper seasons. So he sends his wife to work for me, and his boys run wild. *Very* wild, I'm sorry to say.'

'Mrs Hope mentioned them when she came to see me,' I said, recalling it. 'She implied that they were wild.'

'They are. I am supposed to teach the children of Chenston, teach them their letters and figures, if not much more, but I never could get the Orchard boys to attend lessons. Joan and Will try to keep the lads occupied on their smallholding.'

'Does Jacky Dunning attend your lessons?' I asked, causing Mildred and the Brockleys to look at me in surprise. 'You weren't there when Mrs Hope talked about the Orchard boys and Jacky Dunning,' I told them. 'He threw stones at her filly.'

'Yes, Jacky comes. His mother makes him. He's still a horrid boy,' said Dr Atbrigge dispassionately. 'I'm always worried that my son, Benjamin, will get in with some of those lads. Though he's got good sense and anyhow he's only thirteen. The Orchards are older; twins nearly twenty, and one seventeen and one fifteen. The twins ought to get themselves married soon; there's one empty cottage with a good-sized holding behind it, going spare. An old fellow died and left no one to inherit. They could have that and divide the cottage.'

Brockley said: 'Perhaps there aren't any girls of suitable age in the village.'

'Oh, there are, but I'm trying to discourage the villagers from marrying each other. In the past they've intermarried so much that I reckon every single one of them is a cousin of some sort to all the rest. You look at them; they're all alike. Flaxen hair, round faces, round blue eyes, same set of the shoulders. We have a simpleton or two, alas. Say what you like about the old religion, its priests did at least keep kin-books. But all that's been swept away now and from all I've heard, the priests here never were very particular. Inbreeding's a bad thing, in man or beast.'

'Felix Armer isn't flaxen with blue eyes,' I said.

'His mother married a man from Salisbury. He came to live with her here and Felix takes after his dad. His wenches are flaxen, though. Felix is no fool; he says he's going to see that the girls wed away from the village.' He smiled again. 'But this is a pleasant place, really. When I needed a quiet living and was offered this one, I accepted and I've been glad. Although . . .'

His attitude suddenly changed. He sat up straighter and set down the slice of pie that he was eating. 'To business. Are you by any chance the people that Etheldreda Hope angrily shouted she was going to fetch to look into what she called goings on? Or was that just a fit of temper and you're simply court friends of Sir Henry Compton, here as his guests, and she met you on the road? That you have arrived just as Mrs Hope reappeared does suggest the former.'

I sensed the others wondering how I would answer and considered insisting that we were merely Sir Henry's friends, here by coincidence, but there was an air of intelligence about Atbrigge. Besides, his help could be valuable. 'Yes, the former,' I said, and waited.

Daniel Atbrigge sighed. 'She went all the way into Surrey to find you, did she? She's as obstinate as her own mule, that woman. If she once gets an idea in her head . . . just what did she tell you?'

I repeated the tale to him, using Etheldreda's own words as far as I could remember them. He steepled his fingers and nodded a thoughtful head. When I had finished, he said: 'Well, it's true that this village has a traditional feast and ceremony in the forest at midsummer. At the solstice, I mean. They hold a revel on the night before the longest day, which is the twenty-first of June. Very unchristian. They ought to celebrate midsummer at the feast of St John the Baptist, four days later. I have preached to them that if they insist on holding such revels at all, they ought to do so on the Christian date, but they don't listen.

'Now, you say that according to Mrs Hope, the leader of these ceremonies – whose identity isn't known – has during the last two years or so been calling the villagers to extra ceremonies on other dates, which are those of old pagan or witchcraft meetings. Apparently, this unknown leader has also been praying to a pagan god to deal with an evil queen. Mrs Hope herself never goes to the Wood – that's a local expression – but she said she was told these things by her neighbour Nicholas White. In fact, I had heard some of it before and I have spoken to Mr White. He told me that it was all true but quite harmless, really just a matter of holding parties in the forest now and then, on dates that were easy to remember. I must say that that was much as I expected. My villagers are simple folk – sometimes almost childlike. Mrs Hope seems to think they're hatching conspiracies but frankly, that's nonsense. They're the most unlikely conspirators you could well imagine.'

Dale said primly: 'But these ceremonies, whatever they are – on the dates of old witchcraft feasts? That isn't very nice.'

'Mr White says that nothing serious happens at these affairs,' said Atbrigge. 'And sometimes it's better not to interfere too much. As long as my flock attend church on Sundays and keep the Christian festivals as they should, I prefer not to be heavy-handed about old traditions. Mrs Hope holds herself aloof from the village and that of course makes her unpopular. It's been worse since her husband died. She resents it, perhaps, and has made up or exaggerated things she has heard about these old customs. The arrival of that filly of hers didn't help. Apparently the animal really was born to the mule. The villagers, of course, were all whispers and mutterings and saying it wasn't possible, it must be witchcraft, but it is possible, on rare occasions. When I was studying Greek as a young man, I read some of the work of a Greek historian called Herodotus and came across a tale of Xerxes, a Persian king who in 480 BC invaded Greece. All went well at first and then a mule in his entourage dropped a foal. It was so unnatural that it was seen as a bad omen. Which it was, for Xerxes. Not for the Greeks! The invasion failed. However . . .'

'However?' I queried.

Dr Atbrigge sighed and let his steepled fingers drop apart. 'I imagine you are thinking that I am too tolerant?'

None of us contradicted him, which was answer enough. He said: 'I was just a child in the days when Lady Jane Grey's parents and parents-in-law were doing their heartiest best to put Jane on the throne and her Protestant supporters were fighting those of Queen Mary, who was Catholic. My father had vivid memories of that time. It came just after the reign of the Protestant boy King Edward. Father said that from one minute to another, no one knew what religion they ought to be following. People were being arrested, beaten, even executed for heresy, for trivial things, for genuflecting in front of the cross one week, and the next week, for not genuflecting. Or for saying the wrong kind of prayers, saying you believed or didn't believe this or that, in the wrong company, things like that. When I said I wanted to go in for the Church, he said he must tell me about that time in detail, so that I understood the dark side of religion. In those days, he said, it was all a horrible screaming mess. It made you want just to go to bed and hide your head under your pillow. A man in bed with a pillow over his head couldn't be accused of anything much worse than sloth which might be a sin but wasn't illegal. And all because too many people were making *too much* fuss about religion. He said, if you do become a vicar, well, as long as your parishioners come quietly to church on a Sunday, don't stick your nose into their private observances. If one or two are hearing Mass when they shouldn't, or making too much of the May Day celebrations, or praying on the quiet to a statuette of Our Lady, let it be. Ride with a light rein.

'When I came here, I had a chance to speak to my predecessor, who was going to retire, and he told me about the forest rituals. He said he'd done his best to put a stop to them but completely failed and he recommended me to leave them alone. So, mostly, except for a few irritated sermons, I have done so. They have other superstitions, you know – the main cereal crop here is barley and every year, when the sowing begins, they always bury a loaf of barley bread at the start of the first furrow. To tell the earth what to do! I've let that alone, too. I am a good Anglican but there is no sense in trying to destroy these old beliefs and customs. Mostly they do no harm and simple people like them.'

He shook a regretful head. 'That was the trouble with Mary Tudor and her heresy hunts; she couldn't bear anyone to think differently from her. Now it's often the same with these earnest Puritans whose attitudes are becoming so prevalent. Though, I grant you, I sometimes think that the Puritans have a point when they study the Old Testament. It is much neglected these days.'

'My parents are Puritans,' said Mildred. 'They used to say the same thing.'

Daniel gave her his dazzling smile, before turning to me. 'Mrs Stannard, let me get straight to the point. I know what Mrs Hope has said to you but believe me, I have no knowledge of any treasonable practices here; I have never heard a treasonable word spoken. I wouldn't expect to. I repeat, these villagers of mine are simple folk and the idea of conspiracies involving mighty powers and affairs of state would just bewilder them. I think all that is nonsense and so I told Mrs Hope, who of course was furious with me. As for the talk of witchcraft, well, I had better use my pulpit to give my flock a lecture on Xerxes. Poor Mrs Hope must have been very frightened indeed, to go all the way into Surrey to fetch you, Mrs Stannard. I evidently didn't realize. I'm sorry that you . . . oh, Benjamin!'

The door had opened quietly and a young boy stood there. He had his father's brown hair, worn long and tied back like Daniel's, but his features were not like his father's. He was a handsome lad, in an ordinary way. He said: 'I am sorry, Father. I didn't know you had someone with you.'

'Have you finished the lesson I set you?' Daniel's voice was suddenly stern. 'Even if you are wondering who my guests are, I told you to complete it before you left the schoolroom, and I do insist on obedience.'

Benjamin held up a book. 'I have finished it as you wished, Father.' He smiled and then I saw that in one way he did resemble Daniel, for it was a smile full of sudden charm. 'I translated that whole page as you said. It's the story about the mule that gave birth, just like Mrs Hope's mule did.'

'Well done!' His father's tone changed at once. 'I hoped you'd like that tale. So now, come in and meet my guests.'

Benjamin walked forward. He addressed Brockley, as the only male among us. 'Are you the people that Mrs Hope said she would bring here because she thinks someone here is plotting treason?'

I appreciated that neat precis. He had made a better job of summing up the situation than his father had, let alone Etheldreda.

'I have told them that there are no signs here of any such thing,' said Daniel. 'This is my son Benjamin, that I mentioned just now. The only survivor of the six my late wife bore to me. I brought her here because she used to grow so tired, being a vicar's wife in a big, busy parish. She said, if she could live somewhere quiet, she and her babes might thrive better. So we came here. We had one living youngster at the time – you, Benjamin, and you did thrive, God be thanked. But the one babe she bore after we came here was stillborn, and killed her. I have been a widower now for five years. Will you stay to dine? I would like it if you would; life here does lack society. Joan will find us something good; she is actually a fine hand in the kitchen.'

'That's kind of you,' I said. 'But we are expected back at Minstead. We must take our leave. This talk has been most enlightening. We are glad to have met you both.' I gave Benjamin a friendly smile and received one back. He reminded me a little of my son Harry.

We left the vicarage and remounted our horses. Then Brockley said: 'So that's that. There's no treason here. The story ends.'

We looked at each other, while Mildred and Dale scanned both our faces. I said: 'Does it?'

'He said it mighty quickly,' said Dale. 'I wondered what made him so sure.'

'It didn't sound as though he'd actually tried to find out,' I agreed. 'He said that when Etheldreda talked to him before she left Chenston to come to me, he dismissed her as just a foolish woman, and that agrees with what Etheldreda told me. It doesn't sound as though he listened to her properly.'

'She is a foolish woman in some ways,' said Brockley. 'But he still shouldn't have brushed her suspicions aside without having a good look at them first. They are too serious.'

'I liked him,' said Mildred. 'He talks so well and his face is so open.'

'Oh, hell!' I thought, although I didn't say it.

# SEVEN

## The Secret Clearing

Just as we were about to ride away, Brockley suddenly said: 'Didn't we really come to call on Etheldreda? Madam, shouldn't we try again?'

'Yes, we should. You are quite right.' I turned Jaunty to face back along the street. 'We ought to see if she's home now. I should think . . .'

I stopped short. My companions had turned their horses as well and Mildred now emitted a gasp, while Dale and Brockley, with one voice, said: 'What's going on?'

At the other end of the village, close to Etheldreda's home, there seemed to be a knot of agitated people. At once, we started back along the street in a canter. The cluster turned out to consist of one man and one woman and half a dozen boys. Two of these were a pair of well-grown, tow-headed identical twins with belligerent expressions on their round, blue-eyed faces. Beside them, were two younger boys who looked like their brothers.

The Orchard boys, I surmised. The fifth boy was a lanky youth about the same age as the twins and the sixth, easily the most truculent of them all, was a thickset lad with a touch of ginger in his hair. He was about Benjamin's age, I thought but quite without Benjamin's charm. He was shouting aggressively about something and pointing at the field where the mule and her foal had fled to the far side and were looking back towards the gate, heads raised; frightened. The disturbance had attracted attention from some of the cottages, where the doorways were now crowded with women, indulging in what I felt must be their favourite occupation: staring. Felix Armer was standing at the door of his inn, arms folded, also staring.

The boys were facing the gate to the two paddocks. The

woman in the group was Etheldreda, who was standing like a creature at bay, with her back against the gate and the man was beside her, a friendly arm round her shoulders. He was very likely Nick White, I thought, though if so, he came as a surprise, for I had somehow visualized him as young and he was actually middle-aged and plump round the middle.

Brockley, who had spurred ahead of us, shouted: 'What's going on here?' The aggressive lad stopped shouting, but turned and stood glowering at Brockley, small jaw thrust forward, small hands on sturdy hips.

It was one of the twins who answered. 'We don't want that there unnatural beast in the village. It ain't got no right to live, coming out of a mule, that's agin the laws of God and nature.'

'They were throwing stones! We saw them and came running!' cried Etheldreda. 'No one else did! Look at all them women, just gawping.' She pointed indignantly at one of the audience in the cottage doorways. 'You there, Cat Dunning, why don't you haul Jacky away by the ear and give him the larruping he needs?' She swung round to glare at me. 'Now you see what I have to put up with. This is Nick White that I told you about!'

'You will be Mistress Stannard and her people,' said the middle-aged man. At close quarters I reckoned him to be over fifty. His short hair was iron-grey and his face was heavily lined. 'I ordered them to go but they wouldn't.'

One of the twins laughed. 'Why should we? We don't fear you, even if you are Old Nick.' All the boys laughed, with abandon. Nick looked as if he had heard the same bad joke too often before.

'We looked for you earlier,' I said, 'but you were nowhere in sight.'

'We were in my shed,' said Etheldreda, 'cleaning some of my spades and trowels and sharpening scythes. But then we went out to do some weeding and we saw them! At the gate here, throwing stones, and my poor mule and Windfall galloping away in fright so we ran here to deal with them and when we got where we could hear them, this brat Jacky Dunning was saying to those Orchard boys, let's climb over the fence. To get at my poor Windfall, of course.'

'Here, who're you calling a brat?' demanded ginger-head.

'Almost anyone who ever met you, I should think,' said Brockley.

'We meant to call on you,' I said to Etheldreda, 'so here we are. As for these . . .' I looked angrily at the boys.

'You had all better go home,' said Brockley, regarding them coldly. 'The Dunning *brat* and what I take to be four Orchards, and you as well.' He pointed at the lanky youth. 'What's *your* name?'

'What's it to you?'

One of the female audience in the cottage doors obligingly called: 'He's Matt Graver and what be you about, Matt, when you ought to be out with your dad on the land?'

'Indeed? Then maybe all of you ought to be out with your dads on the land!' barked Brockley. 'Get to it! Now! We'll be here for a while so don't bother to come back. If that really is your mother there, Jacky, where Mistress Hope pointed just now, then go to her at once and ask her to mend your manners for you. Go! I said *now*!'

He moved his horse towards them while fingering his whip suggestively. Glowering, the boys all turned away and dispersed.

I said to Etheldreda and Nick White: 'We are to dine at Minstead, but we would like to talk with you both before we ride back. Mistress Hope, can we go indoors?'

'There's so little I can do to help Etheldreda,' said Nick, when we were in Etheldreda's parlour. It was south-facing and sunny, and the square-leaded windowpanes cast a chessboard shadow on the floorboards. Both Etheldreda and Nick had slippered feet because they had removed their muddy boots on the way in. They were both dressed for working on the land, Etheldreda in a dun-coloured wool dress with a chemise of unbleached cotton and a somewhat grubby white coif; Nick White in a coarse shirt and dusty black breeches with a sleeveless leather jacket on top. We were once more being regaled with cider. I was beginning to think I had better not empty my tankard, or I might topple out of my saddle on the way back, however well designed the saddle might be.

'I try,' said Nick, 'but one middle-aged man can't do much when confronted by a pack of hefty youths and that hateful brat Jacky. He's got powers of leadership, has Jacky, but if he doesn't learn how to use them properly, he'll end up on a gibbet. We can't keep poor Windfall in the stable all the time. She needs the meadow and the green grass. I just don't know what to do and nor does Mistress Hope.'

'As soon as she's weaned,' said Brockley 'better sell her at the next horse fair. She's obviously halter broken.'

'There are fairs at Lyndhurst,' said Etheldreda. 'But I'd get more for her if I sold her full grown and broken to saddle.'

'If she lives that long,' said Nick White grimly.

'I only advise,' said Brockley.

I said: 'I agree with Brockley. But it wasn't Windfall that we came here to discuss. I want to ask you something. Master White, I believe that you attend these forest meetings – you go to the Wood, as Mistress Hope calls it. Where is the clearing where the meetings are held? Where the Midsummer one will be, in two weeks' time. Master White?'

Nick White looked more unhappy than ever. He avoided my eyes and shuffled awkward feet among the rushes on Etheldreda's floor, while Etheldreda bit her lip. She too looked away from me.

'What is it?' I asked sharply.

'He won't tell you,' said Etheldreda bitterly. 'And I've never known.'

'I can't,' said Nick. 'Not unless I am taking someone to be entered as we call it. The lads and lasses don't start going till they're thirteen or fourteen, just turning into young men and women. You know what I mean. They're not supposed to know of the place till then. Likely enough they do, but everyone knows it's not to be talked about.' He looked at me, sadly. 'I am weary of it all and I think I won't attend any more. But the oaths I swore still hold. I can't break them.'

'What would happen if you did?' Mildred asked, in bright, enquiring tones, and Dale muttered: 'That's what I'd like to ask.'

'Something would happen to me,' said Nick. 'Not then, not at once. But after a while, something.'

'You mean they'd murder you?' snapped Brockley.

'They say not. They say that . . . those who betray them just come to harm. There was a young fellow, a cousin of the Orchards, who thought it was all a laugh and he boasted he was going to tell though he didn't say who. He boasted right out loud, there at the end of one meeting. There'd been wine – I can say that much – and I reckon it went to his head. He had an accident with a scythe, just three days later. Slipped while he were cutting hay . . . the scythe went into his upper leg somewhere and he yelled for help but he bled to death. There were others haymaking, of course, but no one got to him in time.'

'But if no one was near him . . .' I began.

'He were just by the edge of the field, right at the edge of the forest, and some of the others, his father and his brother, said they thought they did glimpse something or someone, just a glimpse, out of the corners of their eyes. They had their minds on their own scything, of course. No one knows if he ever did tell any secrets,' said Nick, 'but if so, *they* haven't passed on what they know.'

I sat very still, feeling a familiar coldness creep over me. Etheldreda had been right. There was something dangerous, about these Goings On, however much Daniel Atbrigge might dismiss them. I said: 'Does Master Atbrigge know any of this?'

'Yes,' said Etheldreda. 'He says it was just an accident; you have to be careful with scythes.'

'We won't ask any more questions,' I said.

'If we're to find out what goes on at these secretive events,' I said as we rode back towards Minstead, 'then we need to see them – to spy on them, I suppose you'd say. But we can't do that, unless we know where they're held. We have two weeks in hand. We must do a little prowling in the forest around Chenston. The clearing will be easy enough to identify, I expect. If there are regular bonfires there, there'll be signs.'

'And you, madam, will not do the prowling,' said Brockley. 'I'll do it. Don't worry; I shall be very careful. I'll go on foot.'

'It's a funny little village,' said Mildred. 'Is it the vicar's entire parish, do you think? He has a very small one, if so.'

'You'll have to ask him,' I said. 'Or else ask the Bishop of Winchester. I should think it's within his diocese. Now we'd better trot. Otherwise we'll be late for dinner.'

'Where has Roger got to? The weather was dry enough when he set out but look at it now! I don't like to think of him out in that. Ma'am, I'm growing worried,' said Dale nervously, peering out of the window of the Minstead parlour, though there was little to be seen through the downpour outside.

The four of us, Mildred, Dale, Hannah and myself, were trying to settle down to some needlework, with the help of candles, which were badly needed. Hitherto, the weather had been good, and today too had started fine. For the third morning in succession, Brockley had set off on foot to search the forest around Chenston. But as the morning wore on, the sky had clouded over, grown very dark and given way to a heavy rainstorm. And Brockley was still out.

Hannah looked up from a small and simple piece of embroidery I had given her so that she could begin to learn the art. 'Surely he'll have taken cover. Wouldn't he find somewhere – a hollow tree or something?' she suggested kindly.

'I hope so. He's been searching so hard and it's very exhausting, going on foot in that forest,' Dale said. 'He says it's all tree roots and ivy and it's so easy to lose your way and go round in circles. What about the first time he went out on this search and wasn't home for hours because he did lose his way? He almost got to somewhere called Lyndhurst before he came to some fields and a farmhand directed him to the track for Minstead,' said Dale unhappily.

'He'll come back when the rain stops,' I said soothingly. 'Hannah is right; he'll have found shelter.'

The wind blew rain against the windows, so hard that it sounded like an assault on the house, an attempt to get in.

There was silence for a few moments, while we all bent our heads over our sewing. Mildred and I put a few more stitches into our cushion covers and Dale went on repairing the embroidery on one of my sleeves. Then Mildred said: 'I asked Sir Henry about the size of that Chenston parish. I thought he might know and he did. He said that Dr Atbrigge had applied for it just because it was small and his wife needed a quiet life. It seems that Dr Atbrigge sometimes replaces Dr Robyns when Robyns is ill and so he and Sir Henry know each other quite well.'

There was something in Mildred's face and voice when she spoke the name of Atbrigge and I looked at her warningly. She laughed. 'Mistress Stannard, if I ever say anything about any man we have met, or show any interest in him, you immediately think I am going to fall in love with him. Please don't worry so. I haven't forgotten . . . well, you know.'

Not long ago, back in Devon, Mildred had been in love, passionately. It was a mercy that in the end she hadn't married the young man in question but she had come very near to it and she was still grieving over him. She made no public exhibition of it, but sometimes, during our journey home, since we often slept in shared beds, I had heard her softly crying.

What troubled me about the business was not the natural grief for a lost love but the alarming suddenness with which she had fallen in love in the first place. It was a disconcerting trait.

But I didn't have long to consider it, for at that moment a worried-looking maidservant appeared in the doorway. 'Mistress Stannard, Mistress Brockley, it's Master Brockley. He has just come in by the kitchen door and he is soaked. He says he can't come upstairs dripping and squelching but . . .'

We didn't hear what else she had to say for Dale at once rushed out of the parlour and the rest of us followed and were hastening down the nearest back staircase, making for the kitchen quarters, before she had time to say it.

We found Brockley in the kitchen, surrounded by agitated servants. He was as wet as though he had fallen into a river. He had taken his hat off and his thinning hair was plastered to his head like strands of pondweed. His jacket and breeches were drenched. His boots were squelching. And he was deathly pale and shivering violently.

'The rainstorm caught me!' he said to us. He closed a damp hand on my arm, drew me aside and in a low voice, so that only I could hear him, he said: 'I've found the place. I can find it again. I was coming back. I'd got to that abandoned village where the track widens out so I was out in the open and all of a sudden the heavens just burst! The coldest rain I've ever felt! And the heaviest! I was soaked in half a moment. It's the month of June and that rain was like liquid ice! So I started to run for home but it seems a long way on foot and the rain just went on and on. I'd best get dry and . . .'

'Get to your bedchamber,' I said. 'Squelch and drip on the stairs, it doesn't matter!' I turned to the others. 'Dale, go with him. I'll arrange a hot bath if I can.'

I addressed the nearest of the servants, a sensible-looking woman with a wooden spoon still in her hand from whatever task Brockley's arrival had interrupted. 'I have no business to give orders here, I know,' I said to her, 'but it would be well if Master Brockley could have a bath. Who can see to that? Who must I ask?'

'The housekeeper, Mistress Daker. Or Hayward,' said the woman and then looked past me. 'Hayward's here!'

'I heard a commotion,' said Hayward from the doorway. 'What is the matter?'

'My manservant, Master Brockley, has been out on foot and has returned drenched from the rainstorm. He is soaked and shivering. I have sent him upstairs with his wife, to get out of his wet clothes but he ought to have a hot bath.'

'Shouldn't Master Brockley have a hot drink too?' said Mildred.

'He certainly should,' I said and Hayward promptly turned to the maids and began to snap out orders about mulled wine and hot water and then went to a door, leant through it and shouted, which caused two manservants to appear. He told them to carry a tub up to the Brockleys' room and then turned to me. 'The bath will be ready within half an hour. I will send some mulled wine up at once and one of the maids will bring up the soap and towels.'

'The clearing isn't so very hard to find,' Brockley said when, eventually, bathed and dressed in warm dry clothes, his feet in slippers and his hair only slightly damp, he had joined us in the parlour. 'Once you know the way, that is! I went wrong from the start. I reckoned I'd have to work round the village, but I didn't know where to begin, so I guessed and started with the eastern side, when I should have tried the west. When I did find it, it was further from the village than I'd thought likely. There is a path, but it's narrow, faint, begins from the village just behind the inn but you'd need to know it was there before you'd see it.'

'You weren't seen, were you?' Dale asked anxiously.

'No, no. I didn't find the path at the village end. I stumbled on it in the forest, halfway along and followed it and it led me to the clearing. You can't mistake the place; there's a great big ring in the centre with burnt ashes in it, and there's a stack of firewood, under a leather cover. At one side of the clearing there's a dais, if you can call it that, made of stones, with an oak chair on top and a patch of flat paving in front. It was stained and I've seen that sort of staining before.'

He paused, and I said: 'When you were a soldier?'

He nodded. 'Yes, in France, long ago, but I haven't forgotten. But about the clearing. Behind the dais affair, there's a little hut, quite pretty – carved with animals, stags and goats mostly – and painted. I looked inside but there wasn't much to see; what looked like a bed frame, up on end, leaning against the wall, and there was a shelf with some big jugs on it. There's a rear compartment, at least, there's a door, but it was locked; I couldn't get in. Then I traced the track back and it came out, as I said, behind the inn. I just peeped out from among the trees. I went back to the clearing and part way round it and found another path, leading south as far as I could tell. I followed it and it came out at the ruined village. I'll use that as my route at Midsummer, when I spy on the ceremony or whatever it is that happens there. I don't at all like the look of that staining . . .'

He shivered and I looked at him sharply. Mulled wine and hot water notwithstanding, he still looked cold. I sent Dale for more mulled wine.

I hoped that Brockley's wetting would have no lasting ill effects, but I was wrong. In the morning Dale came to me, looking grave. 'It's Roger, ma'am. He was restless all night; I've scarce had a wink of sleep and this morning he's burning hot and muttering; he's not in his right mind. He had to come a long way, on foot, drenched and freezing and now . . .'

'I'll come,' I said, scrambling for robe and slippers. 'And I'll ask Sir Henry to send for a physician.'

# EIGHT

## Outcome of a Downpour

Brockley was only really ill for two days, but those days were alarming. His fever ran high and sometimes, I saw, with sorrow and guilt, just how old he was. I had glimpsed it before, yes, but never as forcefully as this. He was in his mid-sixties. He had shared fear and danger with me over and over again; he had undertaken lengthy and exhausting tasks for me, he had had to watch, heart in mouth, at times when I and sometimes his wife Frances Dale were in peril of our lives. I had worn him out, I thought. And now . . .

Fran moved into a truckle bed beside him so that he was free to be restless, which he was. For two days, he could not eat, but only drank well water and sips of small ale and he would not let any woman except Dale perform personal tasks for him, such as changing his bedgown or helping him off the bed to relieve himself. On the second morning, when I tried to offer him a fresh bedgown, he hit out at me before collapsing back on to the bed and I had to wake Dale, who had been up ministering to him for half the night and was now snatching some sleep. I left her trying to help him, though obviously exhausted, and went in search of Sir Henry.

'We need the help of another man,' I said, and Sir Henry granted us the services of a sandy-headed lad called Watt. Watt was amiable and strong. When, a few hours later, Brockley mumbled that he needed the privy, got out of the bed on his own but then fainted and fell to the floor, Dale at once called Watt. According to Dale, Watt picked Brockley up effortlessly, saw to his needs and returned him to his bed with competent ease. For the rest of the time that Brockley was ill, Watt was a blessing.

We were grateful to Sir Henry. 'I cannot approve of a woman leading a life such as yours,' he said to me frankly, 'but I suppose I ought to remember whose daughter you are said to be, and whose sister. I fear that I can't expect a sprig of the Tudors to be a pattern of meek womanhood. And in any case, I have a duty as a man to do right by your manservant.'

The doctor arrived on the first day, having been fetched from Lyndhurst. Dr Stone turned out to be a sensible man with a pleasant countryman's accent. We had brought with us a few medicines of Gladys' making, and were already giving Brockley doses of her willow-bark potion though without much result. Dr Stone approved of this and supplied us with a stronger version of it which he said might have more effect. However, he also wanted to bleed the patient, which Dale and I stoutly resisted. Brockley didn't need to be weakened. I was sure of that (Gladys would have said so; I was sure of that too).

Stone was annoyed, but was slightly placated by our willingness to take his advice about seeing that Brockley had plenty of milk or well water to drink and our assurances that someone would always be in the room with him. He wanted, however, to know how the illness had begun.

We had not told Sir Henry what Brockley was doing when he was out on foot in the forest, but he had guessed that it was something to do with our mission. Somewhat irritably, he said to me: 'I am not asking questions but I know your reputation, Mistress Stannard; I know that you and your – retinue – have run into danger in the past. Please try not to run into it now. I have no wish to find myself with corpses on my hands.'

I sympathized with Sir Henry and I was also grateful to him. We were here on Walsingham's orders, which were virtually the commands of the queen; he had been told to help us and he was doing as he was bid and very competently at that. Before Stone arrived, he said to me that if the physician asked what had happened, and we didn't want to talk about it, we would need a story for the doctor's benefit. If so, he could offer us one.

When I agreed, he said: 'Say the fellow was exercising a horse. It threw him, and that's how he was caught in a cloudburst. He had to walk miles to get home. The horse came back to its stable unharmed but the same can't be said of its rider. How does that sound?'

Brockley, who was proud of his horsemanship, would be annoyed but it appeared to satisfy the doctor and he asked no further questions. Sir Henry, however reluctantly, was proving himself a very good aide.

The stronger version of the willow-bark medicine worked. On Monday night, Brockley dropped into a sound sleep and woke on Tuesday, saying that he felt better. Fran was overjoyed and came to fetch the rest of us. Brockley looked at us apologetically.

'I have been such a nuisance.' He was slightly husky but no worse. 'I am sorry.'

'You're never a nuisance.' Dale perched on the bed beside him. He turned and burrowed his head into her shoulder and said: 'I've been wandering in a mist. The only real thing in it was your voice. You must have talked to me sometimes.'

'Often. Often,' Dale said. And if, as she glanced towards me, there was once more just a glint of triumph in her blue eyes, I didn't grudge it to her. What was between Dale and Brockley was the link of man and wife. What was between him and me was Might Have Been, but nothing more. Otherwise we were lady and manservant and always would be.

I said: 'I'll arrange some broth for you.'

Dr Stone called again that morning, and after noting Brockley's improvement, said he wanted to talk to Dale and me alone. I took the three of us to our parlour. He faced us gravely and it turned out that our pretty tale of a walk in the rain after a fall from a horse had been wasted.

'Mistress Stannard, I know something about you. I know that Roger Brockley is your manservant and that his service to you has at times been demanding – even dangerous.'

Dale cried: 'Indeed it has!' and then stopped, looking apologetically at me. I didn't reprove her. 'It's perfectly true,' I said.

'Exertion of that kind would be most unwise, for quite a long time. I ask no questions concerning your purpose here, nor do I wish to know exactly how Mr Brockley's accident really occurred, but his fever is very like the one that the

Minstead vicar Dr Robyns is suffering from at present. Getting caught in the rain may have started it up but I think it is the same thing and it may recur. I will leave a good supply of willow-bark medicine with you. That's all,' said Dr Stone, and looked at me with warning in his eyes.

It was Tuesday, the seventeenth of June. I thought about it, getting my dates right. I remembered what Daniel Atbrigge had said about the Midsummer feast. According to him, it was only four nights away, since Chenston's idea of Midsummer was the longest day, the twenty-first of June. I had already known that this was called the solstice, as that was something else I had learned from my cousins' tutor. Chenston would hold their feast the night before. That meant that it would be celebrated, if that was the right word, on the night of the twentieth, Friday night. There was no way at all that Brockley could be there to spy on the Goings On in the forest.

'I might be able to get to the Midsummer feast if I rest for two days and then practise riding a little,' said Brockley when we went back to him. 'If I make an effort, I can do it.' He was sitting up in bed, propped on pillows. Dale and I had just brought him some supper. 'I'll ride most of the way,' he said, 'and leave Firefly tethered at that ruined village – Edham, isn't it? I found a good hiding place beside the clearing, just opposite the path that goes to the village; it's a big hollow oak. One could hear and see quite well from there. It's my duty and . . .'

'Absolutely not,' I said, while Dale gave a whimper and added: '*Please* not, Roger. *Please* not!'

'I forbid it,' I said, 'even if we have to lock you up to make sure you stay put.'

'But when will the next opportunity come? We'd better ask that Nick White. If it's Halloween, will Sir Henry want us here that long?'

'It's more likely to be Lammas, and that's only a month and a bit away,' I said. 'I will ride over this afternoon and talk to Master White. Anyway, Sir Henry will have to keep us here if Walsingham orders it.'

'You sound very amenable, madam.' Brockley knew me far too well. 'I know that I'm not fit, but I hope you're not planning to go instead of me. You must not. There is something about this business that I don't like. I didn't like those stains on the paving in front of that dais. And now,' he added suspiciously, 'you are smiling.'

'I am always amused when you address me as madam even when you're bullying me.'

'I bully you, as you call it, for your own good and safety. There's no lack of respect, madam, just the opposite.'

Our eyes met. To look at him, I had turned so that Dale couldn't see my face. I hoped that she wouldn't be aware of the secret messages we were exchanging. It was one of those occasional moments that we had shared through the years. One of those Might Have Been moments. I adopted a brisk tone of voice and said: 'I did think of Eddie, but it wouldn't do. I didn't employ him for such purposes and it wouldn't be fair.'

'I agree there,' said Brockley.

Eddie – his full name was Edward Hale – had been just a boy when he first came to Hawkswood as an under-groom. He was a young man now, full of vitality, good-humoured and often resourceful, as he had demonstrated several times during our journeys to and from Devon.

It had been Eddie, early in his time at Hawkswood, who had recommended that when travelling, if we were taking any kind of wheeled vehicle, we should carry ropes with us. Then, if the wheels were to stick in deep mud and even unloading baggage and passengers didn't work and nor did sacks under the wheels, we could harness our riding horses to the shafts. He was also better than Brockley at successful knots. He had an uncle who was a seaman, he had told me once, and the uncle had taught him about knots.

But in my service, he was a groom. He wasn't paid to take risks, which Brockley was. He and Brockley were quite different anyway. Brockley too had originally been taken on as a groom but from the very beginning, though he was always respectful, he had never hesitated to disapprove aloud of some of the things I did. Until, that was, his latent sense of adventure was awakened and then no one could have been a better comrade.

Behind Brockley's steady blue grey eyes and his high, calm forehead with its spattering of gold freckles, lurked an astonishing lust for adventure and a remarkable gift for surviving it. Eddie, on the other hand, would never dream of criticizing me, and I had not detected lust for adventure in his nature. He was capable and bright but no, I couldn't send him to spy on the Midsummer feast as Brockley's replacement.

Brockley was watching me. 'Promise me, madam, that you will not attempt to go to the Midsummer meeting instead of me. You must not run such risks.'

'I promise,' I said, sounding serious. 'I shall ride to Chenston today, and see what Nick White can tell me about the next meeting, whether it's Lammas or not.'

Our eyes met once more. I smiled into his. 'I *promise*!' I said.

I was lying. However, I would see Nick White first. There was good sense in that. If the next meeting was indeed to be Lammas, I might have to talk to Sir Henry because we might need to stay on for it. But if I learned anything to the point at Midsummer, perhaps there would be no need to bother about the Lammas feast at all.

I took a snack in lieu of dinner and then, leaving Dale and Hannah to look after Brockley, and reminding them to call Watt if necessary, I rode off to Chenston with Mildred for company. The rain was a memory now. This was the world of June, full of foliage and wildflowers and birdsong and the shadows under the ancient trees were not so dark today; they were a deep underwater green, promising not unknown danger, but shade and coolness.

We were concerned, though, as we drew near the village and came in sight of the nearer smallholdings, to see that the rainstorm had done damage. There were broken fences and beaten-down crops and one barley field, which lay at the foot of a slope, was flooded.

'That's dreadful,' said Mildred earnestly.

'More than dreadful,' I said, 'there will be families with no barley to make bread, no vegetables to take to market. They'll go hungry unless their vicar steps in to help.'

'Would he?' Mildred asked innocently.

'Well, they're his flock,' I said, as we trotted into the village street. 'Being charitable is part of his profession, after all. Chenston's been unlucky by the look of things. We've exercised our horses round Minstead and we didn't notice anything amiss there, but the land there may be better cared for and better drained by nature. What's that noise?'

The noise was coming from the far end of the street, and as once before, we could see a cluster of people there. 'Not again!' said Mildred as we broke into a canter.

The gathering this time was right in front of Etheldreda's house and it was frightening. At least half the village seemed to be there. They were bawling abusive things at the house. I immediately recognized the Orchard boys and the lanky Matt Graver and, inevitably, the small but belligerent Jacky Dunning.

But this time the crowd didn't just consist of boys. The Orchard youths and a large shirt-sleeved man with over-long and very untidy yellow hair and biceps bulging through the unbleached linen of his sleeves, very likely their father, were working as a team. They were holding a stout bench between them and obviously intended to use it as a battering ram to open Etheldreda's front door, except that Nick White was on the doorstep, looking terrified but gallantly brandishing a scythe.

As before, there was an audience of women staring from their cottage doors, some with children peering round their skirts. But two women were part of the mob as well. One was young and the other was fifty at least but both their faces were distorted by an identical rage and the pair of them were throwing stones at the house. Looking up, I saw that their target was Etheldreda's frightened face, peering from an upper window. Felix Armer was there, not part of the mob but trying to argue with it, pulling Master Orchard's elbow, shouting at him to step back, to make his sons put that damn silly bench back where it came from, which was inside his inn, and listen to sense. Master Orchard senior was shouting back at him to get off, let us be, we're out to get the witch and you won't stop us. Master Orchard had a carrying voice with a gravelly edge to it; I could hear it above all the shouting of the crowd.

The innkeeper was on the side of the angels, it seemed, but if so he had few supporters apart from Nick. If Felix was the leader of the forest revels, whatever form they might take, he wasn't any sort of leader here. The crowd preferred to follow Master Orchard. Nick was being jeered at and even as we arrived and tried to drive our horses into the crowd to break it up, we saw another group of youths running out of the inn with another bench which they had evidently grabbed from inside it. A moment later I realized that they meant to take it round Etheldreda's house and attack from the rear.

I was shouting *Stop This!* at the top of my voice and someone must have heard me, because the jeers were promptly turned on us, and somebody grabbed at Jaunty's reins to halt him. Felix saw us and bellowed: 'Get the vicar! Get Atbrigge! Damned man's never where he's wanted! Get Atbrigge!'

Without a word, Mildred wheeled Grey Cob and went back along the street at a gallop. I used my whip and the man clutching at Jaunty's bridle yelped and fell away. I went on, pushing Jaunty here and there, trying to reach the Orchards, applying the whip wherever it might do some good and wishing there were two of me (three or four would be even better) because of what the boys with the bench might be doing to Etheldreda's back door. I shouted: '*What are you doing? What's all this?*' at any faces that were turned to me.

Master Orchard bellowed: 'Get away and mind thy business!' and one of the women who were throwing stones, screeched: 'Her's a witch! Her and her familiar, that there unnatural foal! Brought on the rain, flattened our crops, what'll we eat next season? *Witch! Witch!*'

Others repeated the cry, screaming it, hurling more stones and a couple of men bawled: 'We'm going to hang she! Got no pond to swim a witch but we know she'm guilty any how!'

With a sickening lurch in my stomach, I saw that one of these men had a coil of rope flung round his shoulder. He caught my eye and grinned. Half his teeth were missing and the grin was vicious, a row of fangs slashing across his round Chenston face. 'Plenty of trees hereabouts!' he shouted at me and somebody else shouted: 'You'm in the right of it, Pickford!'

Then another man, armed with a long pole, suddenly appeared and thrust his way through the crowd. Before we could try to intervene, he had knocked Nick White off the doorstep. The Orchards, in a chorus, bawled: 'One, two, three!' and charged forward, crashing their bench into the door. I swung Jaunty towards them and swore at them and used my whip again but they paid no heed at all. There were tears of fright and hopelessness in my eyes. Once more, I shouted: '*Stop this! Stop this!*' but no one heeded me. I could hear alarming crashes and bangs from the rear of the house, where the second battering ram had presumably been brought into action.

And then there was a drumming of hooves and there was Grey Cob with Mildred in the saddle and Daniel Atbrigge on her crupper. He added his voice to mine and his voice was much more resonant. When Atbrigge roared *Stop this!* he would have been heard above the worst of thunderstorms. Amazingly, the crowd did stop. The shouts and screeches subsided. Faces turned to him. The women with the stones paused, stones still in their hands. The Orchard family dropped its bench. Staying where he was, because up on Grey Cob's back he had as good a view over his misbehaving flock as though he were in his pulpit, Daniel demanded, in stentorian tones, to know what they thought they were about. 'And what's that noise from the back of the house?'

The battering-ram sounds had ceased but something else had taken its place. A woman was screaming and men's voices were jeering. Then a little group came round to the front, slowly because they were dragging someone. Etheldreda was in their midst, struggling, crying out for mercy and for help. She saw the man with the rope round his shoulder and shrieked louder still, kicking at the shins of her grinning captors. This time Atbrigge didn't stay where he was but sprang to the ground and ran to her. Felix Armer, encouraged by the arrival of reinforcements, did the same. The vicar's presence seemed to abash the men holding her for he and Felix snatched Etheldreda away with little resistance. They brought her to me and heaved her up in front of me. She was shuddering as if with an ague and crying uncontrollably, turning her face into my riding cloak as if to seek shelter there.

'Thank God I found Master Atbrigge quickly!' Mildred said to me breathlessly. 'I didn't know where he might be; in the vicarage, the church, his back garden . . . I started shouting his name before I'd begun to dismount and then he came running out of the church and I said, *Come quick, there's a crowd wants to murder Mistress Hope!* and he was up behind me in a trice . . . oh, look, he's going to *make* them listen.'

Daniel Atbrigge had taken up a stand in front of Etheldreda's gate and was haranguing his parishioners at the top of his voice. '. . . never before have I seen such shameful behaviour. Rainstorms, damaged crops are an act of God. They happen constantly and we must endure them and do what we can to be prepared. As we are! There is a barn where every one of you has stored some of last season's produce against such a trouble as this! Have you forgotten? I told you the story of Joseph in the Old Testament who warned the Egyptians of a forthcoming famine and had stores gathered beforehand. I urged you to do the same. I come of farming stock; I know how fickle the weather can be. Now, cease this nonsense about the mule's foal. You were ready, this day, to kill a terrified and innocent woman because you are ignorant. Let me inform you that mules have given birth before. Not often, that's all. Because something happens rarely, doesn't make it diabolical! Who started this?'

There were mutterings and mumblings and an air of reluctance to answer the question, but finally, Felix Armer said: 'Jem Dunning, he's the one!' and the fellow with the long pole stepped truculently forward and declared that he was Jem Dunning and yes, he had got them all going, by going from house to house, his barley crop was flattened and his vegetable patch was under water, and they all knew that there woman was a witch, whatever reverend might say . . .

'Get back to your home!' roared Atbrigge. 'You wouldn't recognize a real witch even if you found her pushing pins into a wax model of *you*!'

A youthful voice cried out: 'Don't you speak to my dad

like that!' and there was Jacky Dunning, rushing to his father's defence, planting himself in front of his parent, arms folded, and glaring at Atbrigge. There was laughter. And now, at last, the crowd was dispersing. Atbrigge came over to us.

'Thank you, Mistress Gresham, for fetching me. I was at prayer in the church and knew nothing of this till you called my name so urgently. Mrs Stannard, I think you should take Mrs Hope away with you. Take her to Minstead. Perhaps Sir Henry will let you shelter her for the time being. She can return home later, when all this has settled down and I have had a few more words with Jem Dunning.'

Mildred said: 'Where is Master White? He was trying to guard the front door but he was swept aside. He . . . oh, look! He's hurt!' She was still mounted and could see better than any of us. 'He's lying on the ground near the door!'

Atbrigge and Felix ran to him. I pushed Jaunty forward as well. Nick was lying on his back with his knees drawn up and his hands clutched together on his chest. He didn't seem to be injured; there was no blood to be seen but his stillness was ominous. Atbrigge knelt beside him, feeling for a pulse, feeling for a heartbeat. Then he looked up and shook his head.

'*No!*' said Etheldreda. '*No!*'

I held her more firmly and said: 'I think so. I'm so sorry.'

'He sometimes said his chest hurt and he was often short of breath,' whimpered Etheldreda. Tears were running down her face. 'But he can't just have died!'

'I fear so,' said Atbrigge. Mildred clutched her fingers to her mouth and through them, said: 'Oh, how dreadful! The poor man. And he was only trying to protect you, Mistress Hope.'

And this, I thought, was the end of my attempt to coax information out of Nick White. He could tell me nothing now.

'I will have him carried into the church,' said Atbrigge. He looked at us. 'As I said, Mrs Stannard, I think it best to get Mrs Hope out of harm's way, along with her mule and foal. Get them to Minstead.'

Etheldreda was in renewed tears when we set off, towing the foal alongside the mule. She had her essential belongings in her saddlebags or on her back and since Nick White was dead, Felix Armer had offered to look after her chickens and her pig; indeed with some enthusiasm. The prospect of extra eggs seemed to please him mightily. Winfred would make good use of them, he said.

But even through her tears, Etheldreda had agreed when Mildred said, in most fervent tones: 'Wasn't Master Atbrigge wonderful? Getting all that crowd of lunatics to listen to him, and go away!'

# NINE
## Deceiving Brockley

I had begun to think that Mildred was admiring Daniel Atbrigge to a disturbing degree but I had no time to worry about it just then. I had to explain to Sir Henry why I had brought Etheldreda back with me from Chenston, along with a mule and a sorrel and white filly. And, since I could no longer learn anything from poor Nick White, I had reached the inescapable conclusion that, since Brockley was out of action, I must be present at the Midsummer feast.

Which would mean deceiving Brockley. If he knew I meant to go, he might work himself into an outraged fever, or even try to get up and carry out the task himself. At the very least, he would lie awake all that night, worrying.

Meanwhile, Sir Henry was angry when he heard of the near-tragedy in Chenston, and although he had no jurisdiction there, he took three men and rode there on Wednesday to investigate. Exactly what happened, I don't of course know, but when he returned he talked a little over supper and said he hoped he had put the fear of God into the lot of them.

'I told them a thing or two and told Atbrigge a thing or two as well, and Mistress Hope can go back home tomorrow. Neither she nor that foal will come to any harm, I promise you.'

Etheldreda didn't hear this herself. In Sir Henry's mind, she was not of sufficient status to sit at his table. Brockley and Dale wouldn't have been there, either, except that there are certain advantages in being half-sister to a queen. Because of that, I was able to insist on treating them as friends rather than servants. But it didn't apply to Etheldreda who had been accommodated among the Minstead servants and had spent the day helping in the kitchen.

She was reluctant to go home but Sir Henry insisted and

she went back on the Thursday. I sent Eddie to escort her. When he came back, he said that Master Atbrigge had seen them arrive and had met them in the street to tell them that Mrs Hope would be quite safe; Sir Henry had made it plain that she had better be. Master White was to be buried that same afternoon. 'Mistress Hope said she would attend. I think she'll be all right, madam. Looked to me as if Sir Henry gave them and their vicar what for and no mistake.'

'I hope he did!' I said. 'Though I don't think what happened was Dr Atbrigge's fault. He came fast enough to deal with them and he *did* deal with them, very briskly.'

'I'm glad you haven't rushed away to attend the funeral yourself,' Brockley told me that same afternoon. He had not been in a fever long enough to be badly weakened and by now, he was up and had pulled some clothes on. Watt had accompanied him down into the ornamental garden that lay behind the house. Part of it was a rose garden, which reminded me painfully of Hugh, my late husband, who had loved roses so much. Brockley was now sitting on a bench there and I had come to sit beside them. Watt rose tactfully and wandered out of earshot, though he was still where I could beckon to him. Brockley gave me a quizzical look. 'I wish, madam, that I could do my duty this midsummer night. I am sorry.'

'From what Etheldreda has said, there may well be another chance at Lammas, which isn't so very far away,' I said.

'You are very complaisant, madam.'

I sighed a little. 'I'm not young enough for adventures now,' I said. 'And anyway, I can hardly believe that those villagers are entangled in any conspiracies, to do with Mary Stuart or anything else. I feel we should never have come here; that it's all a waste of time. From what Walsingham said when I saw him, he has had enough of Mary and I think he is laying plans to entrap her and bring her to the block. The time isn't quite ripe yet and I'm only here to nose out possible interference. But I seriously doubt that interference, if any, will come from Chenston.'

Brockley looked at me searchingly. 'You mean what you say, madam? I can trust you?'

'Yes, Brockley,' I lied and then we talked of Etheldreda and

Nick White's funeral, which I hoped would take place quietly. I would have liked to attend but thought my presence might in itself cause disturbance. Brockley, with a grim smile, was able to believe that.

The Friday evening was warm, with a clear sky. There was supper, and after that, I played the spinet, to which Sir Henry's minstrel sang. His name, appropriately, was John Singer. Then, as was my habit, though plenty of people laughed at it, I went to the stable to say goodnight to my horse, Jaunty. While I was there I talked briefly to Eddie. I came back to the house and Mildred and I retired at the normal time. Dale and Hannah prepared us for bed, and Hannah went to her truckle bed while Dale joined Brockley in the next room. Then I said quietly to Mildred and Hannah: 'I am going out. You are not, either of you, on any account, to let Dale or Brockley know. You understand?'

'You're going to spy on this Midsummer affair?' Mildred said tremulously, while Hannah sat up in her truckle, looking at me with alarm.

'Yes. I shall ride as far as the ruined hamlet and leave Jaunty there. If I don't return by an hour after daybreak, then you must tell Sir Henry. Otherwise, I'd rather he knew nothing about it. *Much* rather – he might try to stop me. You understand?'

'Yes, of course. But, Mistress Stannard . . .' Mildred began.

'And can I borrow that full-length, hooded cloak of yours?'

'Yes, but . . .'

'If you please, Mildred,' I said, in a stern voice. She looked at me doubtfully and then went to her press. She emerged with the cloak in her arms and said pleadingly: 'Mistress Stannard, I beg you, take care.'

'That,' I said, 'you may rely on.'

Even before we left Hawkswood, I had considered the possibility of something like this. My unconventional way of life had taught me to be prepared for such things and my luggage contained some unusual items for a lady. I had brought with me not only a tinderbox and a lantern that could be adjusted to show only the ground beneath one's feet but also the dagger and picklocks that I often carried concealed in pouches sewn inside my open-fronted skirts. In addition, I had packed a pair of breeches, a man's shirt and jacket, and a cap such as a groom might wear.

My riding boots presented a problem, for I wanted to go downstairs silently and their soles were anything but silent. I put the tinderbox and lantern into a drawstring bag along with a flask of water, and clutching my boots, started for the door in stockinged feet.

'If you go down in slippers,' said Mildred, 'and I come too and carry the boots, you can put them on when you get to the side door. Then I can bring your slippers up afterwards. Hannah, you stay here and wait for me to come back. I won't be long.'

'Thank you, Mildred!' I said.

The two of us crept out of our room and tiptoed down a back stair which was close to our chamber, and went down into a passage that led to the servants' quarters. There was a side door in the passage, and outside, opposite to it, just across a narrow courtyard, was an archway leading to the stable yard. No one was about. I sat down on the lowest stairs while Mildred helped me change my slippers for my boots. I stood up, Mildred whispered *good luck* and retreated with my slippers and I let myself out.

Eddie was waiting for me. He had Bronze and Jaunty saddled in readiness, with a cross saddle on Jaunty and a saddlebag for the things I had brought. He too was in a hooded cloak, though his was not full length. Grooms rarely used long cloaks, which got in the way on horseback. 'It will just have to do,' I had said when I talked to him earlier. 'I trust that neither of us will be seen at all. But if we are, well, I understand that everyone wears cloaks at these affairs.'

Now, I said to him: 'Do the other grooms know why you're not in your quarters?'

'No, madam. It's not their business, anyway. I take orders from you.'

There had been no question of sending Eddie on this mission alone, but taking him as companion was another matter. He was a young man with an engaging grin, short, wiry dark hair that stuck up in spikes, and now and then, a somewhat ready tongue. He was a brawny fellow as well. I would be the better for his company and when invited, he had been eager to come.

The stable yard had a gate opening directly into a side lane leading to the Chenston track. We went out quietly, closing the gate noiselessly behind us, and walking our horses until the lane joined the main track. Then we set off at a canter. To reach the ruined hamlet would have taken perhaps half an hour on foot but on horseback, it took less than ten minutes. Once there, we stopped and dismounted. Eddie had brought halters and long tethers so that we could unsaddle our mounts and leave them secure, but comfortable. The ground was very humpy but there was a long clear space through the midst of it all which had probably been the village street, and we settled the horses there, fastening the tethers to a piece of surviving masonry and putting the saddlery into a nook beneath it, to protect it from rain. Eddie took charge of the bag I had brought.

On the way to Chenston with Mildred, I had taken the opportunity, as we passed through Edham, to look for the path that Brockley had said led from Edham to the clearing. 'I think this is it,' I said when Eddie joined me at the edge of the trees. 'It isn't much of a path but' – I pointed – 'I couldn't find any others.'

'Reckon that's right,' Eddie agreed, looking rather doubtfully at the thread of trodden earth leading into the wood. We set off. I led the way. 'Tread quietly,' I said over my shoulder.

# TEN
## Midsummer

The path was so hemmed in and overhung that until we actually reached the clearing, I wasn't absolutely certain that it was the right one, or even a path at all. As on that first ride to Chenston, I felt that the trees were pressing in on me. I was conscious of them as once I had been conscious of the landscape of Dartmoor when I was lost there on a winter night. Dartmoor was bleak and bare, with granite outcrops and standing stones that jutted from it as though their coverlet of heather had been worn away; the New Forest was a place of ancient trees and impenetrable shadows, but both had the same atmosphere; as though my surroundings were alien entities, as alive as I was, and watching me.

Eddie, at my heels, was silent. I found out later that he had had similar feelings to mine. Well, there were certainly live things around us, sleepy twitterings from birds we couldn't see and once a weasel started out from the left of the path, stopped for a second, turning to show us its white front and stare at us out of fierce black eyes. Then it was gone, vanishing silently into the right-hand shadows.

It was still daylight and we could at least see our way. One moment, we were walking warily along that ghost of a path through trees with clutching twigs and branches; the next, we were in a wide clearing. I could see everything that Brockley had described to me. The stack of firewood under its cover was there, though much of it was now piled up in the middle of the clearing, ready for a bonfire. I could see the chair on its rough and ready dais, and the ornamental hut behind. There were also two things that Brockley hadn't mentioned, for on either side of the dais, there were stone cylinders, about three feet high. Perhaps he hadn't noticed them, because they hadn't then been striking. They were striking enough now, because in each of them stood what was obviously a tall, unlit flambeau.

It was still light, so I said we could risk going across the clearing to look more closely at the dais and the hut. We saw the stain that Brockley had mentioned, on the stone paving in front of the dais. We peeped into the hut and saw that one thing had apparently changed since Brockley was there. The bed he had seen upended against a wall was now set ready for use, with a coverlet of sewn moleskins over it. I withdrew hurriedly, puzzled, and Eddie said: 'Madam, shouldn't we hide now? Dusk is coming.'

'Yes, you're right,' I said. 'Brockley spoke of a hollow oak. Let's find it.'

What we found first, as it happened, was the start of the path that was probably the one leading to Chenston village. I remembered that Brockley had said the hollow oak was on the opposite side of the clearing and I hurriedly led us there.

We found the oak at once. The hollow in its mighty trunk was wide enough for us both. It was a few yards from the clearing and faced partly away from it, but not completely so. We could peep round the edge and have a good view of the chair and the hut. Eddie, like Brockley, muttered that he hadn't liked the look of that there stain on the paved patch.

We sat down to wait. It seemed a long time until at last, the sun set and the warmth of the evening faded like the light. A cool breeze sprang up and I was glad of my cloak. Silence settled round us, except for the rustle of leaves in that restless little wind, and the hoot of a tawny owl, and once, in the distance, the bark of a fox. After a while, Eddie, without saying anything, slipped round to the other side of the tree for a few moments, and after he had reappeared, just as the dusk had nearly faded into darkness, I felt the need to do the same. Just as I returned, we saw lanterns coming through the trees on the far side of the clearing.

By now it was fully dark and there was no moon. It was difficult to make anything out. There were only two lanterns. But presently we discerned two cloaked and hooded figures. They were carrying sacks of something, which they put beside the hut. Then they went to the bonfire. They were talking to each other and a few words drifted to us. One was complaining that the wood was damp, cover or no cover. The second man said soothingly that he had brought the oil flask. Then one of them used the flame of his lantern to light a torch, and thrust it into the bonfire, which ignited with a whoosh, a credit no doubt to the oil. Soon there was a healthy blaze going. The two figures – acolytes? – then lit torches, and used them to light the waiting flambeaux on either side of the dais.

'There's another lantern,' whispered Eddie.

Whoever was carrying this one was alone and when he arrived, the others, who were now bringing some wood from the store and laying it handy, took no notice. This figure, also cloaked and hooded, went straight to the hut and went inside. The flambeaux and the bonfire between them gave us enough light to see him by when he came out again and we both gasped. He was no longer fully human, for he had the head of an animal. He had a snout and . . .

'What's that on his head?' Eddie muttered, sounding horrified. 'Looks like . . . antlers.'

They were a stubby affair; no red stag would have been proud of such a tiny crown, but as the figure mounted the dais and sat down in the throne, the flambeaux momentarily made their outlines clear. In miniature, they were red deer antlers and Eddie actually managed to count the prongs.

'Five each side, madam. Ten-pointer.'

I had recovered myself. 'How mean, for the master of such a grand affair. He ought to have fourteen at least.'

'Who is he?' Eddie wanted to know, but I had to shake my head. 'No one knows. The folk we've spoken to say that no one in the whole village knows. They think it's Felix Armer.'

'Do you think so, madam?'

'Do you know, Eddie, I suspect that it isn't. I've talked to Armer, and besides, when we found the mob attacking Mistress Hope, he was trying to stop them. He just seems to have more . . . more sense than to be playing the fool with an antlered mask on.'

'There are more lanterns, madam,' said Eddie.

There were. The other participants were arriving now though I couldn't identify any of them for they too were cloaked and hooded. There were some slim figures that were probably youngsters, not children, but perhaps in their early teens. One by one they went into the hut and came out with their hoods thrown back, and with faces hidden by animal masks, though not those of stags. Nothing so grand for the mere congregation, I thought. Theirs were goat masks, with straight horns, on a small scale, like the antlers.

The masks, presumably, had been stored inside the locked compartment that Brockley couldn't open. They rested on the wearer's shoulders and they covered most of the face, except for long slits for the eyes and openings for nose and mouth, which were shadowed by the snouts. Even chins were covered. I noticed though that about three of them, the last to come out, had no masks. Probably there weren't enough to go round. But in the doubtful light, with their hoods drawn over their foreheads, their features were still shadowed and I couldn't recognize any of them.

The crowd arranged themselves into a semicircle in front of the dais, between it and the fire and facing the antlered figure on its makeshift throne. When they were all there and standing in silence, he spoke.

I didn't recognize the voice. It was resonant and grating and could have been that of Felix Armer but I couldn't tell. I had only heard him talk at an ordinary volume. This powerful vocal projection had a different quality.

We couldn't hear what he was saying, since up there on his dais, he was too far away. We crept out of our hollow and used the darkness to hide us as we edged to where we could hear better. The Antlered One – that was what I called him in my mind – was apparently welcoming his . . . Worshippers? Flock? Followers? . . . to the clearing, in the name, he declared, of the Horned One, Herne the Huntsman and Lord of the Greenwood, and also in the name of Our Lady – here Eddie gasped indignantly and I trod on his foot to keep him in order – Our Lady Venus, the brightest star in the firmament, goddess of the morning and of the evening, goddess of love and fertility.

That was nearly the end of our mission because in spite of my warning foot, Eddie gasped out: '*The Horned One?*

*That's Satan! And Our Lady was a pure virgin – love and fertility indeed! This is devil worship! Blasphemy – sacrilege!*' and he would have rushed out of our hiding place to bellow his condemnation to the assembly if I hadn't grabbed his arm and yanked him back, so hard that we both nearly fell over.

'It's not devil worship!' I said into his ear. 'It's just pagan.'

'Same thing!'

'No, it's not. Back to our hollow tree. Come on. *Quietly!*'

Somehow I got us both back into shelter unheard and I thanked heaven for the tutor who had told his pupils about the beliefs of our ancient ancestors. I was also glad of the odd legend in my family, of the red-headed king who had died at the hands of pagans, in the year 1100. A part of me was already halfway accustomed to these peculiar ideas.

The Antlered One was continuing. By leaning out of our shelter and straining my ears, I made out that he was speaking of unnatural rains, of flooded fields and ruined crops. He freed both hands from his cloak and raised them, invoking the ancient gods to intervene 'for all our prayers to the Christian god have availed us nothing'. That came out in such a resonant boom that I heard it perfectly well. There were murmurs of *Aye Aye* from the crowd. The Antlered One dropped his hands but, again in that powerful voice, implored his congregation to '*pray too for the safety of a beleaguered queen, and for the confounding of her evil adversary for we fear that while the evil queen lives, the discontent of the gods will continue to trouble us.*'

This time the response came in vigorous shouts and the gathering threw its hands in the air. The Antlered One clapped his hands and from the crowd, four people emerged. I thought they might be female but the long cloaks made it hard to tell. They went into the hut, came out again carrying jugs of what I supposed was wine, and went round the crowd filling cups that were held out to them. The worshippers had presumably brought the cups with them. The Antlered One held out a cup like the rest. Then he announced that they must drink to declare their pledge of loyalty to Herne of the Greenwood and the Lady Venus. '*Raise your cups high and cry their names, and then, my friends, drink the wine of worship!'*

Once again, there were shouts, and people held up their cups and clinked them together before tossing the wine eagerly down their throats.

'Blasphemy! He makes fun of the Communion wine!' muttered Eddie, shuddering and thumping a clenched fist against the wall of the hollow.

'Be quiet! It may be blasphemy but we can't do anything about it. We are here as witnesses and nothing else!'

'And now,' roared that powerful voice, when the sacrilegious toast had been drunk, 'let us give the damaged world the benison of blood, to put life into the fields, to bring forth our crops. And prepare our feast!'

I don't know what I expected then; my imagination was suggesting frightful things. What actually happened, however, was that two people went into the forest, passing uncomfortably close to our hiding place as they did so. They returned after a pause, leading a billy goat. He bleated plaintively as he was led to the paved patch. Whereupon, without any more ceremony, the Antlered One left his chair, stepped down from the dais, took a big knife from under his cloak and while the other two held the goat, swiftly slit its throat. It died before it could bleat again. The Antlered One deftly produced his empty cup and filled it with the goat's blood. The two others laid the carcass tidily down and stepped back, one to each side.

The Antlered One stepped off the paving and stood in front of it, facing the crowd. He held the cup high.

'*Behold! This is the libation of blood, that gives warm, rich life to the earth!*' He upended the cup and the firelight was good enough to show that what streamed from it, to fall on the packed earth below, was red. And the crowd cheered.

It was an ugly sound, savage, fierce and without joy. Beside me, Eddie whispered: 'I feel ill,' and I felt him trembling. I was trembling too. Those people in the clearing were no longer individuals; they had welded into one dreadful creature. A creature that I did not think would be gentle with a pair of spies.

But the ceremony had not ended; far from it. The Antlered

One gave the cup to somebody, who came forward to take it. Meanwhile, the Antlered One resumed his seat on the dais and laid his hands on his knees. And spoke again.

*'That is the offering of blood. Herne's hunt is completed. He has run his quarry down and it lies dead at his feet. Now we turn to a happier offering. This too is a sacrifice; this too is meant to inspire fertility, not through death but through the chance of life. Bring forth the Maiden!'*

I had not noticed that in the front of the crowd, there were three figures seated close together and in front of the rest, but it became evident as they rose to their feet and walked forward. The outer two seemed to be escorting the one in the middle. They came to the foot of the dais and then the escort stepped back, leaving the third one alone. It – I could only think of the cloaked and masked figure as It – looked slender, as though it were young. The Antlered One, however, rose and once more descended from the dais. He lifted the mask off the waiting figure and then turned it round and held the hand aloft.

Eddie and I both peered intently, getting in each other's way, trying to see better. We couldn't make out the figure's features but we could see that it had two braids of light-coloured hair, hanging forward. It was female.

'It's just a young girl!' whispered Eddie angrily. 'What's he going to do with her?'

I didn't answer because The Antlered One was speaking again.

*'Behold! I take the hand of the Maiden, for the sake of the spring and the summer and the harvest. But first: Maiden, do you give yourself willingly, offering your maidenhood as though it were incense, to touch the hearts of Herne and of Our Lady Venus, to enrich the land? If you fear, if you are unwilling, speak. The gods accept only willing sacrifices. Do not fear to speak your mind, for no harm will come to you if now, facing the moment of surrender, you find you cannot endure it, and say no. Have no fear. I desire to give you only joy but if you wish, you may leave this place a maiden still. Speak freely. Yes or no.'*

For a moment there was tense silence and then, though

faintly because of the distance between us and the fact that the girl's voice was not loud, I heard her say: 'Yes.'

'Then you and I will withdraw for a while. While she and I are gone from your sight, prepare the feast!'

Eddie had grasped the point by now. He was trembling with outrage as though he were Vesuvius about to erupt. And then, before I could stop him, he did erupt, rushing forward, bursting into the clearing before I could stop him. But if there were any gods presiding over this appalling ceremony, they were on our side. As the Antlered One, holding the girl's hand high, led her away to the hut and the infuriated Eddie dashed into the clearing with, I think, the intention of pursuing them and attempting a rescue, the whole gathering erupted too, leaping about, cheering, embracing each other. Eddie, cloaked and hooded, simply found himself entangled in the midst of it and in the flickering light, no one noticed that his cloak was short.

I stood for a moment, shaking with fright, and then remembered that these were only villagers, whatever else they might do, they surely wouldn't murder me, and I went after him. For an awful moment, I too was part of the excited crowd. Swirling cloaks brushed against me, half enclosed me, swirled away; then someone caught my hands and swung me in a circle, shouting '*for the god of the forest and the goddess of the heavens!*' and then let me go, and now I had lost sight of Eddie and heaven alone knew what he would do before I could stop him . . .

The crowd was getting organized; someone was playing a pipe and someone else was tapping a drum and we were forming a ring round the bonfire. Caught up in it as I was, I dared not resist. I simply thanked heaven for my concealing cloak, pulled my hood further forward, allowed my hands to be taken by nameless figures on either side of me and found myself part of a slow dance, circling the fire while chanting what sounded like an invocation. I couldn't join in the chant but I could pick up the dance steps for they were easy and I had done plenty of dancing. Elizabeth trained her ladies ruthlessly. From within the masks, vision must be restricted, I thought, for no one had apparently noticed that my face was bare. Anyway, I wasn't the only one, there were those others for whom there hadn't been enough masks.

In all the hurly-burly, I did manage to identify Eddie. I knew him by the absence of a mask and by his short cloak. There came a moment when someone shouted something and the dance ended. The circle broke up, and in the brief confusion that followed, I kept my eyes on Eddie, made for him, reached him and gripped his arm.

'You bloody wantwit. Let's get out of this.'

'Madam, I couldn't bear it; that poor girl; it was my duty as an honest man to . . .'

'*Damn you, be quiet, and come on!*' I wanted to get us back to the hollow tree but now I realized to my horror, I couldn't. We were trapped in the crowd, forced for our own safety, to do what they did which just then, meant sitting down on the ground. I yanked hard at Eddie's arm and we sat along with everyone else. Around us, people were talking to each other in normal, cheerful voices. I kept my voice very low, but seized the opportunity to do some talking on my own account.

'*Duty as an honest man be damned. It's your duty to do as I bid you! I could have you beaten for this!*'

'Madam, please!' He was trembling again but this time in fear of me. 'I'm sorry! I'm sorry!' He muttered it into my cloak. We had huddled together. 'My feelings overcame me, that poor girl . . . how could her parents allow it? And it was all planned aforehand, that was plain to see. Who came to tell her and her parents, making them ready? There's people in that village as know who that monstrous thing with the antlers is, for all they pretend they don't.'

'I dare say! But just keep your voice down and don't do anything so bloody silly again. We're trapped. We must just pray for our luck to hold.'

Everyone hadn't been dancing, because while it was going on, the goat had been butchered. Chunks of its meat were now cooking on spits round the fire and I think extra meat had been brought to the feast as well. The roasting smell made me hungry and I heard Eddie's stomach rumble. I could see that two figures were fetching things – yes, loaves of bread – out of the two sacks beside the hut and slicing them up.

Then one of them came round to offer little pots of something. We levered the lids off and sniffed at the contents, which were liquid and spicy, some sort of dip. There was a picnic air. People were human once more. The whole business seemed to be a weird mixture of the lurid and the everyday.

But I couldn't forget that moment when they seemed to have turned into a single monster. They had been like that, I remembered, when they tried to murder Etheldreda.

Cooked meat slices, on thick rounds of bread, was handed out. People were removing their masks so as to eat more conveniently, but they were resuming their hoods. Identities were still to be kept secret, it appeared.

The food was good; the meat hot and tender, the spicy dip tangy on the tongue. Sausages were being cooked too, on toasting forks. They were brought round, on more bread platters. If I hadn't been so scared, I would have enjoyed that feast much more than I did but even as it was, it was enjoyable. The sausages were being handed out when the Antlered One reappeared, with his arm around his victim or lover or whatever the girl felt herself to be. Both were cloaked as before. At the sight of them, there was some more cheering but this time it sounded more normal. The girl was given her mask again and then the Antlered One led her on to the dais and once more took his chair. She sat down at his feet. His cloak, perhaps resumed in haste, had fallen a little open and I was near enough now to see that the firelight, glinting on his upper chest, showed that he was sweating. Food and wine were brought to them and they seemed to partake with zest. They talked to each other as they ate and I heard her laugh.

'The Maiden seems happy enough,' I said through a mouthful of sausage.

'Reckon that antlered brute's in practice,' retorted Eddie. He added: 'Wonder if he took them antlers off. If so, *she* knows who he is.'

'Why should he?' I said, and then imagined lying down and seeing that masked and antlered face above me, and shivered.

The night deepened. There was another serving of wine.

Someone produced a lute and started a singsong. The songs, mostly familiar to us both, varied from the sentimental to the ribald to the simply comic. Again came that strange juxtaposition of savage emotions with commonplaces.

Then it was over. The drinking and singing and feasting had ended and the Antlered One was addressing his audience for the last time. From where we were, we could now hear clearly. He was bidding them depart for their homes and begging for the blessing of Herne and Venus to keep them all safe until next time. '*And next time is the night between the last day of July and the first day of August. Here in this clearing, when the sun has gone down and the dawn will bring that beloved day of Lammas, we will gather at midnight to hold the Lammas feast, the last blessing of the crops before harvest time is upon us. Yea, on that midnight, we shall meet again.*'

The fire was dying. People were getting to their feet. The gathering formed itself into a rough and ready file, leading into the hut. Some were already emerging from it, hooded now instead of masked, and carrying lit lanterns. I gripped Eddie's arm. 'We don't know how things are in the hut. It could be well lit. We mustn't go in.'

In front of us, two people quietly dropped out of the file into the shadow of the trees, and further ahead, someone was coming back out of the trees. 'Calls of nature, madam,' whispered Eddie, and it was he who took my hand and slipped us quickly aside, into the forest.

Under the trees, it was utterly dark; I could feel Eddie's fingers round mine but we couldn't see each other. Once, someone brushed past me and knew I was there, but only muttered an apology and was gone.

We waited, aware of movement and murmuring in the clearing behind us. Eventually, I turned to look and saw that lanterns were bobbing away into the path for the village, on the opposite side. I could hear people talking to each other; the voices sounding natural, cheerful.

When I was sure they had all gone, I realized that we must be near to our hollow tree. I whispered this to Eddie and we moved warily into the clearing, where the dying fire, down to embers now but still giving some light, let us see where we were going. We could edge round and get our bearings. We found our tree and there was our bag of useful things, awaiting us. I brought out the tinderbox and lit my lantern to help us find the path for Edham.

The dawn chorus was beginning as we started out. Eddie said: 'I thought they'd stay to welcome the sunrise. I thought they'd chant some blasphemous hymn to the sun!' He sounded as though his own words tasted foul in his mouth.

'I wondered that too,' I said. 'But I fancy that antlered fellow doesn't want to risk being recognised.' I looked back into the clearing. 'What a mess they've left behind.'

'I dare say they'll come back by day and clear up after themselves,' Eddie said disparagingly as we went on into the darkness of the path. 'When they've slept their revels off. Never seen such a disgusting business.'

'I should hope you haven't,' I said austerely, and then noticed that I could now make out his face. 'High time we got back to our horses,' I said.

# ELEVEN

## In Sickness and in Love

Despite my strictures, Eddie talked persistently and indignantly, all the way home, about the shocking things we had seen, until I halted us, so as to add importance to what I was saying, and told him sternly that he was not on any account to speak of our night's adventure to anyone.

'To *anyone*, do you understand, Eddie? What we heard and saw in the forest last night you may mention only to me or to Brockley and to nobody else unless we ask you to.'

'I understand, madam. I wouldn't speak of it; I couldn't . . .'

'Then don't!'

'I wouldn't talk about such indecent things. I never saw such goings on . . .'

'Nor I, Eddie, and you *are* talking about them. Stop! Let's get home!'

In the stable yard I left the horses to Eddie and slipped in through the side door. As before, the passage was empty and though I could hear the house stirring, no one saw me as I hurried upstairs.

I was very tired but I wanted to talk to the others and tell them all about it. I also wanted to tell them that although I had heard talk of an evil queen, I had heard nothing whatsoever to suggest who she was or that anyone in Chenston meant to do anything about her. However, neither Mildred nor Hannah was in our room. I got my boots off myself, and with relief. The walk between the ruined village and the clearing had made my feet very tired of those boots. I then exchanged my male attire for a loose gown. I kept some gowns with their sleeves permanently attached, so that I need not always be dependent on Dale. I thrust grateful feet into soft slippers and set about combing my hair and coiling it under a cap. I had just finished when Mildred and Hannah came in.

I turned to them at once, full of my news and expecting them to be full of questions but instead, Mildred burst out: 'Oh, Mistress Stannard, thank dear heaven you're back; Master Brockley's in such a state, oh dear, oh dear . . .!' and Hannah simultaneously cried out that it had been such a night, even Dale hadn't known what to do . . .

They both looked even more exhausted than I was and while we were all staring at each other, Dale came in. She ran to me and knelt down, clutching at me. 'You're back safe! It's been such a night! He's asleep now but, oh, dear God, I can't abide such a night ever again . . .'

'Dale,' I said, 'get up, sit on that bed and explain. Quiet, Mildred. Hannah, hush.'

'He found out you'd gone,' said Dale breathlessly, sitting down as I bade her. 'Almost at once. Mistress Gresham came upstairs quiet as a mouse, I never heard aught, but Roger did. He heard something and he sent me out and I came face to face with Mistress Gresham and I insisted on coming here into this room with her and you weren't here and I didn't need to be told where you'd gone; I could guess and Mistress Gresham didn't have to answer when I said as much; I could read her face. So I went back and told Roger – well, he asked me what was going on and I can't lie to Roger and – he demanded to see Mistress Gresham, and then he wanted to go after you . . . he was in such a state! He's fallen ill again, he's so feverish and . . .'

I too sank on to the side of the bed. Dale was in tears. I put an arm round her and said: 'Mildred, tell me the rest, but slowly.'

'Dale came and said Brockley insisted on seeing me. She took us back to him and I told him don't worry, you had only gone so secretly because you didn't *want* him to worry, but he said he must go after you. Then he sent me away but Dale says he got out of bed for all her pleading with him not to, and he tried to dress but his strength left him and he stopped with one leg in the breeches and one not, and said he couldn't; he couldn't do it but we must send after you at once.'

'I told him that you wouldn't like that!' Dolefully, Dale took up the tale again. 'He said we must tell Sir Henry, and I said no, you wouldn't like that either, and he shrugged and tugged the breeches off, and turned away from me and fell on to the bed just as he was and seemed to fall asleep. I got into bed beside him but all night long, he was so restless and he started to feel very hot again, and then he began talking in his sleep and throwing himself about, and seemed to be half awake but rambling and I wanted to go to the kitchen to make him a posset but I dared not leave him alone and so I called Mistress Gresham and Hannah and Hannah went for the posset while Mistress Gresham and I sat with him but it was frightening; he kept half waking up and trying to get out of bed and when Hannah brought the posset he wouldn't drink it – oh, we've had such a time with him, for hours, and thank God you are back; he's asleep now but when he wakes, he'll be in a state again for sure, only perhaps you can quiet him . . .'

Dale stopped for a much-needed breath and then from the next room, we heard a hoarse cry of: *Fran, Fran.* I said: 'Dale, you and I will go to him. Hannah and Mildred, stay here.'

I felt almost too tired to stand but I had no choice. In the next room we found Brockley clutching at the sheet, muttering to himself and breathing harshly. His eyes were closed and there was sweat on his forehead.

'Brockley!' I said. 'I am here. I am perfectly safe. There never was much danger; do you really think the Chenston villagers would have harmed me, a guest under Sir Henry's protection, and a sister of the queen? I was far safer than you would have been. And I took Eddie with me as an escort. I didn't find out much and nothing about any conspiracies. But the next meeting is Lammas Eve. I did learn that much.' There was no response. '*Brockley!*' I repeated, much more loudly. 'This is Mistress Stannard. *Ursula!* I am here!'

His eyes opened. 'Madam.' His voice was hoarse. 'You went! I feared you would! But you *promised*! You broke your word! What time is it?'

'After daybreak,' I said. I don't know if he heard me. He said again: '*You broke your word!*'

'I only gave it to keep you quiet,' I said and let myself

sound irritable, because it somehow made everything more trivial. 'And as you see, I am safely back. Nothing happened to me.'

He didn't answer. His eyes closed and he turned on his side. He appeared to fall asleep. Dale drew the coverlet over him. Across his unheeding body, Dale's eyes met mine, and I saw that she was frightened. 'He's so *hot*!' she whispered.

I said: 'We must tell Sir Henry. Not that I went to the Midsummer meeting, but that Brockley is ill again.'

Sir Henry came himself when I told him. He did so with an air of impatience, as though he were finding his guests a trial and wished he could order us away, except, of course, that Walsingham wouldn't like it. But when he saw Brockley, and the state that Dale was in, his expression changed.

'I thought he was mending. Mistress Stannard.' His hand was on Brockley's sweating forehead. 'This is more than just being caught in a rainstorm. Didn't Dr Stone say it might be the malady that has stricken Julian Robyns down? His fever keeps returning. I will call Dr Stone again.'

'Dale,' I said, 'can you remember what else Gladys used to recommend for fevers, as well as that willow-bark potion of hers? I'm sure she sometimes uses other things but I can't remember what they are.'

'Basil, ma'am. And yarrow.'

'Can we try them? There must be basil in the herb garden here. What about yarrow?'

'If it's not in the garden, then I know how to find it. I know what it looks like!' Dale was suddenly eager. 'Easy to find, on heathland, like we crossed on the way here. Be in bloom this time of the year.'

'Go and look for some. Take a groom – not Eddie, he's been up all night – but go on horseback, waste no time. Do you know how to infuse it?'

'I think so, ma'am. Flower tops and leaves, but you have to dry them first. Gladys makes a drink with the dried flowers in boiling water. It's bitter, but she says it works, for fevers and some female things.'

'Get it,' said Sir Henry commandingly. 'Set it drying by the kitchen fire, and if you know how, make a basil medicine as well. Tell Hayward it's my orders.'

Dale fled. Mildred and I stayed with Brockley, watching over him. He was still sleeping, but restlessly and just by stooping over him, one could feel his heat. Dale was back sooner than we expected, flushed with hope and information. 'They have dried yarrow here in the kitchen; there's a maid here who gets nosebleeds and she takes a dose of yarrow every day and she's been better since she tried it, and they use it for headaches, too. No one thought of it for a fever! And there's plenty of basil. Hannah's making up a drink from both of them, with some honey to sweeten.'

Hannah was with us a few moments later, bringing the combined drink, steaming hot, in an earthenware cup. Gently, Dale woke Brockley and persuaded him to take it. Despite the honey, he made a face and had to be coaxed. But once he had swallowed the drink, he said thank you to Dale and then looked at me and said: 'I'll get better, madam, don't you worry. Now I know you're safe. You shouldn't have done it; you know you shouldn't. I wish I didn't feel so tired.' He was asleep again within minutes.

'Do you know,' said Mildred, 'I think it was worrying over you, Ursula, that threw him back into a fever.'

Mildred meant no harm, but I saw Dale's face. I thought furiously for a few moments, found a solution if not a very probable one, crossed my finger out of sight and stepped in.

'I think I know why he worries so. I have been remiss. I have never told you of the provision I have made for you and Roger in the event of my death. I keep meaning to and then forgetting. I am sorry, Dale.'

'Ma'am, I'm sure we never . . .'

'But you must have thought of it sometimes. It's all right. I have put it in my will and Sir William Cecil, who is my executor, holds a copy of the will. It states that you shall both, always, have a home at Hawkswood, even if you grow too old to work, and it provides for you – and old Gladys too – to have pensions.'

'*Thank* you, ma'am,' said Dale, and I heard relief in her voice. I had never before thought that Brockley might be afraid for his or Dale's future if anything happened to me and I didn't suppose that he actually was. But it explained his collapse in a way that wouldn't hurt Dale. And I *had* been remiss. I should have told them long ago.

I ordered Dale to rest. Throughout all this, neither she nor Mildred had mentioned Midsummer. Brockley's illness had distracted us all. It was still distracting us. The two things couldn't occupy our minds at the same time.

In any case, Mildred and I were by this time almost too exhausted to stand up. We withdrew to our room and there we removed our outer clothing, lay down with just the coverlet over us, and slept.

It was a good sleep, deep and refreshing. I woke up after some hours to find myself alone. I could tell by the light that it was well into the afternoon. There were voices in the next room. I got myself up, pulled my gown on and went, anxiously, to see what was going on.

However, there was nothing to be alarmed about. Brockley, still looking feverish but not so badly as before, was sitting up and without assistance, was drinking another cup of medicine and once more making faces over it, while Mildred and Daniel Atbrigge, sitting on opposite sides of the bed, were watching him, smiling and talking to each other. Dale, looking bemused with a sleep that she had taken on her truckle bed, was sitting up and rubbing her eyes.

Daniel turned to me as we came in. 'Because Dr Robyns is ill, I came over today to conduct a christening here. I heard of Mr Brockley's illness and came to see him. Mistress Mildred says he is better, which is good news. It seems that you knew what to do for him.'

'This one is willow bark,' said Brockley, making more faces. 'It's bitter enough to shrivel one's tongue, honey or no honey.'

'He had another basil and yarrow drink about half an hour ago. I made them this time,' said Mildred. 'Dale told me how.'

'Has Dr Stone been?' I asked.

'Yes, and gone again,' Mildred said. 'It seems that yarrow isn't on his list of useful medicines. Basil is, but not yarrow. I think he was annoyed! But he said that Brockley should soon recover, and that the combination of a severe wetting and the same fever that is afflicting Dr Robyns is the probable cause. Then he left. I don't see how Brockley can have caught anything from this Dr Robyns. We've never met him.'

'On one of our walks round Minstead, we went into the church,' said Dale. 'Roger saw a black gown lying about in a careless fashion and he picked it up and folded it and left it on a bench. Perhaps the vicar had been wearing it just before.'

'Very likely,' said Brockley. 'But I *have* caught it, never mind how. If yarrow was in that other tongue-shrivelling drink I've now been made to swallow twice, it's no wonder that Stone doesn't use it. His patients might object!'

'But you're better already,' said Mildred reassuringly. 'You shall have another basil and yarrow drink tomorrow morning.'

'You are a gracious nurse,' said Atbrigge with approval.

I might have known it. Mildred, who had been so reserved and dowdy under her parents' puritanical cloud, had emerged into the light as – or so I have read – a butterfly hatches from a chrysalis. During our long journey from Devon, I had told her about choosing colours to bring out the colour of her blue-green eyes and the lights in her fine brown hair. I had also shown her how to wear her hair coiled within a net, or else letting it show its curls in front of a small embroidered hood, and I had instructed her in the making of ointments to keep her hands smooth.

She hadn't had much time to put my recommendations into practice, but during our short time at Hawkswood, I had lent her a couple of suitable gowns in the light shades of blue and green that did so much for her eyes and lent her a little jewellery and a silver caul for her hair. And here was the outcome. The very sight of her new self in a mirror had given her a new confidence and a new maturity. Not to mention a new attraction.

Before, in the presence of a man that she liked, she would have been shy and apt to blush. Now, and I realized all this in one suddenly wary moment, she was attracted by Daniel Atbrigge, yet she was smiling at him in a perfectly collected fashion and turning away from him to take Brockley's empty cup. She adjusted the pillows with care and gave Daniel another smile, before she took the cup downstairs.

And Daniel gazed after her in a wondering manner, as though she were an unexpected vision. I looked at him sharply and I began to do some wondering myself.

Another two days passed, during which Brockley made a steady recovery and Mildred never spoke of Atbrigge though I sometimes caught her smiling to herself. By the end of the two days, when Brockley could once more walk about the room, Master Atbrigge rode over from Chenston on the pretext of visiting him. But he didn't stay with Brockley long. Very soon, he came out of the bedchamber, came to pay his respects to me in the West parlour, and then asked to speak with me in private. 'I mean, not in the presence of Mistress Mildred,' he said.

I knew that Mildred had gone down to the kitchen to brew another basil medicine and that Hannah was helping her. Either of them could reappear at any moment, however. I took Atbrigge downstairs and into the garden, and there, I asked what it was about.

'I feel shy,' he said. 'But it's important to me. I have been a widower for five years. I have done my best to bring up my son Benjamin, and he is a fine boy and I love him dearly but I have always known he lacks a mother. At first, I couldn't dream of another woman in my Helen's place but time wears things away, even if it never quite heals. I know I ought to marry again but so far I have never found a woman I could love. Until I met Mistress Gresham. May I have your consent to pay court to her?'

I sat plump down on a bench. I should have seen it coming. In a shadowy way, I supposed that I had. Well, if Mildred had gone and fallen in love again, the feeling seemed to be mutual. But all the same . . .

'Mistress Gresham is my gentlewoman companion,' I said. 'But not my ward though as she is still very young, I feel I must watch over her. But it's her parents who should grant permission for her to marry.'

I felt harassed. I had still not described the Midsummer feast to anyone. Brockley's illness had dominated all our minds.

But Brockley was recovering and we would have much to say to each other, including how much if anything, we should tell either Atbrigge who was after all the vicar of Chenston, or Sir Henry Compton, our host. And meanwhile, I must also consider how to protect Mildred's interests. Dear heaven, what a tangle.

# TWELVE

## Old Roots are Wrenched

I rose to my feet and we began to walk. 'To begin with,' I said, 'I have to ask: if you marry Mildred, will you be good to her – will you *promise* to be good to her? Her parents are in Devonshire and if she weds you, I too will be far away, in Surrey. And, I repeat, even if I am satisfied with our talk now and Mildred herself says yes to you, I must give you her parents' direction so that you can write to them. As I said, you will need their consent as well as mine.'

'I gladly promise to treat her well,' said Atbrigge. 'And I will gladly write to her parents.' He looked at me straitly. 'I understand that they are of the Puritan persuasion and probably dislike even maypoles and may well have a fear of witchcraft. Such people often have. For that reason I would prefer not to mention fertile mules or forest feasts to them and I trust you can see why. I will also add that, as my wife, Mistress Gresham will not be asked to go to the Wood, as the Chenston saying is. Is that acceptable to you?'

I thought about it. Mildred had been disappointed in love and badly hurt only a few months ago. I had seen her quenched once already and I didn't want it to happen again. I must be careful. 'I would wish her,' I said, 'to have absolutely nothing to do with such things.'

'I wish her the same. Mildred will be the wife of a respectable vicar, and a stepmother to a young boy who needs her!' Daniel's voice was sharp. 'Other than that,' he said, 'although mine is a small parish deep in the New Forest, I have an adequate stipend and can support a wife very well.'

'One thing worries me,' I said. 'This is all very sudden. How well do you really know Mistress Gresham? How many times have you met her, after all?'

'It's not quite as strange as you suppose.' And there was that astonishing smile, that lit up his narrow features as the sun lights up a landscape. 'The very first time I set eyes on her, I felt drawn to her and I think it was the same for her too. These things can be sudden, Mrs Stannard.'

I couldn't argue with that. With me and Gerald, my cousin's betrothed, it had been instantaneous. Poor Mary lost him between one breath and the next. But I was still cautious.

'You say you have been many years a widower. In all that time, did you never feel drawn to anyone else and if so, why did it come to nothing?'

'I have never felt it in such strength, Mistress. There have been hints of it, an occasional feeling that this or that lady was attractive. But the shade of my dead wife was always beside me. It is only during the last two years that her shadow has faded . . . not vanished but it is as though she has given me permission to begin anew. I find myself turning again to the living world, to the future, and to Ben's future too. Helen is gone and her place is empty. Mistress Gresham, dear Mildred, has come into my life and I believe she is the one to fill that empty space.'

Once more, he gave me the full benefit of his smile. 'My son agrees. I asked him what he thought about having a step-mother and he said he'd been expecting one so I asked him what he thought of Mistress Gresham. He said that what little he had seen of her, he had liked.'

'I see. And has Mildred told you of her previous and very brief betrothal and its tragic ending? And of her parents' attempt to make her marry a man she didn't like at all, and her own resistance?'

'She has. We have talked more than you perhaps know, Mrs Stannard. When Mr Brockley had his relapse the other day, there were those hours while you were asleep and so was your maid Dale, but Mildred and I were sitting with Brockley. We talked then. I asked many questions, for I wished to know her better. She says that she is conscious of being an undutiful daughter, only she couldn't bear the man they had found for her, and was frightened of the kind of life she would have to lead with him – helping sheep to have their lambs, and being expected to take charge of a big house when she had not been reared to do so.'

'I know,' I said ruefully. 'I was there when the wretched man showed her round his home and his animals, and I saw how horrified she was.'

'She admits she felt imprisoned by the Puritan beliefs of her parents. I could understand. I am no Puritan – though I do feel that the Old Testament has much to teach us. I consider that it's sadly neglected. Still, just because of her parents' beliefs, she almost has it by heart, so there we would share a common interest. I can see very well though that such an upbringing wasn't to her advantage when she was faced with a big house, sheep at lambing time and – she told me this and I laughed but to her it wasn't amusing – she said that one of the things that frightened her most was being expected to know all about complicated recipes when in fact she knows only simple ones because at home all their food was plain.'

'So it was. We stayed in their household for a time,' I said, with feeling.

'Well, plain food suits me and Ben, and Joan sees to the cooking anyway. Mrs Stannard, please do tell me her parents' direction. I take it that they wouldn't hold it against me that I am not a Puritan?'

'I shouldn't think so. The man they chose for her, that she wouldn't accept; he wasn't.'

'I can get a letter off today. There's a man in Chenston who acts as a messenger for me. Mark Appleyard, his name is. You won't have seen him; he wasn't part of that mob that attacked Mistress Hope. He will manage the journey very quickly.'

'It must be over a hundred miles.'

'Mark knows every inn in the south of England that has horses for hire available and he is capable of riding for sixteen hours a day. If the answer is favourable, the banns can begin the next Sunday. That is, assuming that I ask Mistress Gresham for her hand and she is willing. I promise to take care of her, to be kind to her and generous; to love her as a husband should. May I speak to her? Please don't ask me to wait until I have her parents' reply. I shall tell them nothing to alarm them and there *is* nothing to alarm them. Please, Mistress Stannard.'

I ought to make him wait for her parents' reply but from his expression, from his voice, I knew that he wouldn't. The declaration inside him was bursting to escape; he would never keep it in.

'You may speak to her,' I said, 'though the two of you must still wait for her parents' agreement.'

They would agree all right. He would word his letter to make sure of it. I took him back to the house and called Mildred to join us in the parlour. Then I left them together. Half an hour later they came to see me, hand in hand.

I gave him the Greshams' direction and he and I both wrote to them, Daniel to ask their consent, mine to say that for my part I had already given it. Then Daniel left for Chenston to find Mark Appleyard and get the letters on their way. I wondered just how long it would take Appleyard to get to Devon and back. Meanwhile, I had Brockley to worry about. And talk to, as soon as possible. There were things that I knew now I must say to him. They didn't concern Midsummer.

The day after Daniel's declaration, I seized a moment when Mildred was sewing in the West parlour, apparently lost in a daydream of love, Hannah was busy with refurbishing Mildred's ruffs and Dale was refurbishing mine, and went to talk to Brockley alone. It was a wet day and he had stayed in his chamber, where I found him sitting by the window and looking at the sky as though willing it to clear up. I sat down on one of the two chairs in the room, and he turned to face me. 'Mistress Stannard! Good morning.'

'You look much better, Brockley. I think you are almost well again and I do hope so. Brockley, was this relapse just natural, as Dr Stone says has happened with Robyns, or . . . well, what do you think brought it on?'

'These things happen.' He was fully if casually dressed, in an old doublet and breeches and an open shirt. He looked at me and then looked away and then looked back again and I saw defiance in his eyes.

'Brockley?' I said and he knew I was repeating my question. This time, he answered it.

'You did!' He almost spat the words at me. 'You broke your word! You promised me that you wouldn't go off to spy on the Midsummer goings on, and then you did go, to watch the Lord knows what indecent things in the forest and very likely put yourself in danger if you were caught and all because I happen to catch cold after being half drowned in a rainstorm. Even if I did pick something up in the church, along with that gown, I'd probably just have had a day or two out of sorts, if I hadn't got wet through – and I wouldn't have had a relapse but for you. We could have waited; Lammas isn't far off.'

'So you weren't really asleep when I tried to tell you the next meeting would be at Lammas. I only know it for certain because I was there to hear it announced.'

'I know,' said Brockley angrily, 'because when you were out in the garden yesterday, talking with Atbrigge, Eddie came to see me. I know everything that happened! Eddie has been shocked half out of his wits and he was too upset with himself, as well, to hold his tongue any longer. I gather that he lost his head and very nearly got both of you caught. He told me himself and begged pardon, and I know your views on such things, or as soon as I'm strong enough I'd be giving him a belting he'd never forget.'

'You'll certainly do no such thing! I have always forbidden it in my household.'

'There's a few things go on that you don't know about, even inside your household, madam, especially in the stable yard. When Eddie was younger . . . oh well, never mind. He had a tongue that was too pert and Arthur and I decided he needed quelling, more than once. We didn't tell you and nor did he.'

'Good God!' I was sincerely shaken.

'Never mind all that. I know what you saw and heard at that Midsummer meeting and to think of you, there in the forest, seeing it, hearing it and with only Eddie beside you, *Eddie* – I'm ashamed of him. He's no youth any more, but a man in his late twenties yet still he couldn't control himself, failed to obey you . . . I could kill him!'

'Brockley, listen. Forget Eddie for a moment. You could well have been worried about me, but . . .'

'Worried about you! You promised and . . .'

'I promised so as to keep you calm and able to get well again. But it was virtually a promise given under duress, and that kind of promise isn't valid. You know that. I had a duty . . .'

He interrupted me, roughly. 'I know! You would say you had a duty, a higher duty, to the queen!'

'So I had!' I threw anger against anger. 'To a sister and to the queen of England.'

'At least you didn't say a duty to Walsingham.' It was half a laugh and half a sneer.

'Walsingham would throw both of us into a wolf pit if he thought his own duty to the queen required it. We both serve her, as well as we can. And you, Brockley, dear Brockley, I am sorry, but . . .'

I would have to say it. I had come here to say it. This illness of his had shown me that I must. I knew him so well, had depended on him so long. If anything were to happen to him, I would be as grief-stricken as Dale *and I had no right to be*. And if anything should happen to me, he would be as grief-stricken as Harry, my son, and again *he had no right to be*. This state of affairs was wrong and should have been dealt with long ago. I drew a long breath.

'*But*,' I said, 'it's not right for you to worry about me to such an extent that you relapse from a fever, relapse so badly that you frighten your wife and cause Sir Henry to send for Dr Stone. That degree of worry, of concern, of' – I hesitated and then brought out the word as though I were pulling an arrowhead out of a wound – 'of love belongs to Dale and only to Dale. You know it and so do I.'

For a long moment we stared at each other. Then Brockley sighed, and said: 'I suppose you heard the call of the wild geese.'

'Did I? I'm not sure. When we got back from Devon I remember thinking – and hoping – that I would never hear that call again. I went to the Midsummer gathering because it was my duty.'

'You sound like my mother. And my stepfather,' said Brockley. But now his voice was just wry. He was no longer angry, though I thought he was sad, as though he had lost something precious to him, for which I was sorry. To ease the atmosphere, I said: 'Your stepfather? Who were your parents? You have never talked about them.'

'Have I not? In all these years?'

'Not to me, no.'

'My mother was a maidservant in the household of the Duke of Northumberland. Him that was the father of Robin Dudley, the queen's favourite now. She married a groom and he was my dad. I don't remember him, though I think I inherited my love of horses from him. He died, and later, my mother married again, a soldier in the king's army. He was my stepfather. He was good to me, though. I was reared to be a soldier like him, though I always had this feeling that I'd like to work with horses. My mother and my stepfather were always telling me that I should *remember my duty*.' He said the last three words with sternness, imitating the tones of voice he must have heard, so many years ago.

'How did you come to be part of Amy Robsart's household?' I asked, recalling how I had met him when he was a groom in the service of Robin Dudley's first wife.

'When I came back to England, after following King Henry to war in France, and after I'd got over finding that my wife had run off while I was away – well, you know all about that – since my mother and father had once worked in Northumberland's household, I applied to be a groom in his stables. I didn't want to go on being a soldier. After the Duke of Northumberland . . . died . . .'

'Was executed. Yes,' I said.

'I was inherited, so to speak, by Robin Dudley. Later, he passed me on to serve his wife.'

'Have you told Dale all this?'

'Oh, yes.'

'I'm thankful to hear it. It would be a shocking thing if I knew it and she did not. Brockley, my very dear Brockley, I beg you, be content to be just my loyal friend and no more. Dale is your wife and the only one with a claim to be worried about in such a dramatic way. You would be entitled to have a relapse because for some reason you were afraid for her.

But you are not entitled to do the same for me.' I found myself trembling; knowing that I was as much at fault as Brockley.

I had just wrenched something out of me that had deep roots; deeper than I had supposed and deeper than they had any business to be. Wrenching them out had hurt.

Brockley said: 'There's more than one kind of love. Fran finds it hard to understand, I know. My love for you will never change my love for her. But we must protect her from hurt; there I agree. I can't quite promise never to fall ill again out of fear for you, madam, but I'll try. Though God knows, you sometimes run into such danger that your merest acquaintances can't help but get themselves into a lather. You heard the wild geese call, even if you do pretend it was duty. What do we do next?'

It was done. I had been right to tear those deep roots out. From now on, our relationship would, I hoped, be as it should.

'I have come to one conclusion,' I said, 'and that is that we do have to stay on until August. I think we might have to do that anyway, because Daniel Atbrigge is courting Mildred.'

'Is he, indeed!'

'Yes. I have written to her parents about it and so has he. If all goes well, we might have to stay for a wedding.'

'It's a better reason than having to stay so as to attend a midnight gathering where the host is a man wearing a pair of antlers and invoking pagan gods,' said Brockley. He looked thoughtful. 'That's a queer mixture of gods that your antlered fellow seems to be praying to. The horned god of the woods and Venus. They don't go together.'

'No, they don't.' I suddenly realized that the same idea had been in the back of my mind. 'You are right. The Greeks had Pan, who was a woodland god with horns, but they weren't antlers . . .'

'And they worshipped Aphrodite – she was really Venus, but they didn't call her that,' Brockley said, and then grinned. 'Madam, when I was in France as one of King Henry's soldiers, we did some pillaging. I used to help myself to books. I've read all the Greek legends. I feel it's just as well our Antlered One hasn't picked Zeus as his god. The way old Father Zeus behaved . . .'

'Pillaging!' I said primly, 'What a way to get an education! Our Antlered One has probably never heard of Zeus and just as well. I think he just knows about our own old legends and one or two well-known others including the Roman Venus and he's just picked out the ones he likes. His . . . his scheme of things is all his own invention.'

'I don't like it,' Brockley said. 'And madam, I implore you not to go near any of these woodland carryings-on again. If he isn't following a pattern already set – by Greeks or Romans or Vikings or anyone else – then he might do anything. *Anything!* We can't know what to expect. How much have you told to Mistress Gresham or to Fran?'

'Very little. We've all been too busy looking after you!'

And it was there again, one of those flickering moments when unspoken things wrote themselves in the air between us. We shared so many memories. I had once rescued Brockley from captivity in a basement; we had once been imprisoned together in a dungeon, and there had been that wild occasion when we had escaped from pursuit by making missiles of such homely things as pewter plates and pots of pepper, and laying a booby trap by balancing a pot of pottage over a kitchen door and pouring olive oil on a kitchen floor . . .

'I gather,' said Brockley, and from the steel in his voice I knew that he had recognized that shared moment and stepped away from it, 'that you have made Eddie understand that he can only speak of what he witnessed, to me or to you. I shall see he keeps to that.'

'So will I,' I said.

'And Atbrigge wants to marry Mistress Gresham? Have you really agreed, madam?'

'I talked with him. He promised to look after her. He told me about his first marriage and also said that his son could do with a stepmother and had no objection to Mildred. He said all the right things. I think he really is in love with her.'

'Fran doesn't like him. If she'd been with you, she'd probably be saying that the man with the antler mask was him.'

'I have asked myself that, but I can't see it, somehow,' I said. 'He has too much to lose, and besides, he's now arranging to get married. His wife might notice if he's out all night on certain significant dates! Felix Armer is much more likely. Or maybe,' I added, remembering the loud, harsh voice I had heard when we were trying to rescue Etheldreda, 'Master Orchard senior. He has the lungs for it.'

The next day, I found a moment to speak alone with Sir Henry and tell him that I would be grateful if he would extend his hospitality to us until the end of the first week of August. 'My purpose here isn't yet accomplished,' I said. I sincerely wished it was, but whatever I had seen or heard or done at the Midsummer feast, I had not learned whether Mary Stuart came into any of it or not. If at Lammas we still learned nothing, I would report as much to Walsingham and in any case, go home at least for the time being. According to Etheldreda, the next meeting after Lammas would be Halloween and it was a long time from the first of August to the last day of October. During that time, Walsingham's own plans might mature; he might no longer want to concern himself with Chenston.

Sir Henry's response to my request was a curt: 'Very well.' But then I gave him a smile and said: 'There may be a wedding quite soon,' and told him about Atbrigge and Mildred, and his expression changed. Suddenly he was smiling back, and asking me how it had come about.

Mark Appleyard was certainly a fast rider. He had left on a Tuesday and was back on the Saturday evening with replies to both letters. I don't know what was in Atbrigge's but it was apparently the consent he wanted. In mine, the Greshams thanked me for my courtesy in writing to them but said they were happy to leave the matter in my hands. If I thought the match suitable and their daughter was agreeable, then they had no objection.

Daniel Atbrigge came to Minstead late that evening, to tell me and Mildred that the first banns would be called at his church in the morning. He would be so happy to see us there. And would we, Mistress Gresham and myself, care to dine with him at his vicarage on the following Tuesday. He added that his invitation included the Brockleys. He wouldn't wish two ladies to come unattended; they too would be welcome.

# THIRTEEN

## A Civilized Dinner

I expected Daniel Atbrigge's dinner to be an informal affair, since he only had Joan Orchard to cook it. However, it transpired that Joan didn't represent his entire staff, far from it. It seemed that a village couple, John and Bella Sweetapple, called at the vicarage every day, to chop firewood and fetch water from the well. When formal meals were needed Bella helped Joan in the kitchen too. She was there now.

Daniel told us all this while he was taking our cloaks and hanging them up, and then offering us a row of assorted slippers. These were welcome, as riding boots never go well with the gowns suitable for dinner guests. It isn't everyone who takes so much trouble and I have often dined in my boots. I had to do that when we dined with the man that Mildred refused to marry. I hoped that my ward Joyce, who did marry him, was teaching him better manners.

'It was John Sweetapple who took charge of your horses just now,' said Daniel as he showed us into the parlour. 'He'll stable them behind his cottage. He keeps my mare there as well, and Ben's pony, Whitey. Oh, no, they're not Mark Sweetapple's parents. John is a second cousin of Mark's father, I think. And Bella is some kind of distant cousin to Mark's mother. The whole village is a tangle of relationships as complicated as knitting. I would like to forbid villager to marry villager but it would be difficult to maintain. I have started to keep a kin-book, though. The priests of the old religion had *some* good sense. They knew about the dangers of inbreeding. Sit yourselves down. The meal will be homely, of course, for folk who've been to the royal court. We are rustics, here in Chenston. But maybe none the worse for that.'

He turned that beautiful smile of his on to Mildred, and her face lit up as though a lantern had been shone on it. 'I understand that you were reared on simple food,' he said to her. 'That's how it is here. I doubt if the prophets and great men of the Old Testament had elaborate sauces or spun-sugar fantasies at their tables, or marchpanes coloured like the rainbow, either. My dear, I am so happy to welcome you to my home. May I say how pretty you look?'

We had all dressed suitably, by which I mean suitably for a country vicarage, not for Queen Elizabeth's court. Our ruffs were moderate in size, and since we had come on horseback we had dispensed with farthingales. Brockley was in soldierly buff, Dale in dark blue as she always was when she felt herself to be on duty. I had chosen an open-fronted light wool gown of plain tawny, over a cream silk kirtle with a scatter of little embroidered flowers in a deeper cream and sleeve slashings to match. My jewellery consisted of an amber necklace and small amber earrings. At my recommendation, Mildred was in a soft turquoise-coloured grosgrain gown of silk and wool, with a rope of freshwater pearls, and green agate earrings. She did look pretty. The gown enhanced the colour of her eyes and with Hannah's help, she had washed her hair with chamomile in the water, which had given it a new sheen. Hannah had dressed it with the curls showing in front of a small hood with a seed pearl edging.

The air in Daniel's house brought us agreeable odours of cooking and I was intrigued to hear, from the direction of the kitchen, several female voices. As a preliminary to dinner, a bowl of nuts and raisins and a jug of ale was brought in, by two very nice-looking, brown-haired and blue-eyed young girls. Brockley, also surprised, smiled at them and asked who they were.

'We're the Pickford sisters, sir,' said the one who looked to be the elder, curtseying gracefully. 'I'm Jennet Pickford and this is Susie. We're Joan's nieces. We come to help when it's needed.'

Joan Orchard's nieces. And their name was Pickford. During the siege of Etheldreda's house, the man with the vicious grin and the coil of rope slung over his shoulder, had answered to the name of Pickford. Were these pretty things his daughters?

I decided not to ask. I was beginning to see what Daniel meant when he likened the village relationships to knitting.

While we ate the nuts and raisins, I noticed that Mildred, who was at one end of the settle, was shifting uneasily, and also that she was looking at the parlour's unadorned walls. Atbrigge also noticed and laughed.

'Mistress Mildred, you are thinking that this is a Spartan kind of room, for a parlour? No wall hangings! No cushions! I have never concerned myself with such things but if when we are married, you wish to make changes, I will not object. This will be your home, after all. My former wife liked to have cushions about. She made them pretty with embroidery. She made some wall hangings too – small ones, embroidered, not woven. I gave it all away when she died because they were such poignant reminders.' He raised a hand, because Mildred had flushed and seemed embarrassed. 'That's the past. You and I are journeying into the future. You can embroider?'

'Oh yes,' Mildred assured him. Her parents had at least taught her that.

Daniel turned to me. 'May we raise a cup to future happiness?'

We drank the toast and then a tiny little woman, as short as Joan but much thinner, with a tight coif, a small limp ruff and a stained apron over a black dress appeared at the door to announce that dinner was on the table. This, presumably, was Bella. She had eyes as sharp and grey as flint and I saw her pick out Mildred and visibly wonder what kind of mistress the young lady was going to make. All she said, however, was: 'I called Master Ben and he's in the kitchen washing ink off his fingers. How that boy gets ink all over his hands every time he does that writing work you make him do, I can't think. Joan calls him Master Inky Paws.'

Daniel, much amused, said: 'Send him to the table when he's clean enough,' and briskly led us out of the parlour and into his dining chamber. Ben joined us a moment later, very spruce in ruff, doublet, neat puffed breeches and long legs in brown stockings. He bowed politely to us but to begin with seemed shy. However, as the meal began, Brockley started to talk to him about his studies and then got on to the subject of horses, which Ben took up with enthusiasm. Daniel tossed a word in now and then across the bowls of cold fennel soup, and I noticed that between father and son, there was an air of friendship.

The first time we had been here, I had thought Daniel rather stern with Ben over making sure that he had finished his studies for the day, but after all, I had sometimes been the same with Harry. On Mildred's behalf I was sensitive to the nuances in this house. I thought now that the link between father and son seemed healthy.

While we consumed the soup, Daniel told us more about Jennet and Susie. They were indeed the daughters of the Pickford who had been so anxious to hang Etheldreda. 'He's ardent in everything, is Walter Pickford,' Daniel said. 'He's not popular. Walter's too apt to complain to his neighbours if one of their animals strays or dandelion seeds blow over from their land on to his and he has a horror of witchcraft, since one of his aunts and also his only son were born not right in the head, couldn't learn to walk well or talk properly. Neither lived past ten years old and Walter always said they'd been bewitched, that his family had always been hated and this was spite and if he only knew who'd done it . . . well, you can imagine.'

'Do you believe it was witchcraft?' Brockley asked.

'No, inbreeding,' said Daniel. 'There are other poor idiots in the village. Two of them, just now. Not as bad as the Pickford ones were, more just silly, but not normal, certainly. But Jennet and Susie are bright enough, bless them. Their maternal grandmother came from Salisbury; brought new blood in. Jennet is betrothed, in a most sensible way, to a young silversmith from Lyndhurst. Ralph Argent, his name is. I helped there – Walter never thought about it and his wife's dead now. I've friends in Lyndhurst. One of them helped me to arrange a meeting between young Argent and Jenny, and the young pair took to each other, so I shook Walter into taking an interest and we got it fixed up. It's a good match. Argent's parents aren't New Forest folk. His father's family have been in Lyndhurst for generations and his mother's Welsh. Ralph's father travels sometimes, selling his wares, and his wife came from Cardiff. Jenny's children aren't likely to be weak in the head.'

I didn't comment and nor did any of the others. I think we were all wondering what it felt like to be a youngster in Chenston, being encouraged by their vicar to consider potential spouses as though they were all breeding stock. I could well see why but all the same . . . I changed the subject. We had finished the soup and now Joan was bringing in a platter of capons, fresh from the spit. It smelt wonderful and I said: 'Master Atbrigge, you were too modest about the food.'

He certainly had been. The roasted capons were accompanied by a truly delicious white sauce containing mushrooms and – I thought – white wine, and there were side dishes of salad and beans in an aromatic brown sauce which I couldn't identify but liked very much. There was barley bread warm from the oven and later came the choice of almond fritters or cake flavoured with honey and if the marchpane topping wasn't quite all colours of the rainbow, it was coloured bright pink and yellow with the aid of raspberries and saffron (I knew that recipe).

To go with it all, we were served with a pale yellow wine which I thought from its pleasant stony taste must come from a Germanic country. Ben was allowed to have either small ale or wine with water and chose the wine. We drank from glasses engraved with delicate patterns and we ate from attractively glazed earthenware soup bowls and handsome wooden platters of the kind that can be turned over after the main course to accommodate whatever was offered as dessert. I had similar ones at home. There were silver fingerbowls and spoons as well. Daniel might pretend that he was a rustic like most of his parishioners, but he was no such thing.

Meanwhile, to begin with, the conversation ran smoothly. Mildred was shy about references to her future here, and although I would have liked to drop in a few remarks about Mary Stuart and see what resulted, this didn't seem to be the right moment or a likely one, either. The conversation could not have been more innocuous. Daniel had begun to talk to Mildred about his favourite Old Testament stories, while throwing a word in now and then to Brockley and Ben, who by this time were well into their discussion about horses. Dale and I had turned to each other and begun to talk about some new dresses we were planning to make. And then, towards the end of the roast capon stage I heard, in the half-an-ear way one does catch bits of other people's conversations at dinner tables, that Ben had turned his attention from Brockley to his father and was challenging him about something, and Daniel was answering, once again in that stern voice.

So stern, that I detached myself from Dale and began to listen with my full attention. I didn't know what Ben had said to upset his father but Daniel was staring at his son very intently, and I caught just the end of his admonishment. '. . . very wrong to forget that. You have to bear it in mind all your life. I say it again. When you hear God telling you to do something or not to do it, you must obey. Even if you don't understand; even if it gives you pain.'

Ben subsided, looking embarrassed, as well he might. It seemed to me that like a careless musician, Daniel had struck a false note, wrong for a sociable dinner such as this. Even if Ben had said something to annoy him, Daniel should not have corrected him like that in the presence of guests. I tried to change the atmosphere by giving Ben a smile and asking Daniel whether he intended to send his son to school. 'I thought perhaps Ben might want to follow in your footsteps.'

'We have talked of that, yes.' Daniel was once more the sunny host. 'I have been Ben's schoolmaster up to now but I think he would benefit from a few years at a good establishment. I am considering it, am I not, Ben?'

'Yes. I think I would like it,' Ben said, brightening. Only to be dampened at once as his father said: 'But I will have to trust you not to bring home outlandish ideas.'

In a village where most of the population seemed to have very outlandish ideas indeed, and expressed them in extraordinary antics in the forest on the nights traditionally given to pagan festivals, I wondered how Ben could avoid them. School would be a protection rather than a temptation.

However, I could hardly say so, and meanwhile, Ben just said: 'Yes, father,' in a suitably submissive tone and then the talk flowed on. Dale spoke to Brockley, I think about the knot garden in front of the house; Mildred began making friends with Ben, her possible future stepson, asking what sports he liked and describing the mews at Hawkswood, where I kept one or two merlins for my own amusement and as part of Harry's training. Daniel turned to me and said: 'I don't keep hawks but Mark Sweetapple does and I get a few small birds from him now and then; Bella barters eggs for them. I have a poultry run, that she looks after.'

Jennet came in to take away the sauce boats and the serving dishes. Susie brought in napkins to wipe our platters before we turned them over. The sweet course arrived. And at the end of that, when Bella and Joan came to clear the dishes once more, Daniel asked them to bring the Pickford girls in again, gave them all glasses of wine and then, standing up, raised his own and said: 'This is a happy occasion. Mistress Mildred and I are now betrothed. Mistress Mildred's parents have given their consent and so has Mrs Stannard, who is in the position of her guardian, and Mistress Mildred herself declares that she is willing. The first banns have been read. I therefore make declaration in my turn, that if it pleases you, Mistress Gresham, the ceremony can take place on Monday the twenty-eighth of July.'

'It pleases me very well,' said Mildred, and Daniel at once raised his glass and said: 'Please, will you all now drink to our joy, and to the happy future before us.'

We all drank the toast, and then Daniel produced a ring and put it on Mildred's finger. She laughed delightedly, blushing rose-red, showing it round, a silver band set with an amethyst. 'It belonged to my first wife,' Daniel said. 'But now, Mistress Mildred, it is yours, your betrothal ring.' Only once before had I seen Mildred look so animated but that had been the forerunner of disaster. I shook myself. There was surely no need to expect a disaster this time. For a girl reared as Mildred had been, by Puritan parents, with religion a powerful force in her life, this was a most suitable match.

So why this sense of uneasiness? I pushed it aside. It was born of the fear and distrust I had lived through in Devon, nothing more.

# FOURTEEN

## Linseed Oil and Beeswax

On the morning after the vicarage dinner, I went, as I had formed a habit of doing, to walk round the Minstead rose garden. It was so well kept and so much resembled the one that my late husband Hugh had cultivated at Hawkswood. It reminded me so strongly of Hugh that when Sir Henry came into the garden in search of me, I didn't notice he was there until he came up beside me and cleared his throat.

I turned to him, apologizing. He smiled and paced beside me for a while, making a few comments about the roses, but then said: 'You have told me that you need to stay through the first days of August. But what then? You are welcome to stay as long as you find necessary, of course. Those were Walsingham's orders. But may I know more about your plans? Will you be going home in August and if so, will you be coming back at any time? Oh, and has a date been decided for Mistress Gresham's marriage?'

'My plans are doubtful,' I said. 'I don't yet know. But as for the marriage, it is to take place on Monday the twenty-eighth of July and please will you come?'

Sir Henry paused to cup a bloom in his hand and sniff the scent. 'This rose has an exquisite perfume. It's a new variety; I have a clever gardener. He grafted one variety on to another and this is the hybrid.'

'My late husband did things like that,' I said. 'He created two hybrids himself and was so proud of them! At the wedding, would you consent to give the bride away? Mistress Gresham has asked me to ask you.'

'I would indeed!' Sir Henry looked pleasantly surprised. 'It would be appropriate since she is a guest in my house and her parents are not here. I am glad that Daniel Atbrigge is to wed again. A vicar needs a wife. Who is to conduct the ceremony?'

'I believe Atbrigge means to ask the vicar here, Dr Robyns, to perform it, in the Chenston church, given that Dr Robyns is well enough.'

'Very suitable and yes, Robyns has now recovered. I am sure he will be pleased to officiate. I say yes to everything.'

'Mildred will be delighted. That is most kind of you, Sir Henry,' I said.

He smiled again and then, like a rapier, shot out a question I didn't expect. 'A queen's messenger came for you this morning. I saw the letter he left for you, on the breakfast table before you came downstairs. It had Walsingham's seal.'

I was taken aback. I had been slow in rising that morning and the messenger had come and gone before I reached the breakfast table. Hayward had put the letter by my platter and Sir Henry had seen it and, naturally enough, his curiosity had been aroused.

He said: 'According to Walsingham, you are here on business connected with the danger posed by the Stuart woman. Well, as I have already said, I find it strange, and stranger still that a woman should be employed in such work but here you are, all the same. And although you may not have understood this, I worry about you. I have not asked questions but I have as it were remained alert in case I am needed, and I have been watchful. Since you are here because of suspicions involving Chenston, I very naturally wondered if you would be interested in what they call their Midsummer feast – I know all about that – and I wasn't surprised when on Midsummer morning, chancing to be early awake and looking out of my dressing room window, I glimpsed you slipping indoors, wrapped in a cloak, at daybreak. Had you been out spying on the Midsummer celebrations?'

'Yes,' I said. 'I learned nothing to the point. But there will be another feast at Lammas and Brockley will if possible spy on that.'

'I see. So I am right. You are interested in the Chenston customs. If you had talked to me about them before, I could have told you that whatever high jinks the villagers get up to in the forest at midsummer, there's no harm in them. They are nothing but a feast and a dance to welcome the sunrise.'

'They didn't welcome the sunrise,' I said. 'The gathering broke up before dawn.'

'Having danced and drunk until all they longed for was just to go home to bed,' said Henry dismissively. 'Now, what is this about Lammas?'

'I heard an announcement made, saying that there would be another feast on the eve of the first day of August, which is Lammas.'

'Oh, I dare say. In memory of King Rufus, I expect. They used to have a Lammas feast in days gone by, in Rufus's memory; I suppose they're reviving it. There have always been legends about his death. So that's why you want to stay until after the first of August. Well, I am not supposed to put hindrances in your way but I wish you would take my word for it that there's nothing sinister in these . . . occasions. I doubt if the Chenston villagers would like to be spied on and while you're here I am responsible for your safety and that of your servants. Yes, I did wonder what Walsingham had to say to you, what he might be asking you to do next. I can't protect you if I don't know what I need to protect you from.'

'He asked what, if anything, I had discovered,' I said. 'So far, of course, nothing. But he wishes me to be thorough. These are dangerous times. He is concerned for my sister, the queen. It is his duty to safeguard her and so is it mine. He says that her majesty, though courageous as ever, is afraid.'

I wasn't actually lying, for Walsingham's letter did say those things. It was just that it said a good deal more, which I didn't feel free to repeat.

*. . . I will be relieved if you find nothing for I desire no complications, but I would wish you to be as thorough as you can. The need may soon pass, however. Before long, I hope to have the serpent's head off. I have allowed her to write and receive letters, believing that she does it without my knowledge. But in both directions, the letters pass through my hands. A man called Anthony Babington has written to her with details of a very evil plot. We don't yet know the names of his fellow*

*conspirators but when we do, the net can close on them and as soon as we have Mary's consent to the plot, we will arrest her as well. This is confidential but in view of the work you are now doing you should, I feel, be kept informed. Our present tasks are aspects of each other. If you find traces of any conspiracies, inform me at once. Snippets will do. Snippets sometimes add together to make interesting pictures. Her majesty the queen sends you her love. She hopes to have you in attendance on her as usual in August but will excuse you if it hinders your task. She is courageous as ever, although until all the conspirators are in our net, danger will still haunt her.*

I could not repeat all that to Sir Henry. Walsingham would himself tell those details to those he felt should know them. I said: 'I hardly know why he troubled to write to me, except that perhaps it was at the wish of the queen. It's kind of you to be so willing to house me and my companions for so long. But until Lammas is past, my plans will be doubtful.'

'In my opinion,' said Sir Henry, 'the whole idea of plots being hatched in Chenston is an absurdity and I have told Walsingham so. But I suppose you have your orders, as I have. Did *anything* in the least notable occur at that mysterious Midsummer affair?'

Some aspects of it had been so notable that if I were to tell him about them, his hair would rise on his scalp. 'It was just a feast and a dance,' I said. 'There was a fire and they slaughtered a goat, cut it up and roasted it. It formed part of the feast. It all ended before morning broke. Meanwhile,' I said, trying to turn the conversation and attempting to sound bright, 'we have to organize Mildred's wedding. I intend to take her to Salisbury for some new gowns.'

'If she is to be a vicar's wife, she won't need brocades that stand up on their own,' Sir Henry said with some amusement. 'Certainly not if Atbrigge is the vicar! I think he has Puritan leanings. I haven't met him often but every time I do, he talks about the Old Testament.'

'Mildred's parents are Puritan. But she should still have a new gown to wear for her wedding, and some new sheets and so on.'

'As to that, I will give her a set of sheets as a wedding present. She is truly happy in her betrothal?'

'Very much so, I think.'

'I look forward to the great occasion.'

In Salisbury we found a sempstress who could offer gowns ready-made, and would also create new ones at speed. We found two that fitted Mildred, bought new ruffs in different styles and ordered a silk dress of duck-egg blue to be made for her wedding day. We were only away for a week and on our return we once more dined with Daniel, and then again in the week before the wedding. Mildred and I were accompanied by the Brockleys as usual. On the second occasion, just as we were finishing dinner, Daniel suddenly announced that he had been remiss. 'I haven't yet shown Mildred properly round my house. Round her future domains!'

He gave her one of his beautiful smiles. 'You will be the lady of the house. You should become familiar with it. Let us all go round it together. It's quite big. Ben and I rattle around in it; like a couple of dice in an arrow chest.'

He saw me and Dale both blink in surprise at the mention of dice and said: 'I dislike gambling but winter evenings are dark and long and there are plenty of games that involve throwing dice but need not be concerned with money. I hope Mistress Mildred will share them with me. I play chess and backgammon, too.'

'I know how to play both of them,' Mildred said shyly.

'That is excellent!' The smile embraced us all. 'Come, let us all inspect Mistress Mildred's home to be.'

The man that Mildred had rejected only a few months ago, had taken her on a tour of his home and also of his farm and she had disliked almost everything she saw. I wondered how this expedition would turn out.

The tour began downstairs, with Daniel's study, which was behind the parlour. He was obviously proud of it. It was his very private place, he told us, where he didn't allow things to be disturbed. 'If it needs dusting, I dust it,' he said.

I looked round the study with interest. It had a desk and writing things, with a cupboard below which Daniel said held paper, and there was a shelf of books, arranged between book-ends which hadn't been pushed up tight so that the books leant casually against each other. Also, to my surprise, I noticed that in one corner was what seemed to be a small workbench. I moved a little closer and saw that there were woodworking tools there, and a couple of shallow boxes, one containing pieces of wood, of different kinds, and one full of small wooden animals. I asked about it.

'Oh, that's an amusement of mine,' Daniel said. 'I like carving things. The potter in Minstead takes his wares regularly to Lyndhurst market and he takes some of my little wooden animals too, and sells them. They make toys for children or ornaments for the home. He brings me the money and I can use it for charity. There's old Granny Dunning, for instance – she's the grandmother of Jacky Dunning of whom I think you have heard . . .'

'We have,' I agreed.

'She doesn't live with Jacky's family. She has her own cottage and a little maidservant, but she gave her smallholding up years ago and it's let to someone else now, so she's poor. She still has a vegetable patch and some fowls and a few goats, and the little maidservant lass sees to them, with the help of Jacky's father – he's Granny's eldest son – when he feels like it, which isn't often. Granny Dunning can just about pay her rent and buy ale and flour for bread. Mr Dunning grudges his help. She's one of the ones I use my whittling money for. Poor soul, she's very old now, and ailing. However, about this study of mine. I dust it and I let Joan sweep the floor but that's all. I won't even let her polish the panelling and she is strictly forbidden to move anything on my desk or my workbench.'

The dining chamber, of course, we knew, so we went on to look at the parlours.There were two, both at the front, one on each side. The one to the east was smaller than the room we had seen and just as plain, but Daniel told Mildred that if she wished, she could have it as her own private parlour and of course she could do whatever she liked with it.

We saw linen closets and Joan's stillroom, a proof of her industry, for its shelves bore rows of bottles containing fruit preserves and medicinal remedies. Then we had a glimpse of the kitchen, where Joan and Bella were busily plunging our dinner dishes into hot water. They clearly didn't want our intrusion but we stayed long enough to admire the pans hanging on the walls, the shelf of serving dishes, the hams hanging from the beams, and the bunches of culinary herbs hanging alongside them; the stockpot and the tub of water. 'John Sweetapple fills that for us every morning, from the well,' said Daniel.

We moved on to a small room evidently devoted to prayer: one candlestick on a small, plain altar and a prie-dieu set before it; another shelf of books, like the one in the parlour, a little writing table at one side. It was all very clean. 'Joan can dust here all she likes,' Daniel said when I commented. 'There's nothing that can get lost. Now I must show you the room where I hold the bigger parish meetings and so forth. I use my hall for the smaller ones. This one is where I shall welcome our guests on the wedding day and where we shall hold the feast and afterwards dance. I am not opposed to dancing. The queen herself enjoys it, so I have heard.'

He glanced at me as he spoke, raising an enquiring eyebrow and I nodded. 'When I attend on her, I often take part,' I said. 'She likes to practise steps with her ladies on most mornings. Her musicians are always kept busy.'

'I hope you'll admire my parish room,' Daniel said and showed us into it. It was beyond the study and it ran from one side of the house to the other. It was twice the size of the hall and more than large enough for dancing. It held a central table with benches on either side and a chair at each end. Tall windows at both ends and along the rear wall gave it an excellent light. It was handsomely panelled and the floor was made of polished wood but there were no rushes or rugs, and, of course, no wall hangings. There was a good-sized fireplace, though. The parish council wouldn't freeze in winter.

Upstairs came next. Here there were several bedchambers leading in and out of each other, a schoolroom for Ben, with more books and writing things and a whitewood table indelibly stained with ink, and an awkward, narrow set of stairs into an attic which was like most attics; dusty and full of discarded objects, broken stools, hampers with damaged wickerwork and old clothes poking from under their lids, an ironbound chest with nothing in it at all, and rust on the iron hoops.

Every room was panelled, though in the bedchambers the panelling only went halfway up the walls, with white plaster above. 'I sometimes think I should paint all the panelling white,' said Daniel. 'It means so much work for Joan as it is. It's kept polished, as you see. Not that I insist that she does it; I think that panelling can be left to look after itself. Joan's the one who insists.'

'How does she polish it?' Dale asked. 'I mean – what with and how can she reach the high panels?'

'She has a long-handled sponge and she uses a mixture of linseed oil and beeswax. I buy such sponges for her at Lyndhurst market. You'll soon get to know where to get what,' he added to Mildred. 'When in doubt, ask Joan.'

'I think the panels are beautiful,' Mildred said. 'I can help Joan look after them. I know how to make beeswax and linseed oil polish.'

'It's a good mix,' Brockley observed. 'It brings saddlery up glossy as if it were new and a deal more pliable than new tack ever is.'

'And it has a good clean smell and yes, it does make my panelling shine,' said Daniel. 'Ben wishes we had a panel that slides aside to reveal a hidden room containing something lurid. He has heard of priest holes, of course, and secret rooms with skeletons in them. The sort of tales that boys delight in. A couple of years ago, I caught him going round the big parlour, tapping panels to see if they sounded hollow. He was quite disappointed because they didn't.'

'Where is he just now?' I asked. Ben usually joined us when we visited, but this time there had been no sign of him.

'He has been slack with his Latin,' said Daniel. 'I told him he couldn't dine with us today, but must stay in his room and finish the work he should have done yesterday. I allowed him a tray of buttered bread and small ale. He was much disappointed, Mistress Mildred, for he wished to join us at dinner. He has taken to you and is happy about the wedding. I said though that when he had finished his task, he could go out and ride his pony and I imagine that he's doing that now.'

'I'm sorry. I would have liked to see him. If I had been here and known in time, I would have pleaded for him,' Mildred said.

'I would probably have forgiven him and let him dine with us if you had! A boy needs a firm hand but in future you will guide me as to how firm that hand needs to be.'

Once again, I experienced a twinge of uneasiness and I now understood it, or thought I did. There was a hard facet to Daniel and though he was in love now, later on, would Mildred one day come up against that hardness? The marriage was now a settled thing. I wished I didn't have that cold snake of misgiving inside me.

We went down to the larger parlour where there were more refreshments to round off our visit, and at length, we set out for Minstead, letting our horses move at an easy walk. Brockley and Mildred were a little way ahead; though still near enough for me to hear Mildred saying to Brockley that on her wedding day, when she rode to Chenston on Grey Cob, he ought to have his mane and tail trimmed. I was riding beside Dale. We were halfway there, when Dale suddenly said: 'Ma'am, I just hope all this goes well. May I say something I keep thinking?'

'Of course you may, Dale. Go on.'

'I don't like that man, ma'am. It's his eyes. They're too intent. When he looks at me, I feel I'm being skewered. And his face is all taut, as though he's holding something inside that's boiling and bubbling to get out.'

She had done it. Dale had had another of her unexpectedly percipient moments and she had found words for my feelings. But the date was set, banns were being read, Mildred was wearing his betrothal ring and she at least seemed happy.

'He does have an intent gaze, Dale, but I think it's just because he concentrates on whoever he's talking to. And as for his face, well, he can't help that! I don't think he's handsome, myself, but Mistress Gresham does.'

'I wish her well of him,' said Dale and sighed. 'Time will tell. I hope it tells good things, that's all.'

It was Monday, the twenty-eighth of July, and July was behaving well. We had woken to sunshine and a few harmless white clouds, and a light breeze chasing their shadows across the cornfields round Minstead. The harvest had recovered from the rainstorm and was growing vigorously now. Poppies and cornflowers glowed amid the crop; and in the grass of the paddock where our horses had grazed overnight, grasshoppers were chirping. We set out early for Chenston, with Sir Henry as one of our party, but to begin with, went to the inn where Felix Armer regaled us with cider, until the moment came when the church would be full and the bridegroom waiting for us.

And there, suddenly, the things Dale had said, and my own secret unease about that strange hardness in Daniel, came forcefully into my mind. Abruptly, I said to Mildred: 'It's not too late! Even now it's not too late! Mildred, if you have any doubts, any doubts at all, tell me. I will do the rest.'

Mildred, beautiful in her duck-egg-blue gown and the chaplet of cornflowers that Dale and I had made for her hair, gazed at me in amazement and so did Sir Henry, who looked quite appalled. He started to say something, choked on it and then stopped. Mildred, however, smiled at him and said: 'I have no doubts. I would have said, long since, if I had.'

'That's all right then,' I said and Sir Henry took out a handkerchief and wiped his brow, remarking that the morning had become very warm. I gave him a glance of commiseration. If Mildred had asked to be rescued, we should have had to do it but it would have been a horrid undertaking. And then it was time to remount and to ride the last short distance to the church, where Sir Henry would lead Mildred to the altar.

Felix Armer, on foot, led our little procession to the church, where John Sweetapple and another man were waiting to take charge of the horses. We dismounted and went in, out of the sunlight, into the cool, shadowy interior. I looked about me.

A row of seats had been left vacant for us at the front and

as we walked along the aisle, I saw Daniel's housekeeper Joan Orchard, seated beside a big tow-headed man who was presumably her husband, with the four Orchard boys just beyond them. Two benches further on, I saw Pickford, and beside him were Jennet and Susie, having a giggly conversation with a row of three young girls behind them and also with Jacky Dunning who was there with his parents. I realized that Etheldreda wasn't present and wondered why. I hadn't seen her of late. I only hoped that Sir Henry really had put the fear of God into the villagers where she was concerned.

We settled on the front bench. Daniel Atbrigge was waiting by the altar and we smiled at him, as much as to say: '*Don't worry, your bride is coming.*' Ben Atbrigge was already seated on our bench, looking serious and slightly ill at ease in a stiff new doublet and what looked like a painfully starched new ruff. We exchanged quiet greetings. And then there was a stir at the back of the church and we turned to see that Sir Henry was escorting Mildred in.

She held his arm as they came up the aisle, not a lengthy one, in this small church. Daniel turned his head to watch as she came towards him. He had abandoned his clerical black for a doublet of russet, with puffed hose of russet and cream, russet stockings and a ruff, stiffly starched like Ben's. Dr Julian Robyns, awaiting them before the altar, was the one in the official black gown.

The service proceeded. The vows were exchanged. Daniel placed the wedding ring on Mildred's hand. They were pronounced man and wife and Daniel was invited to kiss his bride, while the congregation cheered.

The couple were last out of the church and we were all waiting for them as they emerged, blinking a little in the brilliance of the sun. There were more cheers and then everyone turned to follow the new-wedded pair the short distance to the vicarage, where the wedding breakfast would be served.

It was then that I saw Etheldreda. She was standing by the wayside, looking utterly distraught, her hair slipping from under her coif; bits of grass clinging to her skirts. So much so that I stepped out of the procession and said to her: 'What is it?'

'Not now. You must go to the vicarage. But later. I wanted to see you, to beg you to let me speak to you, before you go back to Minstead.'

'Tell me quickly what's the matter. And then,' I said, troubled by her white, wan face, 'better straighten your coif and brush your skirts and come to the feast with us. The whole village has been invited so that includes you. And you look as though you need something.'

'It's Windfall.'

'You mean . . . Windfall . . . the filly?'

'She's gone! She was in my paddock. But this morning she wasn't there! The gate was shut and she's not big enough yet to jump out. I think she's been taken! There're signs. She's big enough to eat grass and fodder; she's not suckling much now, she can survive without her mother but she's still just a baby, she'll be frightened, so bewildered!' Etheldreda was crying. I had never liked her all that much but now I wanted to put my arms round her. She said: 'There were *footprints*. She's been snatched, by *them*; you know who I mean. And it's only three days to Lammas.'

# FIFTEEN

## The Madness of Fools

Daniel's council chamber had looked big when he showed it to us during our tour of his house, but when the whole village crammed into it, it dwindled. The crowd at his wedding feast packed it solidly and we could hardly get through to the table where the food was laid out. Extra supplies had been set out in the hall.

The wedding breakfast was substantial. 'Everyone in Chenston has contributed something,' Sir Henry remarked. 'Atbrigge has just whispered it to me. It isn't all the work of Joan and Bella.'

Jennet and Susie were on duty, helping the guests to choose, and little Hannah was assisting them. Sir Henry very chivalrously pushed through the throng on my behalf and returned with a tankard of cider and a filled platter for me. It was heaped with cold chicken, cold pork sausages wrapped in bacon, radishes, a chunk of white bread, and a spoonful of pickled cucumber on one side. I caught sight of the Brockleys, ploughing sturdily through the crowd with dishes containing what looked like cold chops and bread rolls and slices of fruit tart; Brockley was coping with the platters while Dale grasped two earthenware goblets of drink of some kind. Whatever their capers in the forest, the villagers had good hearts, I thought.

I had brought Etheldreda in but had somehow lost touch with her in the crowd. Joan came past me, bringing fresh supplies for the table, and I caught at her sleeve. 'Have you seen Mistress Hope at all?'

'The Hope woman? Eating in the kitchen, out of the way,' said Joan contemptuously. She apparently shared the villagers' unfriendly attitude to Mistress Hope.

I would have gone to the kitchen to find her, but at that

moment, Sir Henry, who had gone back to fill his own platter, returned to me, wanting to talk and the opportunity was lost. I was caught up in it all, part of the happy buzz as I fell into conversation with this person and that, until the feasting ended and the table was pushed back. Half a dozen villagers with musical instruments struck up the melody for a dance, and Daniel led Mildred on to the floor, which was the signal for other couples to follow.

The Pickford sisters came out from behind the table and at once found partners; they were guests now like everyone else. It went on for a long time, until dusk was falling, and Joan and Bella were lighting candles. I danced with Brockley, with Sir Henry and John Appleyard, and then found myself being invited to take the floor with the gap-toothed Master Pickford, who when the mob wanted to hang Etheldreda was so anxious to point out that there was no shortage of trees. I wasn't very willing but accepted because it was polite. I tried to make conversation to him about his lovely daughters but he made few replies. He just leered into my face and his breath smelt dreadful. He was a poor dancer, too, and kept getting the steps wrong.

On the other hand, Master Orchard senior, who was my next partner, danced with surprising grace, and made conversation that was almost courtly, despite his broad country voice. All the same, while I was dancing with him, and listening to those gravelly tones, I kept thinking that the harsh and resonant voice of the Antlered One in the woods was unquestionably similar. Somehow, Felix, who had fought against the mob that attacked Etheldreda, had never struck me as a likely candidate for the Antlered One. But more and more, Master Orchard did.

When that dance ended, there was a mild stir and then ten or twelve young girls, including the Pickford sisters, formed a ring and began a set dance, traditional to the village, Sir Henry whispered to me. As it ended, I saw that the bride and groom had vanished from the scene. So had Hannah, no doubt to look after Mildred's toilette. There clearly wasn't going to be any noisy business of escorting the bride to her bedchamber or any horseplay when the groom went to join her. Daniel Atbrigge had probably forbidden it.

My feet were aching. Guests were being invited to take partners for another dance, but this time no partner had presented himself to me, for which I was thankful. My stamina was no longer what it used to be. With considerable relief, I subsided on to a settle. A few moments later, Etheldreda suddenly appeared, and joined me.

'Didn't want to make a fuss when that Joan Orchard told me to eat in the kitchen. I did, for the sake of peace but the whole village was invited, and that meant me as well, and who's Joan to be so high and mighty? Those boys of hers are the worst louts in Chenston,' she said resentfully.

'I know,' I said. 'About your filly. Mistress Hope, just what happened?'

Etheldreda's face was woebegone. 'I woke up this morning and looked out of my window and the mule was in the paddock but I couldn't see Windfall. So up I got, quickly like, and rushed down and outside and looked and she weren't there. I went to the gate and looked at the ground, both sides. It's trodden, not grassy, and there was a shower last night so there was moist ground this morning. There were prints all right and more like boots than hooves though I think I made out Windfall's footprints – she's not shod, of course. She's been taken, that's what. *Taken.* And for what, I asks myself. Like I said, the Lammas is nigh and there's going to be a forest gathering then. Maybe they want her for summat then. Felix Armer told me about the Lammas feast. Asked if I felt like joining in for once.'

'What did you say?' I asked her.

'I said no, thank you kindly, what else? I want no part of those goings on. But what do they want with my Windfall?' She sagged, suddenly stricken with exhaustion. 'I get lonely now Nick's not there to talk to,' she said. 'I've been to London to see my daughter Edith. Stayed a week, got back two days ago. Sir Henry's had words with the chief villagers and Dr Atbrigge; I thought it would be safe to leave Windfall in her field and she were all right when I came home.'

In her usual fashion, she was wandering off the point. She seemed to expect me to say something so I asked if she had found her daughter well. 'What family has she?'

'Her man and their four chicks as they call them: two boys, two little maids. All well, but there's a bit of gossip going round where she is. Thought you'd like to hear it so I been wanting to see you anyhow. Her man's sister, Cath, she's called, she's housekeeper to an artist, a fellow that paints portraits. You pay him, he draws a picture of you and paints it so you can hang it on a wall in your house.'

'Yes, I know.' I had once had a portrait done of my daughter Meg.

'Well, while I was there, this Cath came visiting and she had such a tale to tell. This artist that she works for, he's busy painting a group of men and it's a great nuisance because he can never get them all together; he has to work piecemeal. But the thing is, he's a Catholic though he keeps quiet about it mostly, and so are all the men in this picture. And the one who arranged it, who's paying, is a fellow called Sir Anthony Babington and he let out one day that they are all sad for the plight of that Mary Stuart that there's been whispers about here, like I told you when I came to see you . . .'

The name of Anthony Babington made me jump so much that I barely stopped myself from jumping physically, which might have put Etheldreda off her stride, just as I needed to keep her to the point. 'I remember what you said,' I told her, restraining myself. 'What about this picture?'

'Him that's arranging it; he's in it himself, he's been painted already and he sometimes watches when one or other of the men it's to be of . . .'

'He sometimes watches while one of the others is being painted.' I said helpfully, before Etheldreda became impossibly entangled in her own confused grammar.

'Yes, well, sometimes they talk, quiet like but once in a while the artist that's doing the painting overhears and Cathy does too, because she's sometimes about at the same time. If a room needs dusting, she dusts it and the artist never stops her. And once . . .'

Etheldreda paused, but her pale eyes suddenly became big and round. 'What?' I asked.

'She were dusting and the man that's paying, said to the one that was being painted, that it would be a fine present one day for this Mary Stuart; it would remind her of the band of loyal followers that did so much for her, and the fellow that was being painted, said back that he was glad they were having this portrait done because that way posterity would know what they looked like. They were talking soft like, but all the same, Cath did hear them and the artist did too and he got angry and *don't talk in that fashion; it's not wise. You pay me to paint, I paint. I don't ask what you want this picture for and you don't need to tell me.* Cath said she just got on with her dusting but it all sounded sinister like to her. And since you're here at all *because* there's been talk of Mary Stuart, to do with what goes on in the forest, I reckoned you'd be interested.'

I was. Walsingham had mentioned Anthony Babington in his letter to me. This was assuredly a snippet that would interest him. I told Etheldreda that we would do all we could to find her lost filly. And I sent Eddie off with a letter the next morning.

We had been invited back to the vicarage for dinner two days later. Before we set out, when we were in the stable yard, about to mount, Brockley suddenly asked me: 'When is Lammas, madam? I mean, which night is the feast to be held? The one before, when it turns the first of August at midnight, or is it the next night, the night of the first?'

'It's Eve of Lammas,' I said. 'The night of the 31st. Thursday night.'

'Are you sure, madam?'

'Quite sure, Brockley. I heard the announcement. I remember the words.' I certainly did. I would never forget any detail of that terrifying night. *And next time is Lammas, the Eve of August the first, and here in this clearing, on that Eve, we will hold the Lammas feast, the last blessing of the crops before harvest time is upon us.*

'Good. This is Wednesday. I shall have all of tomorrow to prepare.'

'You had better rest all tomorrow,' I said. 'I wonder if you ought to go. I don't like sending you into danger, Brockley.'

'Do you think the villagers of Chenston would murder me, madam?'

'I don't know,' I said. 'I was afraid, that night. It was so weird. They all had goat masks on. I couldn't tell one from another and they didn't seem to be properly human. I don't suppose Eddie would ever admit it but he was frightened, too.'

'I know. He told me so. He was scandalized and petrified both at the same time.'

'I remember,' I said, 'what Nick White had to tell us, about the accident with the scythe. *If* it was an accident.'

'I still have to be there,' Brockley said with resolution. 'I shall take no risks, believe me.'

'I shan't sleep that night,' I said. 'I'll be awake until you get home safely. If Eddie's back in time, will you take him with you?'

'You surely don't want to risk us both, madam!'

'Brockley! How can you jest? This is so serious!'

I said it so sharply that Jaunty's ears went back and he stamped a hoof. But the sharpness ended in something like a sob. Very gently, as he helped me to mount, Brockley said: 'Fran is honest and loving and often very wise and Fran is my dear wife. To us both, you are our gallant lady and since you are ready to risk yourself for the protection of your royal sister, then we are ready to share that risk so as to protect *you.* It is necessary that you should understand what happens in the Wood, in case it bears on the safety of the realm. Therefore, this Lammas, I shall be there as your deputy.'

Ever since I had rebuked him for letting concern for me go too far, there had been a constraint between us. We had been too polite to each other, too careful of what we said. But now Brockley was smiling, and when Brockley smiled like that, it changed his face just as thoroughly as Daniel Atbrigge's smile changed his. I was glad to see it. The constraint was gone. We understood each other now. I said: 'Take care. Hide in that hollow oak but for the love of heaven, *stay* in it; don't go rushing out as Eddie did. Dale and I will see the night through together.'

But before that, came the dinner at the vicarage in Chenston, and I for one was anxious to go. I wanted to be sure that all was well with Mildred.

But she and Daniel together greeted us all at their front door, and I never saw Mildred look happier. Her hair was coifed but her light brown curls showed in front, glossy with washing, and she was dressed in the gown in which she had been married, which picked up the blue in her eyes to perfection, and those eyes were sparkling. Daniel too, although he had resumed his clerical black, had an air of great self-satisfaction. Just this first sight of them told me all I wanted to know.

They ushered us inside, and there was Hannah, curtseying and evidently proud of her elegant mistress. Ben was waiting to take our riding cloaks and bring us slippers. Once more, he seemed to be worried by his stiff ruff and Joan, emerging from her kitchen to greet us and bring us cider in the parlour before we dined, said ruefully that she'd likely put a bit too much starch in it. 'It's just that Bella and me like to keep things spruce.'

Laughing, we repaired to the parlour and accepted the cider. Daniel and Mildred were clearly on the best of terms. Their first nights together must have gone well. There was general talk for a while and then Daniel said: 'I hear your man Eddie Hale has been away to London. I wouldn't be rude enough to ask why but I do hope all is well.'

'All is well. It is a private matter. How did you come to hear of it?'

'Oh, John Appleyard, who looks after my horse, is a cousin of one of Sir Henry Compton's grooms. They get together in the William Rufus and the groom told him of Eddie's journey. Then John told me.' He took a draught of cider, casually.

'I correspond with friends in London,' I explained. 'Eddie carries messages now and then.' And then, feeling that I had just been too obviously putting a stone wall in his way, I added: 'Why do you ask?'

'I wondered if it had anything to do with the tale that Mistress Hope has been putting about, about a portrait being painted, of some of Mary Stuart's supporters.'

'Oh yes. I have heard that she brought some gossip back from London. I can't attach much importance to it,' I said dismissively.

'Really?' Daniel said. 'It sounded to me as if some of the lady's supporters might be making dangerous plans and meanwhile, behaving like madmen. Poor lady, to have to depend on such frail crutches! If they're plotting, they'll be caught before it can go an inch further! Having a portrait painted! The madness of fools!'

'Well, it may be all for the best,' said Mildred. 'We have all prayed for the queen's safety; perhaps this is the answer to the prayers.'

Daniel leant over to pat her hand. 'That's my dear Milly. You are right, of course. I just can't bear stupidity, even the stupidity of an enemy! My own villagers can be foolish and then I grow angry with *them.* Though it's not their fault; they are simple people, easily swayed by emotion. As you saw when they tried to seize poor Mrs Hope, accusing her of witchcraft!'

Wishing to change the subject and seeing my opportunity, I said: 'Is there any news of her filly, Windfall, that disappeared?'

Daniel grew sombre and Mildred shook a sad head. 'Nothing,' she said. 'And there has been a very thorough search.'

'*Very* thorough!' Daniel agreed fervently. 'The loss has been cried in Lyndhurst and Minstead – did you not hear it?'

'Yes, we heard it,' I told him. I had sent Brockley to arrange things with the criers and I had paid for their services.

'There have been search parties out, going through everyone's fields and holdings, prying into outhouses, searching through the woods,' Mildred added.

'The footprints that Mrs Hope found did look as though the filly had been taken, but it isn't certain,' said Daniel. 'Mrs Hope says she can't yet jump gates, but perhaps she can, after all. People do go and stare at the animal, after all. Any boot prints could have been made by folk doing that. My feeling, though, is that she *was* stolen, taken away and put up for sale somewhere. There was a horse fair near Salisbury yesterday, I think.'

'Mrs Hope is so distressed,' said Mildred. Evidently she had adopted Daniel's preference for the modern Mrs instead of the traditional Mistress. 'I saw her earlier this morning,' she said.

'My new wife is already learning the work of a vicar's lady, visiting parishioners who are in trouble,' said Daniel proudly.

Ben said: 'I think Joan's coming. I can hear her footsteps.'

A moment later, round and red as ever, and flushed from her kitchen tasks, Joan was in the doorway, bobbing a curtsey and then abandoning formality to announce that the soup tureen was on the table; best hurry afore it got cold, it was hot soup this time, chicken broth with parsley in and cumin and just a touch of saffron. We repaired to the dining chamber.

# SIXTEEN
## Lammas

'I rather wish you *would* consider taking Eddie with you,' I said, as I watched Brockley preparing for his vigil in the forest on Lammas Eve. Eddie had returned the previous day. I had told him where he could change horses and the court was conveniently in Richmond. He had delivered his letter to Walsingham on Tuesday, been given the reply at once and returned to us late on Wednesday evening. I wasn't at all easy about letting Brockley go alone. 'I am not giving orders, but . . .'

'No, madam,' said Brockley, fastening his belt. Dale was on her knees, making sure that his sword and his belt knife were properly attached. She was like a squire of bygone times, making the knight he served ready for battle. 'Eddie must not be endangered,' Brockley said, 'or be the cause of danger, again.'

Dale finished and Brockley turned to pick up a small sack that was lying on his bed. He said: 'I can't imagine needing this any more than I'm likely to need Eddie, but I intend to go fully armed. I'm taking Tommy Reed's toy bow and his quiver-full of arrows with me. I'll give it back to the boy when we get home. Madam, you did right to take Eddie because you are a woman and it was right for you to have a man with you as you went into danger. But a man should be able to take care of himself.'

'Is there really danger?' Dale was alarmed. '*Roger?*'

'Not if Brockley stays safe in his hollow tree and doesn't dash forth to interfere in anything that goes on in the clearing,' I said. 'The tree is easy to find and the hollow is deep. Even if they go quite mad and have an orgy, or there's the ceremony of the Maiden and you think she's a distressed damsel and you long to rush to her assistance, Brockley, *stay put!* The one Eddie and I saw seemed perfectly happy about it all and in any case she was offered a chance to withdraw. Don't try to rescue her. I must ask Atbrigge what the villagers do or say when young unwed girls unexpectedly produce babies nine months after one of these forest meetings.'

'I know the answer to that,' Brockley informed me unexpectedly. 'When we went to Mistress Mildred's wedding, I helped John Appleyard lead the horses to his stable and he told me that there'd be another wedding soon, as Jacky Dunning's sister was marrying a man from Fordingbridge; the other side of the forest. All fixed in a hurry, he told me, vicar saw to it. Seemingly, the lass is having a baby next winter; best have it born in wedlock. *We don't turn our noses up at what's natural*, that's what he said to me. *We just tidy things up and good luck to the wench.* That's how it's dealt with, madam. Appleyard didn't go into any more details but the timing is about right if it happened at Walpurgis. But if it looks as though there's to be murder done, what am I to do then?'

'No one looked like being murdered when I was a witness,' I said. 'If such a thing should happen, I leave it to your good judgement.'

'Thank you, madam,' said Brockley. He was at the doorway when he turned back to say: 'I beg that neither you nor Fran will sit up for me. Please go to your beds and sleep. Only if I am not back soon after dawn, should you begin to worry and of course I *will* be back. Don't fear for me. Sleep well.'

Then he was gone and Dale and I were left looking at each other. 'May I share your room tonight?' Dale asked. 'I don't want to be alone.'

'You can share my bed,' I said. 'I expect it's more comfortable than a truckle bed.'

'I suppose we ought to sleep,' said Dale dolefully. 'But . . .'

'I know,' I said. 'We ought to try.'

We retired as usual and to begin with, we did sleep. But just before dawn, when the first birds were piping but daybreak was only a faint greying of the eastern sky, we woke and after that there was no question of trying to go back to sleep. We rose and lit candles and without a word, Dale brought me my clothes. Without even discussing the matter, we got ourselves dressed.

By then, the sky was really lightening. We blew out the candles and sat by the window, which looked towards the track to Chenston. We watched as the grey dawn warmed to gold, the dew beginning to glitter in the grass just under the window; the sky turning to eggshell blue; somewhere, a lark's ascending song.

The track to Chenston stayed empty.

'Perhaps he has come back but didn't want to disturb us,' Dale said, and went to the next room to see. She was back in a moment, shaking her head. 'No, ma'am. He's not there. I knew he wasn't. I'd have *felt* him come back.'

To sit doing nothing was unbearable. Brockley should have returned by now. I had been back only just after dawn, and that had been the shortest night of the year. I looked at Dale and she at me, and without words we knew that the fears we had told ourselves were unreasonable, were justified after all.

'What do we do?' Dale asked. 'Should we tell Sir Henry?'

'Not until we must,' I said. 'But sitting here . . . no. Let's go down to the stable and see if . . . well . . .'

'If Firefly has come back without him?' ventured Dale.

'I hope not! He's too good a rider. Well, Eddie knows where Brockley's gone; he saddled Firefly. I saw him doing it when I went to say goodnight to Jaunty. He'll be in a terrible fuss if the horse has come back on its own. Yes, let's go down.'

It was still very early, though I could smell bread baking and when we reached the passage at the foot of the back stairs, we saw one of the maids opening windows. She wished us good morning but showed no curiosity. We went out through the side door and made for the stables. Sir Henry's grooms were always abroad early, getting the horses fed and their stalls cleaned, and there was Eddie, busy with Blue Gentle, but looking anxious all the same and relieved to see us.

'Madam, there's no sign of Master Brockley. Oughtn't he to be here by now?'

'We're worried too,' I said. 'But we don't want to speak to Sir Henry yet. I think . . . yes.' I made up my mind in that instant. 'Eddie, saddle Jaunty for me, and a horse for yourself and Blue Gentle as well. Let us all go part of the way to Chenston and see if we meet Brockley.'

'Oh, ma'am, what if we find him and he's hurt?' Dale sounded petrified. 'What if we find him lying somewhere?'

'I hope not!' I said bracingly. I was thinking the same thing. I had been hoping with all my heart that Brockley would suddenly ride in through the gateway but he did not. We mounted and started out, making haste, and were very soon at the ruined hamlet, where Brockley should have left Firefly tethered. Firefly wasn't there. Nor was Brockley. They had surely been there recently, for we found horse droppings. But where were either of them now?

'What now?' Dale quavered.

'We go on,' I said. 'Only . . .'

I considered taking the path to the clearing. It was too narrow and heavily overhung to be a good track for horses and I hesitated, wondering if we shouldn't try the broad main track to Chenston instead. I looked at it. I couldn't see far, as there was a bend just ahead.

'Listen!' said Eddie suddenly.

Somewhere on the main track, there were hoofbeats. We were all alert, and then we drooped with disappointment. 'That's not Roger,' said Dale miserably. 'Something's creaking and there's people talking. And chickens clucking and something's snorting.'

'But perhaps whoever it is may have news,' I said hopefully and we all sat still, waiting. Then they rounded the bend and there they were: Brockley on Firefly and behind him, in a little cart drawn by her mule, was Etheldreda Hope with a pile of hampers, a snorting and irritated pig and several coops containing protesting chickens, and tied to the back of the cart, a chestnut and white filly, rolling her eyes as though frightened, and straining against her halter. There were leaves in her golden mane.

'What in the world?' I gasped. Dale said: 'Oh, Roger, you're safe!' Eddie exclaimed: 'Thank dear heaven!'

The strange little party reached us and stopped. Etheldreda said: 'I'm sorry. I'm right sorry for all this. But Master Brockley said I'd got to come and it might not be safe to leave my chickens and pig behind; maybe they'd be sacrificed next.'

Brockley said: 'I've quite a tale to tell, though not until after I've dressed that wound on Windfall's haunch. I have the right salves with me, but the wound is deep – in fact, it's two wounds, in the same place. Poor little thing, she's in pain and scared half to death. It was all I could think of as a way to save her life, but it'll be a while before she stops being frightened. After I've tended her, I'll give you my tale.'

And it is, indeed, Brockley's tale. This part of the narrative is his. I must report it as he told it to me.

Everything began well. Brockley set off in good time and, just as Eddie and I had done, tethered Firefly where he could graze in what had originally been the main street of the lost village, and hid the saddlery under some partly fallen masonry.

He was cautious on the way to the clearing, pushing overhanging branches aside with the least possible noise. He reached the clearing without incident. The bonfire had been built and the stack of firewood was there at one side but nobody was present as yet. He found the oak with the wide hollow and sat down to wait inside it.

It was a long wait, but night fell at last. Like me, he heard the sounds of wild things in the wood: the calls of owls, rustlings among the leaves. Just before darkness had quite fallen, a fox ran across the clearing. Not long after that, the first voices and lanterns came, and two cloaked and hooded figures emerged from the path on the opposite side. Soon, the bonfire sprang into life and lit the whole scene.

Presently, a new figure arrived, went into the hut and came out with the antlered mask in place, as I had described. This antlered being sat down in the chair on the platform, and by then, many lanterns were bobbing into the clearing from the village path. Brockley watched a stream of shadowy shapes going to the hut and coming out again, nearly all of them with goat masks on, and he saw them gather in front of the dais. Then the Antlered One spoke.

Seated there with the stag's head mask where his head should have been, the Antlered One was curiously frightening.

Brockley felt it. He was far from being a timid man but he put a hand on the edge of the hollow to feel the rough wood, reassuring and normal, under his palm, and then placed his hand on his sword hilt. That too was reassuring.

The business began as I had related. The Antlered One spoke in his harsh voice and Brockley inched out from his hiding place so as to hear better. The gathering was welcomed, and the Antlered One spoke of the Horned God whose title was Herne, God of the Greenwood, and Venus, the lady of love and fertility.

He didn't this time have anything to say concerning flooded fields and spoilt crops, but begged his followers, or congregation (at this moment, Brockley tried to find a suitable description for the audience but failed), to consider the terrible plight of a beleaguered queen, whose evil enemy might at this moment be moving against her, to the anger of the gods. His voice at this point became full of anger too and it gained an extra resonance, dominating the crowd, who answered it with an outcry that made the hair rise on the back of Brockley's neck.

'It was so . . . so *animal*,' he said. 'It wasn't like the noise even of the mob that had attacked Etheldreda. It wasn't human. It was horrible. As though the crowd had become all one being.'

'I know,' I said.

'I was afraid,' Brockley told me. 'And yet I was in no danger and could hardly believe that even if I were caught, I would come to serious harm, yet still I was afraid.'

So had I been afraid, and so had Eddie.

The next thing to happen, however, was not alarming. When the noise of the crowd had quietened, the Antlered One quietened too and then the wine was served. Watching this made Brockley thirsty. All three of us were in his and Dale's chamber to hear his narrative and we were all sipping wine. At this point, Dale refilled his glass.

The toast to Herne and Venus was drunk as before. And then the business diverged from what I had witnessed and Brockley crept back to the hollow and stood straining his ears and gripping the edge of his refuge to keep himself from trembling. For the Antlered One had once more begun to speak. His voice suddenly acquired a new resonance and Brockley could make out most of the words.

'Soon,' said that grating, powerful voice, 'the evil queen must be disposed of and if she is not, then stronger measures must be taken. We have tried, at every meeting, to invoke the powers of the gods to do it for us, but we have not tried hard enough. Our next meeting will be on the Eve of All Hallows, and if the gods have not answered our appeal by then, we must make it stronger. If by Halloween, the evil queen still lives, then the Great Sacrifice must be held. For tonight, all may proceed as usual except that this time, the sacrifice is not a goat. The village has for too long tolerated the presence in its midst of a witch and her familiar. Sir Henry Compton has reviled us for our fears and our good vicar has counselled calm and told us we are foolish to be afraid, but we have had enough. Tonight, we pray for the death not only of the evil queen but of the witch as well, and her familiar shall be the sacrifice.'

As he spoke, someone came out of the forest, passing so close to Brockley that Brockley feared his pounding heart and anxious breathing would be heard. But they were not, and then it was apparent that whoever had just passed him was leading an animal and having some trouble with it; Brockley heard the sound of stamping hooves and muttered cursing.

Then, as they emerged into the firelight, Brockley saw that what the figure, goat-masked like all the others, had brought with him was Windfall, Etheldreda's filly. The firelight was good enough to show him the chestnut coat and the white splashes. The little filly, who after all was still little more than a foal, was nervous, not liking the goat mask, trying to sidle away from it, pulling at her halter. The light flickered on her white-encircled eyes and her laid-back ears. The figure holding her suddenly declared: 'She'll break away if someone don't give me a hand here,' and someone came out of the crowd to help. Between them they made the filly stand still, though she was trembling. She had sensed danger.

And she was right. They had taken her to the stone floor with the stains that Brockley so disliked. The Antlered One was on his feet, descending from the dais, and a knife was in his hand. He was announcing something to do with strengthening the earth and pleasing the gods with a sacrifice of blood, and her handlers were trying to make the filly raise her head, to expose her throat.

'I didn't even think about it,' Brockley said to me. 'I just did it. I groped for the sack with the toy bow and quiver inside it, got them out, put a shaft on the string and loosed.'

He was aiming for the filly's haunch, and Brockley, who had been taught archery as a boy and had a soldier's trained eye as well, hit his target. Windfall reared and plunged. Brockley shot again and with that, squealing, swinging from side to side and then rearing again, she broke free and bolted, halter ropes flying, into the forest. One lunging forehoof caught one of the men trying to hold her on the thigh and sent him reeling, and her shoulder knocked the other man off his feet, leaving him on his back on the stone floor, right in front of the Antlered One.

'Who was standing there with his knife. I thought for one mad moment that as the filly had run away, that . . . that antlered *thing* would cut the man's throat instead,' Brockley told us. His voice shook.

But someone in the crowd was shouting: 'Let's get after her!' and for a moment, Brockley said, it looked as if the whole lot of them were going to pursue the fleeing filly. 'I was so glad that she *was* fleeing. I hated to hurt her, but it was all I could think of, to make her fight them, to make her break free. I thank God that it worked. I don't think anyone realized that there was a bowman among the trees; in the firelight no one saw the arrows.'

It was the Antlered One who stopped the pursuit. His voice rang out.

'*Halt! Be still!* The gods have refused the sacrifice. So be it. But the rite must be completed! I understand now why the gods have refused our offering. For it was created from devilry, from the unnatural birth of a foal to a mule. I see now that sacrifice must be innocent, as animals are innocent. Well, we keep goats at hand, do we not? Let one be found and let the rite proceed. We will deal with the witch ourselves. We need no gods for that. Tomorrow she shall hang. Meanwhile fetch a goat! And while we wait let another serving of wine be made.'

Brockley stood rigid. The wine was duly served and there was time for it to be drunk as it was quite a long time before the replacement sacrifice was found; presumably there wasn't one anywhere at hand. But a goat was brought eventually and slain and the Antlered One emptied a cup full of blood into the earth before he announced what he called the Happy Sacrifice, by which he meant the loss of some girl's maidenhood, and from the front row of the crowd, a hooded and – so Brockley said – shrinking figure was led forward.

But when invited to refuse, she didn't take the opportunity. The Antlered One took her hand and led her to the hut, and meanwhile, the goat was being butchered and made ready for the spit and other meats were already on it.

It was then, while the meats were cooking and the gathering had started to dance round the fire and in the hut, the Antlered One was presumably bedding the girl, that Brockley called to mind the words *We will deal with the witch ourselves. We need no gods for that.*

Then, horrified by his own remissness, he muttered a prayer that the firelight would not catch him out, and crept away, making for the path that would bring him to the ruined hamlet, and his horse. He had heard no word of any plots and could not linger in the hope of hearing any. He had got to warn Etheldreda. And fetch her away to safety.

# SEVENTEEN
## Royal Terrors

The reply that Eddie had brought from Walsingham was brief but instructive. Walsingham was very pleased indeed with the snippet about the piecemeal portrait. Sir Anthony Babington was already known to be scheming on behalf of Mary Stuart, but so far there had been no progress on identifying his co-conspirators. I gathered that Walsingham was grimly pleased to learn that Babington and his foolish friends apparently wished to immortalize themselves in paint to commemorate their usefulness to Mary Stuart.

*If they are commemorating a conspiracy, then they are somewhat premature. Are they quite blind to their danger? However, turning to your own task, if you learned nothing at Lammas, do not trespass longer on Sir Henry Compton's hospitality, but be prepared to return for Halloween if necessary. I do not concern myself with what happens in the forest unless it involves conspiracies to aid enemies of the realm. But if it does, I wish to be informed . . .*

After that, came polite enquiries after the wellbeing of us all, and a courteous signing off. 'Well,' I said. 'We now know what to do.'

Etheldreda was safe for the time being. It seemed that in the past she had met and made friends with Mistress Robyns, the wife of the Minstead vicar, and now she took shelter with the Robyns family. Sir Henry was presumably aware that Brockley had been to the Lammas meeting, but he had asked no questions. He might well come to hear that Etheldreda was in Minstead, having once more fled from an accusation of witchcraft, and that might make him angry, but he wouldn't be unduly surprised.

Dale couldn't understand why we didn't just tell him everything. 'He can call on the sheriff of the county, can't he? They could just go into Chenston and question everyone till they find out who was there last night and what all this talk of evil queens means. Or wait for Halloween and then descend on them and charge them all with blasphemy because blasphemy is what it was, from what Roger says. Why not? If there's a conspiracy, that would smash it. It sounds disgraceful!' Dale was seething. 'A young girl being violated, too!'

'She appeared to consent,' I said. 'She was invited to say no. Anyway, we now have our orders. Home for the moment, back for Halloween if we are told to. Walsingham doesn't care what is done in the forest, unless it's actually a cloak for a plot to help Mary Stuart. If there has been blasphemy, he thinks the vicar should deal with it. I'm not sure that there has.'

'What?' gasped Dale.

'There were no Popish practices, and no direct insult to any Christian beliefs. I don't know where invocations to pagan gods stand, legally. Do any of that crowd really believe in them? I can't credit it – not after they get home and take their cloaks off and commonplace daylight is pouring through their windows. Walsingham wanted me to find out quietly – he seemed to think that I had more chance of finding out than a whole squad of soldiers.'

Dale sniffed. 'From all I've heard, that Richard Topcliffe in the Tower could get the truth out of anyone.'

'Truth – or lies just to stop the pain?' Brockley said. 'And he could hardly hale the whole village into the Tower.'

'He could hale that vicar!' snapped Dale. 'I can't abide that man and that's the truth.'

'Poor Mistress Mildred,' said Brockley. 'It would come hard on her if Atbrigge were dragged off to the Tower! I fear that a good many innocent men may have died because Topcliffe's rack made them confess to things they hadn't done.'

'For the moment,' I said, 'we are to go home and I think we had better take Etheldreda with us. She won't be safe in Chenston and the Robyns won't want her as a guest for ever. Certainly not with all that livestock. Since I'm leaving Chenston for now, I may well be called to attend on the queen after all. Meanwhile, Sir Henry will be relieved of our presence for a while.'

'But the blasphemy!' Dale protested obstinately.

'That's for Daniel Atbrigge to deal with,' I said patiently. 'It's a matter of religion. I must ride over to say goodbye to Mistress Mildred, and then we can start for home tomorrow. Brockley, you had better catch up on your sleep today.' I added: 'We are all so glad to see you safely back.'

If that mob of pagan worshippers had caught him trying to get Etheldreda away . . .

It was as well we didn't delay in leaving Minstead. We took four days to get to Hawkswood, for travelling with a carriage and a young foal really is very different from riding hard and changing horses, and a summons to join the queen for six weeks arrived the morning after we did.

'I will set off for court tomorrow,' I said to Wilder. 'Please look after Mistress Hope and see her pig is looked after too. And keep her chickens separate from ours.'

The queen was now at Hampton Court, an easy journey. Being at court also gave me the chance to see Walsingham, who in turn wished to see me. He saw me arrive, along with the Brockleys and I had hardly been there for an hour before he sent for me.

'The queen will want me soon,' I said doubtfully to the page who came to fetch me from my rooms on the eastern side of the first floor, where the Ladies of the Bedchamber slept.

'Her majesty knows Sir Francis is anxious to see you, Mistress Stannard,' said the page. 'You are to go to her as soon as you have spoken with him.'

Dale quickly helped me out of my riding dress and into apparel suitable for the royal court, and I went with the page, leaving the Brockleys to finish the unpacking.

Walsingham was as usual in his office at the other end of the palace, amid his usual array of papers, scrolls, books, maps and the smell of dust and ink. He looked wan, and did not rise to greet me. 'Forgive me, my stomach has been troublesome again,' he said. I knew he had bowel trouble; he had had it for years and there was a privy attached to his office, for the times when he needed it in haste.

'I am sorry,' I said.

'No matter. My plans are ripening – with your help. The snippet you sent me about the portrait of a group of young men who apparently think Mary Stuart may like it as a memento of something was as valuable a piece of work, my dear Ursula, as you have ever done. It wasn't too hard to find the artist who was painting them and he was glad enough to speak. He didn't need persuading; he had been worried about the business himself but he isn't all that worldly and had no idea who to approach. As I think I told you, we already knew Sir Anthony Babington was plotting with Mary; we'd been allowing them to exchange letters and we've read them with great interest, but Babington is annoyingly coy about naming names. He didn't even give their names to the artist – or not their right names. The artist may be unworldly in many ways but he had the sense to realize that Mr Brown and Mr Black and Mr Green and so on probably weren't what they seemed. But now we have a chance of identifying them. I made the artist lend me the picture for a day or two and I showed it round, to the queen and many others. A couple of faces have been recognized and I have an idea that I have seen two others though they don't seem to be at court now. Once we have named them all and Mary has definitely agreed in writing to their plans, we will scoop them all in, the lady with them. All the same, I am still wary of possible events down in Chenston. Are you any further forward?'

I told him about Brockley's alarming adventure at Lammas. 'Brockley paid great attention to everything was said, and all that was said concerning queens, was – these were the exact words that he repeated to me: "*the terrible plight of a beleaguered queen, whose evil enemy may at this moment be moving against her*."

'That wording sounds as though her majesty is the beleaguered queen, which she is, and in that case, those words are positively patriotic. But it's not certain,' I said doubtfully. 'The words *could* apply to Mary.'

'Was there any suggestion, either way, that men of Chenston would themselves try to do anything about it?'

'No, unless you count the Antlered One's statement about

holding a mysterious Great Sacrifice at Halloween. I didn't like the sound of that and nor did Brockley.'

'Nor do I but it doesn't sound at all like a plan for a conspiracy,' Walsingham said. 'I am feeling reassured. It begins to seem as though whatever is going on at these feasts is thoroughly improper but not treason. Let the vicar deal with his objectionable parishioners. When the queen releases you, you can probably just go home. I think I was mistaken in ever taking that Chenston woman seriously.'

I opened my mouth to say *thank you* and *yes, that's what I'll do* and instead I heard myself say: 'But something ugly is going to happen at Halloween; I'm sure of it. The vicar doesn't want to take these things seriously and if something terrible occurs at Halloween, it will be too late for him to change his mind because whatever it is will already have happened. And my friend Mildred Gresham, who was more or less my ward, has married him. If I don't pursue this, I shall be leaving her alone in that village where there has already been some grave unpleasantness and there is the threat of more. We brought Mistress Hope back to Hawkswood. Chenston isn't safe for her.'

'You want to go on?'

No, I didn't, but some other person, who lived inside me and could on occasion control my tongue, apparently did. I said so.

'I won't try to stop you,' said Walsingham slowly. 'You have the instincts of a bloodhound. Once on the scent, you follow it to the end. I'm not paying you a compliment; it's a most unwomanly characteristic.'

'That's what Sir Henry Compton thinks,' I said.

Wild goose and now a bloodhound. Dear heaven, such terms to apply to a lady! And I was inclined to agree with both of my critics.

'Sir Henry Compton is quite right!' Walsingham said. 'Your peculiar gifts have proved useful, but I am chagrined to admit it. It isn't in the nature of things that the queen and her council should be beholden to a woman for the kind of services that you sometimes render. Oh well. Your late father had a nose for trouble, too – for danger, for any kind of threat. It was how he and his father before him, and our own queen now, held – hold – their thrones secure. Not that her majesty needs to be clever at detecting danger when it comes to the Stuart woman; *her* intentions are all too plain. I am fairly sure now that Chenston isn't hatching out a conspiracy on Mary's behalf though you are probably right that something unpleasant is going to happen there at Halloween. Well, if you want to hunt that business down, you are free to do so. But take care. I really don't want you to come to harm. So, do whatever you think you should do. You probably will anyway.'

He seemed to be washing his hands of it all. Perhaps with relief; for he really did look ill. 'But take care, as I said,' he told me. 'And see that Brockley does, too.'

I left him and made my way to the queen's apartments. It was nearly evening, and I was surprised as I went into her apartments, to hear the sound of music and the click of dancing feet. She and her ladies usually practised dancing in the morning. When I was shown in, the dancing stopped and Elizabeth said: 'Ah, Mistress Stannard. Welcome. You can take over at the spinet. You play better than Jane.' A nervous maid of honour left the spinet. The queen had acknowledged my arrival but for the moment, it seemed, there was to be no private conversation.

Nor was there any private conversation the next day or the next, though I found out why dancing practice had now been moved to the late afternoon. Elizabeth was sleeping badly and rising late. I noticed that she seemed remote and on edge. She several times snapped at her ladies and during dancing practice behaved as though she were thinking of something else, yet was still liable at any moment to turn on some unfortunate lady who had made a faulty step or got out of time or played a wrong note, and berate her as though the poor thing had committed a serious crime, such as murder or at the very least, theft of royal jewellery. I avoided censure; which was recognition of a sort, I supposed.

Meanwhile, I concentrated on settling into my own place among her ladies, always a delicate task. They were never sure what to make of me. Walsingham's daughter Frances, who was a darling but was absent from the court just then, and a pretty young thing called Bess Throckmorton were friendly but one or two were hostile, not openly, but it was there. I had privileges that they did not, a room of my own, for instance, and stabling for three horses. All the rest were wary. *She's the queen's sister; not quite the same as us; keep watching her in case she tries to take advantage; when she talks alone with the queen, does she say things about us?*

I never did any such thing but it wouldn't have been any use to tell them that. It wasn't until the fourth day that I would have had the chance, anyway.

The third day was a Sunday and that day I was acknowledged just a little. I was required to carry Elizabeth's prayer book when we attended divine service in the royal chapel. The queen and her ladies were in the royal pew, which overlooked the chapel. The pew wasn't spacious, and with our spreading skirts and big ruffs and puffed sleeves and her majesty's colossal farthingale in particular, it seemed cramped. For the first time, I was close to her and this time, she smiled at me. And then, on the Monday, I was bidden to join her and the other ladies for a walk in the garden.

It was a perfect morning, sunny, with a soft breeze. We were a fair-sized crowd, consisting of not only Elizabeth and most of her women, but also many court gentlemen. That morning Elizabeth had risen early, having slept well for once, and we went out while there was still dew on the grass. The queen told us how when she was a child, she had once run across a stretch of dewy grass and then stopped and looked behind her at the green footprints she had left behind.

Bess said shyly: 'I am always charmed by the webs of hammock spiders when I see them spangled with dew. When I was small, I had a nurse who believed the old tales about the fairy folk, and she said those webs were the hammock beds of fairy kings and queens.'

Some of the gentlemen laughed politely, amused by this childish fancy, and the queen laughed too and bent her head to catch the scent of a late-blooming rose. Somewhere at the back of the crowd, a man said: 'Perhaps we all sometimes long to be innocent children again,' and the queen turned, smiling, to see who had spoken. And then went rigid.

I mean rigid. On the instant, she seemed to turn into a pillar of stone. Then she came back to life, spun on her heel, and started back towards the palace, nearly at a run. I did run, trying to keep up with her. Someone, close beside me, kept calling out: 'What is the matter?' and Bess Throckmorton three times cried out: 'Madam, what is it?' but Elizabeth took no notice. She rushed on and on and some of the guards, who were never far away, started towards her in alarm.

She shouted 'Seize him! Seize him!' to them in a wild voice, but no one knew who she meant. There was a muddle of people asking and no one knowing the answer. Two of the guards came running with us, back into the palace and up to the royal apartments. When we got there, Elizabeth stopped at the door to her inner chamber and we could see that she was trembling. She said: 'Ursula, come with me. I must speak with you alone,' and then marched forward with me at her heels, through the inner chamber and into what, essentially, was her private parlour.

It was actually half parlour and half study. Here, Elizabeth had her books and writing materials and a wide desk where she could work at the translations she so much enjoyed, to and from Latin, French or Italian. I knew that this was a pastime that both stimulated and soothed her, taking her mind away from the worries of state. But here too was a generous fireplace, though that warm August day it was not in use, and there were cushioned settles, little tables, rugs of bear and goatskin on the flagstoned floor, and on the walls, tapestries of noble lords and ladies riding through sunlit forests, all pale gold and springtime green. Here, in fact, was comfort and a sense of safety.

Elizabeth threw herself into one of the settles and waved at me to take another. She said: 'Ursula, my sister, I have not welcomed you as I ought. Yet I am glad to see you. That was a terrible moment.'

'In what way, madam?' I asked cautiously.

When I first knew Elizabeth, before I knew that we were sisters, she had been young, fiery, sometimes a terror to her ladies and her councillors, but capable also of relaxing into the informality and merriment of youth, and approachable by any troubled subject who might accost her when she was out riding for pleasure, or hunting.

With the years, however, she had acquired great dignity, a mighty presence, a fearsomeness. Encased in ruffs the size of cartwheels, in stiff buckram-lined bodices and billowing sleeves and the vast skirts that hung from her enormous farthingales, she no longer looked approachable, although inside her carapace, she still wanted to be. It had been the pride of our joint father, King Henry, that when he was out and about in his kingdom, any of his people who had lawful complaint might come to his horse's head and beg him to hear a plea. Elizabeth, I knew, had always desired to be the same. But it rarely happened now, because she no longer *looked* approachable. I was wary of her.

'There was a portrait,' she said to me now. 'A portrait of several men. You know about it. Sir Francis Walsingham made the artist lend it to him and he showed it to me. He asked if I recognized any of them, if I had seen any of the faces about in the court. Well, I recognized Anthony Babington! And one or two others. But not all. So many young men attend my court; I scarcely know some of them. I don't keep their faces in mind. But today, looking back at the crowd behind me, I *saw* one of them. Just a face among many. But he was there, one of the men in that portrait of conspirators who want to kill me! He might have had a knife under his cloak this very morning!'

'Your grace!' I said. My own stomach was turning over and over as I thought what might have happened.

'You may call me Elizabeth. It warms my heart sometimes to hear my own name spoken. Since you came to court this time, Ursula, I have held aloof from you because I didn't know what to say to you. Because I feared that alone with you, because you are my sister, I would let my guard fall, let down my drawbridge, as it were, and all my real thoughts, my fears, that all day, and sometimes all night, I keep so sternly hidden, would rush out and shame me.'

'Elizabeth, my dear sister, I . . .'

'And now they have. You saw it, just now in the garden. I gave way to terror. Ursula, Walsingham wants to bring Mary Stuart to the block. He has had enough of her and indeed, so have I. If she could – God knows she has tried often enough – she would make a treaty with any prince willing and able to provide her with an army to enter England, set her free and place her either back on the Scottish throne or, *preferably, preferably, my* throne, and place me either in a dungeon or, again, *preferably,* a grave. An unmarked grave, at that,' said Elizabeth grimly.

I said nothing. My sister looked at me out of golden-brown eyes in which I read the terror of which she had spoken.

'Her real preference would be rescue by Spanish troops, sent by King Philip,' she said. 'And at this very moment, Sir Anthony Babington, who is so proud of himself that he has had himself and his collaborators recorded for all time on canvas, is gathering supporters from among the English Catholics to make ready for the Spanish invasion by murdering me and getting Mary out of her captivity! My God! I have not persecuted the English Catholics! I have guarded them from the danger of massacre, more than once. They share in my peace, my prosperity, as any other subjects do. And this is their gratitude!

'Walsingham lets Mary and Babington correspond. Mary has been induced to trust a man called Gilbert Gifford, a Catholic plotter who has turned his coat as an alternative to execution. He sees that all the letters pass through Walsingham's hands. Walsingham wants to identify the men in that picture but most of all, he is waiting for the moment when Mary puts in writing, in plain words, that she approves Babington's plans and wills him to proceed. Once she has done that, she can be arrested and so can Babington, and *then* he will name his collaborators fast enough. Oh yes, he will!' My sister's voice was savage. 'But the moment isn't yet here,' she said. 'Mary still withholds her *fiat* and while she does so, the plotters remain at large, and at any moment, one of them may attempt my life. And one of them is here now at Hampton Court and was in the garden with me this very day.'

'My sister!'

'Ursula,' said Elizabeth simply, 'I am so afraid. I often fear to sleep at night because I'm listening for the stealthy footfall of the assassin. Sometimes in the morning, I awake feeling as though my limbs will not obey me; I want to cower in my bed like a mouse when the shadow of a hawk passes above it. Every day, I wonder, is this the day when death will strike? Have I seen my last daybreak?'

'Walsingham won't put you at risk,' I said firmly. 'You are guarded, day and night.'

'The guards were not close to me this morning, when I saw that face, one of the faces in the portrait.'

'But in such a public place, with all your friends round you . . .'

'And maybe others, not my friends, ready to defend him; there in the crowd with him, those who had the sense not to be painted for the world to see.'

'Oh, my dear!'

Court gowns notwithstanding, crushing our ruffs, denting our mighty puffed sleeves, shoving our farthingales aside, creasing our skirts, I held her in my arms while she cried.

But very soon, it wasn't Elizabeth for whom I feared, but Brockley.

# EIGHTEEN

## Be My Witness

I could stable three horses in the queen's stables, but not four. There was accommodation for my Jaunty and Brockley's Firefly and Dale's Blue Gentle, but not for Bronze, who had pulled the carriage with the luggage. So, I had decided, Bronze and Joseph Henty, who had driven the carriage, should spend one night at an inn in Hampton, the nearest village, and go home the next day. Joseph knew on what date he should return.

This plan, however, went awry because Bronze went lame during the last mile of the road to Hampton Court. Joseph had to get down and lead him, slowly, and when we stopped in the palace stable yard, Robin Dudley, the Earl of Leicester, chanced to be there and came over to look at the injury for himself. He was still the queen's Master of Horse, and if he happened to see a lame horse in the royal stable yard, he wanted to know what was wrong with it.

'Just a strain,' he said, feeling Bronze's hot foreleg. 'A daily poultice and a rest at grass, nice and soft for his feet, that will cure him in a few days. Poor old fellow,' said her majesty's favourite earl, patting Bronze's sweating bay neck. 'Struggling with that carriage in this warm weather, too. You have enough baggage there, mistress, to sink a barge. Why do women wear such immense dresses?'

'The queen wouldn't like it if I attended her wearing brown homespun with tight sleeves and no farthingale,' I pointed out.

Dudley grinned and I laughed back. I was still as indifferent as I always had been to his dark good looks; for some reason they had never moved me. But the days had long gone by when I considered him untrustworthy; had feared that he might betray the queen. I knew now that he was her best friend and her best support, much as Brockley was for me.

He said: 'Henty, put him in the field with the three other overflow horses we've got there as well. Put him in the small sectioned off part until the others make friends across the fence. Horses are so childish, always suspicious when you put a new one in with them. We don't want this fine fellow kicked. Unload that luggage and I'll send a groom to find quarters for you.' He knew all the palace grooms by name and he also knew the names of all the grooms whose masters came regularly to court. He had even been known to ask after their children. It was one of his attractive traits.

During my first week at Hampton Court, therefore, Brockley was often with Joseph, exercising our horses and seeing to the poultices for Bronze. It was three days after that conversation with Elizabeth that I returned from the morning dance practice, free for an hour before dinner time, and found Dale awaiting me, not with the fresh gown that I expected to find laid ready on my bed, but in a state of high anxiety, with Joseph beside her.

'What's this?' I said, stopping short.

'Oh, ma'am, it's Roger, he . . .' But Dale was too close to tears to go on.

Joseph, who was usually taciturn, took over with a flood of words. 'We brought Bronze into the stable yard to groom him and look at his leg. He's sound now, or so we think, but it's best to be careful. Then we took him back to the field. He's in with all the others now. I turned, madam, to say to Master Brockley how quickly Bronze has got better, and Master Brockley was lying on the grass beside me! I thought he had fallen, and I stooped over him saying, *let me help you up* and then I found he wasn't conscious.'

'What? What happened to him? Where is he now?' I demanded.

'It's that fever again!' said Dale, snuffling.

'His brow was wet,' Joseph said. 'He was sweating. It's a warm day but not so warm as that. Madam, I ran for help and two of the grooms brought out an old door that they use if anyone has a fall and has to be carried, and between us all we brought him up here and I helped Dale here to put him to bed. He's come round but he seems to be in a high fever.'

'Dale!' I snapped. 'Willow bark, basil and yarrow! Did we bring them?'

'Yes ma'am, and all what's needed for your migraines, too.'

'Go to the kitchens and get the potions made up. Say it is by my orders, Mistress Stannard's orders. Make haste.' I turned back to Joseph. 'You did well, just as you should. I must see him. Come with me.'

Brockley was in bed but awake. He greeted us with a wan smile. 'I don't know what happened. I've not felt well for two days and then, suddenly, I was so hot, so hot, and then the next I knew, I was lying on something wooden and being carried. And now . . .' he plucked at the bedsheet. 'Now I feel cold. It's the fever again; it was like this last time, feeling hot and then cold and even shivering and all my strength is gone . . .'

His voice faded. Then he rallied and with another wan smile, he said: 'This isn't due to worry over you, madam. I don't know what it's due to. Dear God, my head does ache. I know now how you feel when you have one of your sick headaches, madam . . .'

Again his voice faded and this time he just closed his eyes and seemed unable to go on.

'I hope Dale hurries with those potions,' I said. 'You had best get back to your work, Joseph. But thank you for looking after him.'

'Hadn't you better call a physician?' Joseph asked.

'Yes, I will, as long as no one tries to bleed him. They always want to bleed their patients and *that* won't help him.'

The queen sent me her own physician. His name was Roderigo Lopez and I already knew him slightly. He was a tall man in late middle age, with no grey as yet in his dark hair and beard but deep lines in his long and serious face. I knew of his past; he was a Portuguese Jew who had had to flee to England because he was in danger from the Inquisition.

'They fear all new remedies,' he told me now, after he had examined Brockley. 'I wished at times to try new ideas out but they think anything new may be allied to witchcraft or else perilous because it has its origins among those they call infidels.'

Now, having examined Brockley with great care, asking a few questions, and then testing his pulse rate and peering into his eyes and throat, he said: 'These recurring fevers do happen. Mostly they burn themselves out in time, if the patient is given the right care. I will not bleed him; I would do so if he were of a choleric nature but he is not. I would recognize that. I have seen him often when you come to court. The potions you are giving him are the best for reducing the fever. Make them a little stronger, though not too much. When the fever is reduced, he should be coaxed to swallow some broth and an egg beaten into milk and I recommend aniseed and sumac to flavour the broth, as both have a calming influence and will help his digestion. I have them here in my bag.'

He had brought a medical bag with him, a bulging affair, and when he opened it to get out the little leather drawstring bags in which he kept the ingredients for his medicines, I glimpsed steel instruments and preferred not to imagine how they would be used.

He was attentive, visiting Brockley every day and watching over his progress. The fever did begin to drop after two days and from then on, the improvement was steady. On the third day, Brockley tried to get out of bed but Dr Lopez forbade it. 'Getting up too soon as I understand you did before, will set you back,' he said sternly.

Not until the fifth day did he allow Brockley to get up and dress, and only after ten days did he permit him to go to the stables, and then, at first, only for an hour. Brockley was impatient but Dr Lopez was adamant.

'You can't go back to working all day, until a fortnight has passed since the beginning,' said Lopez. 'And three weeks would be better still.'

That evening, Brockley told Dale that he wished to speak to me alone and when I came to him, he said insistently: 'I don't believe that I *ever* fell ill or relapsed through worrying over you, madam. I don't worry about you when you're at court. I got wet and perhaps I was already unwell after handling that gown in Dr Robyns' church and that's how the thing got its grip on me.'

I said: 'But what I said to you then, Brockley, still holds.'

'I know it does, madam, and nevertheless, I shall worry about you for ever. Whatever you may say.'

'I'll try to keep out of danger in future,' I told him soothingly.

'I doubt you'll ever do that. Whenever her majesty is in danger, you'll say it's your duty to run into danger with her. I know it is, and mine as well. Just, please, be cautious.'

All this time, I had tried to attend Elizabeth as usual. On the day when Brockley was at last allowed to spend an hour helping Joseph to groom our horses, she called me once again to her private room.

'You have had a hard time of it, between my megrims and your man Brockley's illness,' she said. 'And have borne up as I would have expected.'

In private, she dropped the royal We, unless she felt – as sometimes happened – that she must remind me of her royal status.

'I think Brockley is well again now,' I said. 'I must thank you for sending Dr Lopez to us.'

'He is a clever doctor. I knew he could make Brockley well. Ursula . . .'

'Yes, majesty . . . Elizabeth?'

'One of the terrible things at this moment is that I have no power,' Elizabeth said. 'I, the queen of this realm of England, have no power over my own fate. In the past, I have at times saved myself through my own wits. Once in the days of Mary my sister's reign, I was challenged about my opinion of the sacrament and I feared to answer. I could say one thing and lose my life; say the other and save it but lose the trust of those who relied on me to be there for them when Mary died. If I had given that answer, it would have been bruited abroad, a triumph for Mary, the end of my integrity. But words came into my head: *His was the Word that make it. He took the bread and brake it and what that Word doth make it, I do believe and take it.* Falteringly, I spoke those words and evaded the trap that Mary's councillors had set for me. But now! All I can do now is wait, trembling, a deer in its covert, hearing the horns of the hunters, wondering: is it my scent the hounds are on? How long before they reach me?

'Time goes on and still, it seems, the Scottish queen has not replied to Babington's last letter. Walsingham has the names of the other conspirators now. He is only waiting for the letter in which Mary gives her consent to their plans. At the last moment, has she feared to take that last, vital step over the edge, from the safety of dreams and hopes and imaginings, into the world of real armies, real bloodshed, and a real throne with all that occupation of a throne must mean? There is that, too. A realm to be cared for and defended – yes, should the times ever be so desperate – to be defended at the expense of one's own life! That is no light burden. As a young queen in Scotland, she never understood that. Perhaps she has had time to consider it by now. And still I wake in the night and think: can I hear the feet of an assassin?'

'Elizabeth, you are well protected; your ladies are around you; several doors lie between you and any intruder and armed men guard them day and night. And surely it can't be long now.'

'She may refuse to accept Babington's plot.'

'He can still be arrested and so can his fellow conspirators.'

'But Mary will then survive to create more plots,' said Elizabeth with a sigh. 'Walsingham is wild to get her head upon the block and that will relieve us all of her devilry. Yet that, when it comes, if it comes, will be a terrible thing. A woman, my cousin, and an anointed queen, to be executed like a common felon! If one queen can be executed, then why not another? Why not me, if the times turn against me? Ursula, I wish to lay a new duty upon you.'

'Yes?' I felt nervous. It sounded like the introduction to a new assignment and I didn't want one. Elizabeth read my mind.

'No, Ursula, I am not sending you into a dangerous mission this time. When – if – Mary comes to the block, it would not be fitting for me to be present, nor would I wish it. And yet I *would* want to know what happened. I would want to know how Queen Mary died, so that I may know – just in case –

how, if the same thing should one day happen to me, how I should or should not, comport myself!'

'Elizabeth . . . majesty! I beg you, don't . . .'

Her golden-brown eyes were fixed on mine. 'It could happen. Mary's death won't make me safe. Philip of Spain may wish to avenge her. He was once king of England – more or less – and with Mary's prior claim gone may fancy pursuing his own, and avenging the murder, as he will see it, of a Catholic queen. Ursula, if Mary ever faces the block, will you agree to be a witness on my behalf?'

'Elizabeth . . . your grace . . . there will be many witnesses who will be able to tell you all you wish to know.'

'Men,' said Elizabeth dismissively. 'I would want to know how a woman sees it. How a sister of mine sees it. Will you do it, Ursula?'

As ever, I could not deny her. 'If it comes to it,' I said, 'yes, I will.'

That was on the twenty-eighth day of August. During the following week, Mary answered Babington's last letter and gave her assent to his plans and so signed her own death warrant. On the third of September, just six days after my alarming talk with Elizabeth, Anthony Babington was seized, and his fellow conspirators too were swept into Walsingham's net.

On the fourth, I was called to Walsingham's office. 'Your term of attendance on the queen ends at the end of September so you can go home then. You will be needed at court when the time comes to deal finally with Mary Stuart but that day is still well ahead. The evidence against her must be amassed and put in order ready for her trial. Her treasonous correspondence, her attempts to suborn this person or that, all those things must be at the lawyers' fingertips before the trial can begin. And then we still have to have the trial itself. Meanwhile – do you still intend to return to Minstead for Halloween?'

'Yes. I am afraid of what may happen then.'

'Very well. I will see that Sir Henry Compton is at home. He has been back in Warwickshire for some weeks. Well, you will have two weeks at home, I suppose. You haven't seen much of Hawkswood this year; not a good thing for the lady of the manor. Your stillroom will need attention, no doubt! However, once in Minstead, use your own judgement. I no longer believe that any dangerous plots are being created in a place like Chenston but, thinking it over, I didn't like the sound of the plans for the Halloween festivities, if one can call them that, any more than you do. Great Sacrifice indeed! If the vicar won't act, perhaps you may learn something to make him act. Have Brockley spy on it if you think that best.'

'Sir Henry won't approve,' I said, though with some amusement. 'He is very obstinate about refusing to believe that anything sinister happens during these forest feasts. I wish he had been with Brockley at Lammas!'

Walsingham smiled, a sinister spectacle in its own right. 'I know. And now I know why he is obstinate.'

'You know why?' For a wild moment I had a vision of Sir Henry, with the antlered mask on his head, presiding over the forest festivities. Walsingham was still smiling.

'I saw Compton only a week ago,' he said. 'He was at court for only two days and you have been in such close attendance on the queen that I suppose you didn't encounter him. But I have talked with him. He told me how shocking it was to use women as secret agents. We became quite good friends. In the course of that, he became quite informative.'

'About what?' I asked, surprised.

'He told me frankly that he couldn't take your mission seriously,' said Walsingham. 'He explained that he had always known that the villagers of Chenston had this custom of celebrating midsummer with a midnight feast in the forest. Three years ago, when Daniel Atbrigge took over the parish, the innkeeper . . .'

'Felix Armer?'

'Yes, that was the name. He thought that the new vicar should be informed of the local customs. Anyway, he told Dr Atbrigge about them. What he said disturbed Atbrigge a good deal and he sought Sir Henry's advice. So the two of them, in person, decided to do what you have been doing – to spy on the next Midsummer.'

'They did *what*?' I was really staggered.

'They spied on the next Midsummer,' said Walsingham.

'They heard the man with the antlered mask announce that the proceedings had begun, but after that he apparently did nothing worse than declare that this was a feast to mark the longest day of the year and offer their gratitude to God for the sunshine that would ripen the crops. Then a goat was slaughtered and the master of the revels, if I may so phrase it, asked for the Maiden to be brought forward. He began to ask her if she were willing to play her traditional part – those were the words used that time, apparently – Atbrigge and Compton were so horrified by what they feared was about to happen that they ran forward, shouting *stop* and were seized.'

Walsingham was smiling like a death's head. 'What *happened*?' I demanded.

'To them? Nothing,' said Walsingham. 'They were made welcome, amid roars of laughter, were invited to join the dance and the feast, and were assured that the part the Maiden was to play was only to be their Midsummer queen, and sit in the Master's throne while the Master became for the time being just another reveller. Compton and Atbrigge found themselves prancing round the fire, drinking some very strong wine, eating new barley bread and roasted goat's meat and then like everyone else, going home through the dawn. They both found the whole business thoroughly embarrassing. Sir Henry didn't tell you because of the embarrassment and he said to me that Atbrigge feels the same. Neither of them feel that dancing round bonfires at midnight is the sort of thing a titled lawyer and a respectable vicar should ever admit to doing. But I think you ought to know.'

'And Sir Henry is now assuming that the goings on are as harmless as they used to be? He supposes that he knows all about them?'

'Yes. In the present times, with priests being smuggled into England for the express purpose of making converts and inflaming Catholics, there would be nothing odd if the order of these midnight services, so to speak, were to include a few prayers about getting rid of an evil queen. Both Compton and Atbrigge assume that it must mean Mary Stuart, and that the troubled nature of today's world could explain why the meetings are now more frequent. Neither Sir Henry nor Daniel

Atbrigge see anything sinister in the talk of old gods or the dates of ancient festivals. They think it is all in line with maypole dances and hobby horses and the like. Just ancient practices that have been handed down among the simpler folk, and also among some scholars, of course. All the preaching of the priests has never wiped that knowledge out but these ancient customs are harmless enough.'

'What Brockley and I witnessed,' I said, 'wasn't harmless.'

'No, I know. But Sir Henry doesn't believe that, and he certainly can't believe in any political plots in Chenston. He has said to me that villagers in remote places, folk whose hands are full with work on the land or in their crafts, don't waste time conspiring against their queen. They wouldn't know where to start, anyway. It's wild young men with heads full of romantic dreams and hopes of rich reward, young men with money, political knowledge, swords at their sides and no work to do beyond giving orders to their stewards and bailiffs, who go in for such follies. I agree. Yet I have thought it over and now, just in case, I think that yes, we need to find out what happens on Halloween. Sir Henry won't hinder you and he'll be there in case you run into danger or need help. In case something needs to be stopped.'

I said: 'From what you say, it sounds as though Daniel Atbrigge is clear of suspicion. I think Felix Armer is our man. If I can identify him at Halloween, we can lever open the door to the truth. Which may well be nasty, but with luck, nothing to do with conspiracies.'

# NINETEEN
## Tantrum in a Chapel

I remember that year as the one in which I hardly ever saw my home at Hawkswood and never had an opportunity to visit my second house at Withysham in Sussex. I usually did that twice a year, and took the opportunity of visiting my Aunt Tabitha and Uncle Herbert, who only lived three miles away. They had brought me up and if we had no love for each other, nevertheless, I owed them something. But in that year of 1586, I never had the chance to go near them. And my fortnight at Hawkswood, between returning from court and starting back to Minstead, passed as though it were only five minutes.

I took the pulse of my household and nothing more. Wilder said that if young Hannah had now gone to be a lady's maid with Mistress Mildred, then we really would need another maid. Bess was willing but there was only one of her. Etheldreda had proved herself to be such a good hand with poultry that Ben Flood, my assistant cook, who usually looked after the poultry-yard, would be happy to give the job up and let Mistress Hope do it. Wilder suggested that she should be appointed as an official poultry-keeper and paid for it. She could help out in the house as well. Her pig was flourishing and ought to produce piglets before long.

Laurence Miller had a satisfactory report to make about the trotters' stud; Gladys grumbled because I was going away so soon and prophesied danger and disaster. I told her to stop forecasting trouble; she always did it and it was becoming tiresome.

'I do it 'cos it's always true,' retorted Gladys.

In the middle of October, along with the Brockleys and the carriage, drawn by Bronze and driven by Joseph and this time used simply as a baggage cart, I set off again for Minstead.

* * *

'So here we are again,' I said, as we drove through the gateway of Minstead Manor. We had timed our journey neatly. It was now the twenty-second of October, a week and a half before Halloween. It was a wet morning with a cold north wind and although Dale, perched on Blue Gentle, was well wrapped in her cloak, she had a red-tipped nose and looked shivery. 'Let's get inside, ma'am,' she said.

She sneezed and I hoped she hadn't caught cold. As usual, the lodge keeper had come out to meet us and send his boy to announce us, and within a few minutes, we were at the front door, grooms were coming to take the horses and plump, businesslike Hayward was there to welcome us.

Most of our baggage would be unloaded in the stable yard and taken in through the side door, but whenever we arrived anywhere, I liked to see that a separate hamper containing immediate necessities such as changes of clothing and some toiletries was carried in straightaway, and with Dale sneezing this seemed doubly important. As soon as possible, she must shed that damp cloak and get into a fresh dress, with a thick shawl round her and slippers instead of boots. Sometimes, I wondered who was the maid and who was the mistress. I turned to Joseph and said: 'Get our special hamper inside quickly.'

Brockley was ahead of me, however. He was already off his horse and delving inside the carriage, shifting larger items to get at the one he knew I wanted. It seemed to have got itself buried and he heaved and grunted as he got it out. Then, as he backed out of the carriage with the hamper in his hands, I saw that his efforts had pulled his cloak awry and pulled back the open neck of his shirt. Brockley didn't wear a ruff when he was travelling for then he acted more as a groom than as a manservant. I could see the top of his chest. He was sweating.

I always used hampers to hold baggage because they were lighter than boxes to handle. But on this raw morning, Brockley was sweating because he had just pulled two or three pieces of my comparatively lightweight luggage about.

I stared. And then, like sea breakers crashing over my head, I simultaneously realized two things. One was that Felix

Armer could not possibly be the Antlered One. I had seen sweat on the upper chest of the Antlered One when he returned from his assignation with the Midsummer Maiden. On the *bare* upper chest of the Antlered One. The first time I had seen Felix Armer, he had his sleeves rolled up and his shirt wide open while he shifted barrels about and his chest was covered with thick black hair right up to his throat. Whoever had been wearing that antlered mask, it couldn't have been Felix.

The second was that if just moving a couple of hampers, even full ones, could make Brockley sweat on a cold wet morning, then something was wrong with him. I might well worry about Dale catching cold, but with Brockley, I feared something worse. His recurrent fever had come back.

'Yes, it looks like the same malady,' said Dr Stone from Lyndhurst, somewhat breathlessly, after being summoned in a hurry by Sir Henry and making the three-mile ride at a gallop.

'The same treatment as before,' he said. 'Keep him warm, keep him quiet. Broth and white wine when he can take it. I don't think this attack is as bad as it was the first time.'

'Stop talking about me as though I wasn't here,' grumbled Brockley from under a pile of coverlets. 'And don't bleed me!'

'He seems still to have some life in him,' said Stone reassuringly.

Sir Henry had welcomed us with his usual good manners and a knowing smile for me (*poor little woman; I suppose Walsingham is still indulging the queen's sister in her silly notions*) and he sent for Stone on the very day of our arrival. Dale had brought ready-prepared supplies of the willow-bark potion and the combined yarrow and basil one, and during the afternoon and evening, she gave Brockley some of each. But the next daybreak found him rolling and murmuring in a fevered sleep. Dale called me at dawn, in tears.

Brockley's sheets needed to be changed and Brockley himself needed help to get on to a chamber pot. It was beyond Dale and me, but Sir Henry once more sent us the sandy-haired Watt and Watt was a blessing. He was built like a small bull and he was strong enough to lift Brockley on his own. It was also Watt who made him swallow further doses of the two potions. Ignoring Brockley's petulant snortings and turnings of his head, he held the patient's nose to make sure that the liquid went down. Brockley swore feebly at him but Watt ignored that as well.

Dale and I finally left Brockley in Watt's capable hands while we took some breakfast. When we returned, the patient was quietly asleep.

'He's cooler,' Watt said. 'And not tossing any more, Mistress Brockley, madam. If you've things to attend to, I will watch over him. I think he's a bit better.'

From the first, when we started out from Hawkswood, I had been saying that I wanted to see Mildred. I felt very responsible for her; indeed, she was the main reason why I was so determined to be here as a safeguard for her until Halloween was over.

Brockley was safe with Dale and Watt. I could be in Chenston in twenty minutes and I could do without an escort. As soon as dinner was over, I had Jaunty saddled and Joseph was about to give me a lift up on to his back when it seemed that there was no need, for Mildred was riding in at the gate and talking volubly to me before she was well inside. Grey Cob was blowing, as though he had done the whole journey from Chenston at full gallop.

'Oh, Mistress Stannard, Ursula, oh, I am so glad. He said you had come . . .'

'Who did? Mildred, what is it?' She seemed distraught and I was alarmed.

'John Appleyard had an errand to Minstead; he saw you riding in yesterday. I was so glad, I wanted to see you so much.'

'Be calm, Mildred,' I said. 'Get down and come inside. I was about to visit *you*. Come along, now.'

'That's right. Madam . . . allow me . . .' said Joseph, moving across to Grey Cob and holding out his hands to steady her down from the saddle. I left him to see to the horses and led Mildred indoors. I took her to our parlour and as we went, called to a passing maid to bring us some wine. In the parlour, we both sat down, but Mildred almost immediately leapt to her feet again, seized an ornamental bowl that stood on top of a little cupboard, and threw up into it.

I came quickly to her side, exclaiming, and then said: 'Are you with child?'

'I think so, yes . . . urggh,' said Mildred wretchedly. 'So sorry . . . urggh!'

The maid arrived with the wine, took the situation in at once and went for some water. Between us, we mopped poor Mildred up, gave her water to drink, and after a while, had her calm and clean again.

'You shouldn't have been tearing about on a horse,' I said reprovingly.

'I've only missed once. I wasn't sure and I did want to see you, oh, so much!'

'Mildred, dear Mildred, what's the matter? Something to do with Daniel?'

'Yes . . . no . . . I don't know! Dear Daniel, he's so kind, we get on so well. Every evening he makes hot possets for us – he makes them himself – and we sit and sip them and talk over the day's doings, and I do hope that Ben will be pleased to have a brother or sister. I think he will; he's such a nice boy and he and Daniel are so fond of each other, only . . .'

'Only what? Hadn't you better tell me?'

'I'd rather show you,' said Mildred.

In the curious way of pregnancy, the fit of nausea passed completely within a short time. I made her rest on my bed for a while but she wouldn't rest for long. She was too anxious for me to come with her to Chenston. I sat with her, however, until I was sure she had recovered, and she asked if I had come back to watch whatever happened at Halloween. 'I thought so,' she said when I confirmed it. 'And that makes it more important than ever that you should see what I've found.'

Two hours later, she was so much better that she and I set off for Chenston, though I wouldn't allow us out of a walk. We talked as we went and Mildred said that Daniel was away that day, because he had an ailing friend in Fordingbridge and had gone to visit him. 'He's taken Benjamin with him,' Mildred said. 'Joan and Bella both come every day, now, but they go home after dinner and come back to make supper. We'll have the house to ourselves.'

She seemed to be glad of Daniel's absence but still wouldn't explain what it was all about. We were slightly delayed because just as we entered Chenston we came across Jennet Pickford, sitting by the roadside, under the shelter of a bush, crying bitterly into clenched fists.

'Jennet!' Mildred exclaimed. 'What's the matter?'

Jennet looked up at us and then looked away. '*Jennet!*' said Mildred, quite sternly, now very much the vicar's wife concerned about one of her husband's parishioners.

'I can't say!' Jennet suddenly shouted. 'But it'll spoil everything!' Suddenly, she opened her clenched right hand and with a violent movement threw away something that had been clutched in her palm. 'He'll know!' Jennet shrieked. 'Ralph will know! It'll ruin everything, everything!'

'Jennet . . .' Mildred was going to say something more but Jennet sprang to her feet, picked up her skirts, and fled.

'What in the world . . .?' said Mildred.

I shook my head, and we rode on, perforce. As we did so, I looked down and there in the roadside grass was the object that Jennet had thrown away. It looked harmless enough. It was a wooden disc, perhaps three inches across. In the middle there was a white roundel. That was all. I pointed it out to Mildred, who shook her head in puzzlement. We shrugged and rode on.

When we at last arrived, John Appleyard was working in the vicarage garden. He left his task and took charge of our horses. Mildred led me into the house and made straight for Daniel's study. She shut the door behind us and then turned to me, almost fiercely, as though about to refute some kind of accusation.

'I wasn't prying. I was always taught not to pry, not to be curious, but it was just an accident, and knowing you'd come back and remembering what you said when you came to say goodbye to me, back in August, and Daniel left us alone for our farewells, well . . .'

'If I remember rightly, I said that we might come back for Halloween and that I was sure there was something mysterious and not too healthy happening in Chenston.'

'Yes. Is there going to be a Halloween feast in the forest? Is Brockley going to spy on it?'

'Brockley isn't well. I may have to do it. But yes, we have good reason to watch that gathering. Mildred, if you know anything that could bear on this, please tell me.'

'I don't know that I do, but I don't know that I don't, either. I wasn't prying, I wouldn't!' Mildred was stammering.

'Please stop babbling,' I said. 'Just tell me. Or show me. I don't mind which.'

Mildred swallowed hard and then said: 'Mistress Pickford, the mother of Jennet and Susie, she's got an old mother-in-law, bedridden, but always thinking she's dying though she never does. She's always sending for Daniel, thinks she's going. It annoys Daniel because she's such a nuisance, while Granny Dunning who really is dying, has never called him once. Yesterday, Mistress Pickford came to the door and said the old woman wanted Daniel again. He always goes. He says: you never know. He was in his study. I'm not supposed to go there without him, or intrude on him when he's there unless I must – unless someone needs him – and then I must knock. Well, I did knock, but the door was ajar; and my knock made it open more. Daniel was by the far wall and behind him there was a dark line up the side of one of the panels as if the panel . . . didn't fit, or, or . . .'

'You mean there really is a sliding panel in the study? I'm surprised young Ben hasn't found it. He's been longing to find such a thing.'

'He's never allowed in the study except when his father calls him there and he's never alone in it. He's never had the chance to tap the panels in there. Daniel hurried me out of the doorway at once and sent me to find his prayer book that he'd left in the big parlour. I did that, but when he'd gone off with Mistress Pickford, I went back into the study. It wasn't just idle curiosity . . .'

'I know that. No one is accusing you of anything. Go on.'

'The panelling all looked as usual. While I was fetching his prayer book he probably went back in there and closed it. Oh, dear, I'm sure I shouldn't . . .'

Here Mildred stopped short. I wanted to shake her just as I had once yearned to shake Etheldreda, but once more, I restrained myself. I hadn't wanted to muddle Etheldreda's confused narrative any more than it was confused already, and now I needed to respect Mildred's delicate condition. I merely said: 'Surely, you've brought me here to show me whatever you've found behind that panel.'

'Yes,' said Mildred, swallowing again. To her, this was a confession. 'I wasn't sure which panel it was, because they're all the same. But I knew roughly where it was and I tapped all the possible ones till I found one that seemed hollow. It took me a while to find the trick of opening it, but I did in the end. Yes . . . here we are.'

She had stepped across the room and was using her thumb to press the edge of one of the panels. As I watched, it slid noiselessly aside. Mildred put her hand into the aperture, and pressed something else and a whole section of panelling swung back, like a narrow door, about six feet high, extending from the floor.

I worked out later that the big council chamber at the back of the house didn't in fact extend from one side of the house to the other. There was a narrow room at one end. The council chamber had no door to it; the only door was this secret one behind the back of Daniel's adjacent study. The room had light, from a stained-glass window at the far end, though the light was dull because the window looked as though it was overhung with ivy. However, it was possible to see what was in the room. We stood at the door and I stared.

The room was, or had been, a Popish chapel. The altar, a solid affair with heavy carved panels, was still there and so was the massive rood attached to the wall under the window. Everything else was in wild disorder. An elaborate altar cloth, all gold and silver embroidery, had been hauled off and flung in a heap on the flagstoned floor. Candles, several silver candlesticks, a silver communion cup, a crucifix in wood and bronze that had probably stood on the altar, were strewn haphazardly everywhere. The silver cup was dented. The crucifix had fallen at the foot of the wall and there was a scrape on the wall above it, as though it had been flung there in a rage and had hit the wall first. Benches had been overturned and the shadowed window had a crack as if something had been thrown at it. The predominant colour of the glass was crimson and the light it cast over this chaos was like a veil of blood.

'This is . . . awful,' I said.

'It looks as though someone in here has had a fit of the most terrible temper, has had a tantrum in here,' said Mildred in hushed tones. 'I was taught to detest all things Popish, but this is wrong; it's a kind of blasphemy . . . hurling silver cups, and that crucifix too . . . I was told not to venerate things that were just made by hands, that that was a kind of idolatry, but it isn't venerating something if you just think it's beautiful and ought to be treated with . . . with a little respect and not thrown about. Everything's dusty, but all the same, this doesn't look as if it was done years ago, does it? That altar cloth isn't rotten. Only, who . . .?'

Who indeed? The damage didn't look particularly recent but nor was it ancient history. Benjamin wasn't allowed into the study and even if his boyish desire to find a secret panel had driven him to disobey his father, I couldn't somehow see Benjamin being responsible for this. So how many people, apart from Mildred, knew how to get into this place? I didn't suppose that Joan or Bella did; Joan, I recalled, wasn't allowed to polish the panelling in the study, perhaps to keep her from finding the panel by accident. Bella might have peeped in here out of curiosity, when Daniel was out but I doubted if she would have thought of tapping the panels. Nor could I imagine either Joan or Bella creating this kind of chaos.

That left Daniel Atbrigge himself. Who had apparently been looking at the place when Mildred came to the study door. I wondered why. Had he just found it? Or was he the one responsible for this mess and did he keep returning to stare at his handiwork?

I didn't say any of this. There was no need. Mildred knew it as well as I did. Instead, I said: 'We had best not be caught here. Come along, Mildred, out of here, close the panel. We'll go to the parlour, talk of ordinary things. Then I must go back to Minstead. I don't understand this, and you, dear Mildred, had better just forget that you've seen it. Is Daniel kind to you, usually?'

'Oh, *yes*,' said Mildred fervently.

'Then do nothing to change that. *Forget* this. It's nothing to do with you. You were right to show it to me, but I can't see what it means, any more than you do.'

'He keeps a diary,' Mildred said as we backed away and she closed the panel. Closing it was easier than opening it. 'I've seen him writing in it,' she said. 'It's a thick book with a leather binding, and once I asked him what it was. He said his diary, and he was smiling, but he also said that diaries were private things and I must never try to read it and I promised not to. But I know where he keeps it. I've had to call him from his study several times, not just that once on account of Mistress Pickford's mother-in-law. I once saw his diary lying open on his desk when he let me in, and I saw him pick it up and put it into the cupboard under his desk.

'I'd very much like to know what's in that diary,' I said.

Mildred at once turned red and then white. 'I knew you would say that. Oh, I shouldn't have told you . . . I did wrong . . . I don't know what made me . . .'

'Perhaps you're wondering if it contains an explanation of that wrecked chapel,' I said. 'I agree with you.'

'Yes, but . . .' Poor Mildred was almost wringing her hands. 'I shouldn't have said it. I shouldn't have! I couldn't . . .'

'I could,' I said. 'And if Daniel's not here, this is the moment. I'll do it; you need not even be present.'

'But he told me never to . . .'

She stopped. We had just heard the sound of the front door opening, and now we heard the voices of Joan and Bella. 'They're early,' said Mildred, half whispering.

'Mistress Atbrigge! Where are you?' That was Joan, we could hear her walking about, looking for Mildred. Quickly and quietly we got ourselves out of the study and into the parlour, where Joan found us a moment later.

There was no question now of investigating the diary. It was in all probability just an account of soul searching, I thought; a record of prayers said, prayers omitted, uncharitable feelings about Mistress Pickford's mother-in-law, anxieties about an ailing friend in Fordingbridge.

Only, that chapel had been wrecked fairly recently, and how was it that such a chapel existed, anyway, in the house of a respectable Anglican vicar?

I said all this to Mildred before I started back to Minstead. She looked at me piteously and didn't answer. I said no more then, but at the last moment, when I was already mounted, I leant down from Jaunty's saddle and said: 'I know. It feels like a terrible betrayal. Whatever happens, don't be caught.'

# TWENTY

## There is no Time

When I returned to Minstead, Brockley's fever had risen again and Dale, pink-nosed and sneezing pitifully, had unquestionably caught a rheum. Watt had sensibly sent her to my room, where, I said, she would have to stay. Brockley mustn't be afflicted with that as well. I was too concerned with the pair of them to worry about myself, but the next day I too began to sneeze.

It wasn't a severe rheum but between the respective ills of the three of us, I had little time during the next few days to think about Mildred and the extraordinary scene in that secret room, and whether or not she had managed to snatch a glimpse of her husband's diary.

I felt guilty about that, for to advise someone to pry into another person's diary, especially that of a husband, is a serious thing. But it now seemed to me that here in Chenston there really was a mystery that needed light to be shone on it. I wished I could have read the diary myself. I was used to privily reading other people's private papers.

Brockley did begin to improve but as the last week of October wore away, it finally became clear that he couldn't go spying on the Halloween feast. I was more or less well by then, and Dale very nearly, but Brockley, though improving, was only just out of bed and by no means ready for midnight excursions.

I didn't intend to discuss my plans with Sir Henry but he decided to discuss them with me. 'Walsingham's orders not to interfere with you still hold,' he said, arriving in the Brockleys' room one morning when I was there, enquiring after the patient's health. 'I will therefore not even ask you if you mean to investigate the Chenston feast at Halloween. I just assume that you do. You attended their feasts at midsummer and Lammas and now you are here just in time for Halloween. It doesn't take much intelligence to work your intentions out. Though I don't understand why either you or Walsingham should want to go on with this. Mary Stuart is under arrest and Babington and his crew are dead. If there ever were any plots brewing here on Mary's behalf, they're dead meat now.'

I felt shivery. Before I left the court, Sir Anthony Babington and his fellow conspirators had been executed, horribly. It hadn't been possible to avoid hearing the details; too many people wanted to talk about them, in tones hushed, in tones horrified; a few with savage joy but most with revulsion. Babington himself and the foremost conspirators had had the worst of it; their agonies had appalled even the hardened London crowd and the rest had died less shockingly. I didn't want to think about it.

I said: 'Yes, that is true,' and then turned my mind resolutely back to Chenston. 'But something unpleasant *is* going to happen at Halloween,' I said. 'Brockley found that out at Lammas. Did you not, Brockley? I have of my own choice, decided to investigate it.'

'I don't know what the world is coming to,' said Sir Henry, as people have probably been saying since the days of the Pharaohs and very likely before.

'Someone must go,' said Brockley. 'I hate it, that I have to leave the task to my mistress, but Mistress Stannard has many times proved that . . .'

'It is unfitting for a woman to be out alone in the forest at night . . . spying on . . . witnessing . . .'

'I've been doing unfitting things for years,' I said, and Brockley and I exchanged looks, in which memories, sad, terrifying and hilarious were mingled and just for a moment, once again, our minds were linked. One of our most glorious shared visions was that of a most unpleasant noblewoman sitting on a slippery kitchen floor with cold pottage splashed all over her and an upturned colander on her head. We had greatly enjoyed some of our shared adventures.

Fortunately, once again, Dale was not there, so there was no danger that she might observe that silent exchange. She was in my room, resting on the truckle bed, and still intermittently sneezing.

'I trust my mistress to do this work and do it well,' said Brockley. 'Please, Sir Henry, let her judge for herself.'

Dear Brockley. When it came to the point, like a good crewman in a small sailing boat, he always threw his weight in the right direction.

'I'll come to the rescue if you need it,' said Sir Henry grumpily and as obstinate as ever. 'But I know perfectly well that whatever goes on at these affairs is just foolish high jinks.'

I did not reply. I hadn't told Walsingham and I didn't try to tell Sir Henry how, during the Midsummer feast, that crowd of cloaked figures, faceless in their inhuman goat masks, had seemed to blend into one huge and horrible animal that might do anything. Every time I remembered that I cringed but I couldn't try to describe it. It had been too strong and too horrible. I couldn't find the kind of words that would make either of them believe me.

By the last day of October, though Brockley was still only convalescent, I felt recovered enough to carry out my plans. I kept asking myself what either the damaged chapel in the vicarage or Daniel's probably very dull diary could have to do with pagan festivities in the clearing and yet the feeling that they were in some way linked, wouldn't leave me. Someone – and it would have to be me – must witness whatever happened at Halloween.

When the time came, Joseph had Jaunty ready with a cross saddle on and once again I was in breeches, and was equipped with a flask of water, a lantern, and the small dagger that I usually carried in the hidden pouches of my overskirts. I knew that I could hide safely in the hollow tree. Nothing could go wrong.

The next part of the story belongs to Mildred, as valiant a comrade in arms as God ever made.

Ever since my visit to her, Mildred had been in a fret about reading Daniel's diary. She knew her parents would be horrified to think that she would do such a thing without his permission; but she could not rid herself of the certainty that she must. Except that she never seemed to get the slightest opportunity. By the evening of the last day of October she was near to despair.

After all, her dear Mistress Stannard was here to investigate what she said was some kind of mystery in Chenston and after finding that secret chapel looking as though a great storm had swept through it, it seemed to Mildred that if that and the mystery weren't connected, it would be a wonder. In little Chenston two such extraordinary things surely couldn't be separate. And Mistress Stannard, dear Ursula, was going that very night to watch the Halloween feast in the forest, and she had said that she feared that something terrible was going to happen there . . .

She hated the thought of reading that diary. She had told Daniel that she thought she was expecting his child and he had been so delighted. She was touched by his joy. He had told Ben and Ben was pleased too. He had said, so wistfully, that he would like to have a brother or sister. Earlier in his life, he had had siblings, but none of them had lived.

And the last one had killed their mother. There was always that fear, of course. Mildred wanted children, as women mostly did, but some women died, and many children failed to survive. Daniel told her not to think about such things and so did little Hannah, who had now become a most devoted, almost motherly, lady's maid. But Mildred would rather have concentrated on her pregnancy, even if it made her nervous, than have to think about . . . prying into her husband's diary.

So here was the last day of October and the diary was still unread. Darkness had fallen and supper at the vicarage had been eaten, and Mildred had given her task up as hopeless, when there came a noisy knock on the door.

'It'll be someone in desperate need of me, for sure,' Daniel groaned. 'And I've spent all day trying out themes for Sunday's sermon. If it's the Pickford woman again, saying her mother-in-law is at death's door, just for once, I'm not going!'

It was not the Pickford woman. It was Jacky Dunning, serious and polite for once, taking his cap off as soon as the door was opened. Daniel left him on the step and came back to Mildred.

'It's Granny Dunning. I think this may be the end. I've expected it for some time. Do you know, even at her age, she's been taking care of a flock of goats – milking them and making cheese and butter to use for herself so that she need be as little of a burden to her family as possible. But not long ago, her best billy escaped into the forest and it was never found and it upset her. She's been slipping downhill ever since. Jacky says she's still conscious and she wants the sacrament. I've made our possets for tonight. Yours is the sweeter one, in the blue cup.'

As he spoke, he was collecting the bag in which he kept the necessities for bedside sacraments. 'I must go, my love,' he said. 'I may be back late. Go to bed and go to sleep. I may have to stay until the last.'

Then he was gone, accompanied by Jacky. Mildred was alone. Now, at last, was her chance and she only hoped that if there was anything to find, she wouldn't find it too late. After all, this evening was Halloween itself. Joan and Bella were still splashing about in the kitchen, cleaning the supper dishes, but they were nearly finished and soon they were calling goodbye and letting themselves out. Hannah was upstairs, setting out Mildred's night things and kindling a fire in the room, for the night was cold.

Mildred still waited for a while, wrestling with her conscience. What she was going to do, was wrong, wicked even. But that wrecked chapel! She had found it because Daniel had been in there. He must have been, or that panel behind him wouldn't have been partly open. And only he could have done the wrecking.

She must be quick, in case he returned after all. She lit a branch of candles, poured a glass of ale and placed it in the small parlour and made her way upstairs.

She found Hannah still in her room, trying to coax the fire, which was sulky, as some of the wood was damp. 'Leave that, Hannah. Go downstairs. In the little parlour, I have left a glass of ale for you. You may sit down to enjoy it. I have to look something up for the master, in his study.'

Hannah knew her work by now and it included doing what her mistress told her and not gossiping to her lady's husband, either. She would have no trouble from Hannah.

Mildred went into the study. She must leave no traces of her intrusion. She put the candles carefully on the flat work-bench and tried the cupboard beneath the desk top. The catch was tricky and at first it refused to open. She fiddled with it anxiously for what seemed like eternity though it was probably about a minute. It gave way suddenly, with a satisfying click. She peered inside, found the leather-bound book and drew it out. She placed it on the sloping desk top and opened it.

The sense of wrongdoing was so strong that it had made her heart pound. Her ears were straining, in case Daniel came home early after all. If he did, she must thrust the book back into its hiding place as fast as she could and then she must be out of the study even faster, going to meet him, with a branch of candles in her hand . . .

She looked down at the pages in front of her. Daniel's writing was plain enough. The first entry was dated about a year before, and was harmless; it was to do with changes he had made to the vicarage since he came to live in Chenston. He had had the thatch renewed and bought new furniture for the parlours. She turned the pages rapidly, just glancing at their content as she went. Details of sermons he had preached, and here . . . yes . . . there was a reference to preaching against the forest feasts, *even if King William Rufus was killed nearby and there are superstitious tales told about his death* . . . nothing of interest on the next two pages or the next, turn the page again and . . .

She felt her whole body stiffen. She read on, intently now, with a dreadful coldness gathering in her stomach and a tremor beginning in her legs. No. Oh, no! *No!* NO!

It was late. Very late. What was she to do? She couldn't go into the forest herself and attempt to intercept Mistress Stannard. She didn't know the way. She had better go to Minstead and seek the help of Sir Henry Compton. But Grey Cob was in the Appleyard stable and she couldn't, she *couldn't* explain this to anyone and besides, it was Halloween and the Appleyards were probably going to the Wood tonight; she couldn't trust them, or anyone and she couldn't get Grey Cob out without them knowing. What was the time? There was a clock on the work-bench. She went to pick it up and accidentally knocked over an untidy pile of wooden animals. Amid the pile were some wooden discs with white centres. Like the one Jennet had thrown away. That must mean something, but what? The clock said eleven. How long would it take her to reach Minstead on foot?

Daniel, of course, would expect her to go to bed without waiting for him. He would also expect her to swallow her posset first. To ensure good sleep. Oh yes, he'd want her to sleep, for sure! She wouldn't like to speculate on what was in that posset.

She must make no mistakes. She must go at once, without delay. She put the book back in its drawer and left the study as she had found it. She went to the kitchen and found the possets waiting on the table, poured ready, with a pan nearby in which to heat them. They were heated separately because their contents were slightly different, on account, Daniel said, of her preference for sweet things. She poured the contents of the blue cup out of the kitchen window.

Hannah was still in the little parlour. Mildred went to find her and spoke to her in tones more decisive than she had ever used before. 'Hannah, I need you to come with me. We have an urgent errand to Minstead. Please ask no questions, but put on your outdoor shoes and a warm cloak, and make two lanterns ready, and come.'

Then she too donned stout shoes, took her cloak from its hook in the hall, remembered to bring spare candles and a tinderbox in case the lanterns needed refreshing. After that, with a bewildered but loyal Hannah beside her, Mildred set off on foot, praying she would be in time.

# TWENTY-ONE
## Halloween

I had to do the journey to the clearing after dark this time. By the end of October, the days are growing short. To go earlier would have meant a long and tedious wait. The forest revels weren't likely to begin till midnight.

It was a clear night which was as well, because although there was a huge, gold-tinged moon, nearly full, it was still so low in the eastern sky that the trees along the track blocked its light. There were glimpses of it now and then and that was all. There was no mist, yet the air had a tang of mist, mingled with the scent of fallen leaves. It was an exciting smell and I think it excited Jaunty too. He got me to the ruined hamlet at a fast trot.

There, I dismounted and tethered him as before, where there was good grass to be had. Then I lit one of my lanterns and by its light I searched for the path to the clearing and almost panicked because in the darkness the path seemed to have vanished. The start of it was such a very slight gap in the trees. I found it at last but even with the lantern it was so hard to follow that the first thing I did was to walk straight into a tree. I began to think that I should have come by daylight after all, and put up with the long wait. Then the lantern light suddenly picked the path out clearly. Relieved, I set forth.

I didn't enjoy that walk. The crowding trees were oppressive enough in the daytime and now, with only the flickering lantern to light my way, they seemed not just oppressive but menacing. Beneath their shadow the darkness was intense, almost palpable; more than ever, I felt that the trees were aware of me and not with goodwill. The rustling of the leaves where the boughs met overhead was like whispering voices, discussing what to do with this impertinent human creature who had intruded into their fastness.

But the unsteady lantern light brought me safely to the hollow oak. I sat down to wait, wrapping my cloak around me and dousing the lantern. Presently, the rising moon penetrated the clearing, and I could see the bonfire ready piled and the waiting torches in their sockets on either side of the dais. I had come on the correct night, I thought.

And sure enough, here came the first lanterns. There were voices, movement, flaring torches and then the bonfire was blazing up, and by its light, I made out the arrival of a single figure which went into the hut and came out again in an antlered mask. Then the other lanterns filed in. Hooded shapes entered the hut, and goat-headed shapes came out again.

I found them even more frightening than before. I remembered those words *Great Sacrifice.* Despite the stout oak at my back, I began to feel very afraid. I was alone here and out there in the clearing, something evil was brewing. I knew it.

It could not, of course, be anything to do with Mary Stuart. I pitied her, after a fashion. I had met Mary; I had even liked her. She had a charm that worked on women as well as men, though what it did to men, admittedly, was excessive. It had worked so well on some of her custodians that Sir William Cecil, Lord Burghley, had said he was determined never to meet her, because he feared the effect she might have on him. I personally wished her no ill and it was most unlikely that now anything said or done here in this clearing could concern her one way or the other. Only, for Mildred's sake if nothing else, I needed to know *what* was going to happen and whatever it was, I dreaded it.

The proceedings began as they had at Midsummer, except that when the Antlered One invoked his pair of pagan gods, his prayers didn't mention crops. He prayed once more and with excessive fervour for the life of a beleaguered queen and, which was very alarming indeed, promised the gods a libation of blood of such great value that it must surely win their help in keeping her safe, surrounded by enemies as she was. That surely had to mean Mary, however useless such a prayer must obviously be. But what was the blood of great value? What did that mean?

It was time for the wine to be handed round. A noisy toast was drunk. Then something new occurred.

'On this night,' declared the strong voice of the Antlered One, 'we have two young folk now grown to an age to enter our charmed circle. Stand up, Jack Dunning and Benjamin Atbrigge!'

*Benjamin Atbrigge?* Had Daniel allowed his son to become mixed up in these pagan revels? Perhaps he didn't know; perhaps Benjamin had stolen out at midnight on his own account. I remembered the wrecked chapel and then silently shook my head, unable to see any connection. The two boys were on their feet. They were still just hooded, not masked. They were summoned to the front of the crowd and I watched with alarm, wondering what lurid initiation rites would attend entrance to this nasty cult.

In turn, each of the boys was asked, loudly, whether he was ready to *enter our company, to honour with prayer and libation Herne, the God of the Greenwood, and Venus, our Lady of purity and light. And are you ready, out in the world, for all the length of your life, to be silent concerning all seen and heard and done at these our feasts, our revels, our occasions of worship?*

Each, in turn, said, '*I am.*' Benjamin said it too softly the first time and was asked to repeat it, more loudly, which he did, though I thought his young voice shook a little. I could barely imagine what Daniel would say to this. Whatever would Mildred say if *she* knew?

The harsh voice was speaking again. '*And now, repeat after me: if ever I break my promise of silence, then may Herne, the Antlered One, the God of the Greenwood, reach out with his fingers of gnarled twigs and strangle the breath out of me and may Venus, the pure Lady of Dawn and Evening, turn her white beams of light into spears to put out my eyes. And may I never hope for forgiveness.*'

The boys, speaking in unison, repeated these dreadful invocations and the grim rejection of forgiveness, and at the end, the whole gathering intoned, '*So be it.*' At the end, the Antlered One declared: '*You have taken the oath. You are one of us now, and may you never be forsworn. You have this night become Sons of the Wood. Be faithful and rejoice!'*

I had been peering round the side of the hollow tree. Now I withdrew into it, shuddering from head to foot, folding my arms hard across my body as if to warm and protect it. I had felt the atmosphere change. Once more, that crowd, that mob, was welding together into that awful composite animal that I had sensed before. I huddled deeper into the hollow, wanting to make myself tiny, invisible, safe from capture. I thought of my bed in Sir Henry's beautiful house and longed for some magical device to carry me back to it.

After a moment, though, I peered timidly out again, and saw that the boys were being solemnly invested with goat masks. Then they withdrew into the crowd and preparations began for the feast, but not, this time, by slaughtering a goat. Extra meat always was brought; both Brockley and I had realized that. With virtually the whole village there, one goat wouldn't go far enough. This time, the slaughter of a goat in front of the gathering had just been omitted. There were some murmurings as though the crowd was surprised. However, the meat was put on the spits and the loaves were set ready for slicing and then the Antlered One ordered the Maiden to be brought forth.

On the previous occasion when I had witnessed this, the Maiden had walked calmly forward between two sponsors, had been offered the chance to withdraw and declined it. This time was different. This time the sponsors had to pull a reluctant Maiden to her feet and drag her forward, protesting. Nor was she offered a chance to say no.

'Usually,' said that resonant voice, 'it is our custom to allow the Maiden to decline this honour if she so wishes, but on this night, she may not. On this night, all the sacrifices must be complete; the gods must be cheated of nothing, so badly do we need their help. Take her to my chamber and make her ready. I will follow.'

'No!' screamed a voice and now, though it was muffled by its mask, I recognized it as the voice of Jennet Pickford. '*No! I don't want this. I didn't want to come here; I was taken from my bed and made to come; I want to go home . . . let me go!*

*Please let me go, I'm frightened . . . I'm soon to marry and what if when we're wed, my man realizes . . . what if he casts me off . . . LET ME GO! . . .*'

It was no use. Weeping, she was divested of her mask and then ruthlessly marched off towards the hut and there was nothing I could do to help her. Brockley had saved the life of the filly Windfall by using an arrow to startle her into breaking free, but even if I had had a bow and arrow, they wouldn't have helped Jennet. I doubted if Reed's toy arrows would have killed the Antlered One, and if they had, what would his crazed followers then have done to me? All these thoughts ran feverishly through my head as I saw the Antlered One start towards the hut.

And then, unintentionally, and in a most commonplace manner, I betrayed myself. I still had the lingering remains of my rheum.

I sneezed.

It was a loud sneeze and at that moment the crowd was silent. Instantly, people were springing to their feet, torches were being kindled at the fire and men were running towards my side of the clearing, looking for the source of the interruption, hunting me out.

Gladys, foreseeing danger for me, had been absolutely right. It wasn't the first time I had suspected that she really was a witch.

My one chance was to abandon the hollowed oak. It was too near the clearing and would certainly be searched. I must plunge into the depths of the forest, find another big tree and hide behind it, flattening myself against the trunk and keeping motionless. Movement attracts the hunter's eye, as Uncle Herbert had told me long ago in one of his pleasanter moments, when he was telling me about falconry and how birds of prey found their victims.

I nearly managed it. But the hunters' torches threw light well ahead and one of them glimpsed movement just as I was taking cover. There was a loud '*Hah!*' and then two masked figures sprang round the tree where I had tried to take sanctuary and with joyous exclamations of *now we have you!* grabbed me and unceremoniously haled me back to the clearing, bringing me to a halt in front of the dais.

The Antlered One had waited. My hood was thrown back and my captors stood me in front of him, holding me fast. They didn't speak. They left that to the Antlered One.

'Well, well, what have we here?' He lowered his voice. 'Mrs Stannard! This is a surprise. What brought you here? You weren't invited, but you decided to come just the same. Tut tut!' I didn't reply. He lifted his head and thundered a question towards his flock. '*We have an intruder, my friends! What shall we do with her? Tell me, what shall we do with her?*' His voice dropped again. 'Here in the Wood, the things of the world no longer apply. Sister of the queen, we will deal with you as with any other intruder.'

I realized, as I stood there between my captors with my knees shaking under me that the question I had just heard bellowed over my head, wasn't just a question, it was part of a ritual. The crowd knew the answer, had possibly, at some time, been rehearsed in it. The answer came at once, in unison.

*SHE MUST JOIN WITH US OR DIE.*

'So there is your choice,' said the Antlered One to me, quite conversationally, though I still couldn't recognize his voice. 'You may take the oath, as you have, I suppose, heard two young boys do, this very night. Or you may take the place of the Great Sacrifice that I must make on this feast of All Hallows Eve, and be slain by the blade I have dedicated to the task.'

He slipped a hand under his cloak and withdrew it with a knife in his grasp. Its blade gleamed red in the firelight.

I was carrying my dagger. It hung in its sheath from the belt of my breeches. Could I be quick enough to snatch it out and . . .?

No, I couldn't, because my own cloak had swung back and one of my captors had seen too much. Even as the thought of my dagger formed in my mind, he was wrenching it from its sheath and casting it away. 'None of that!' growled an angry voice, in my ear.

'*Well?*' demanded the Antlered One. '*Death or the Oath? There is no time to consider. Make your choice and speak it now!*'

All sorts of things rushed wildly through my mind. I remembered the legend that had been handed down in my family, about King William Rufus. It said that he went knowingly to his death. I remembered several tales about holy martyrs who died rather than lose their integrity. I wondered what Hugh would have had me do.

Well, what if I did take the oath? I cared nothing for Herne or Venus. They couldn't harm me and I wouldn't give the villagers the chance to do it for them. As fast as I could, I would flee back to Minstead and the shelter of Sir Henry's house and after that, I would make for Hawkswood and home, far away from this hateful forest and its mad inhabitants. 'I'll take the oath!' I gulped.

At once, there was a kind of bustle all about me. Someone brought me a cup of wine and whispered roughly: 'Here, this'll put heart in you,' and someone else ran to the hut and came back with a goat mask. When he or she opened the door of the hut, I heard Jennet crying. Poor Jennet. I could only hope that the Antlered One would make it easy for her.

I also hoped that no one would realize that to me the Oath would be meaningless.

Only, it wasn't like that at all.

The moment came. I stood before the Antlered One. Two of his aides, each with a flaring torch, stood by, shedding light on the proceedings. He began the ritual.

'What is your name?'

He had already called me Mrs Stannard but I supposed that this was part of the official wording. 'Ursula Stannard,' I said. My voice squeaked.

'*Are you, Ursula Stannard, ready to enter our company, to honour with prayer and libation Herne, the God of the Greenwood, and Venus, our Lady of purity and light? And are you ready, out in the world, for all the length of your life, to be silent concerning all seen and heard and done at these our feasts, our revels, our occasions of worship?*'

'Yes,' I said.

One of my captors nudged me and muttered: 'The right answer is *I am.*'

'I am,' I said obediently.

Then came the worst part of the business. That voice, that grating, resonant voice once more rang out. *'Now repeat after me: if ever I break my promise of silence then may Herne, the Antlered One, the God of the Greenwood, reach out with his fingers of gnarled twigs and strangle the breath out of me . . .'*

I was expected to repeat the wording, so I did. I would have liked to cross my fingers but my captors, still gripping my arms, might have noticed. The fire gave quite enough light for that. The Antlered One went on. *'May Venus, the pure Lady of the Dawn and the Evening turn her white beams of light into spears to put out my eyes . . .'*

The oaths were meaningless to me. I kept saying that inside my head, but something was happening to me that I never expected. It was the atmosphere, the portentousness of it, the strangeness of that firelit clearing with the watchful trees all round, the primeval, animal-headed congregation, the spit and crackle of the flames and the cooking meat, sounds that seemed to whisper words too soft for me to hear. It was knowing that I was far from help and from the normal, daylight world; it was knowing that although surrounded by Beings, I was alone. It was all those things. It seemed that the promises I was making were real, had force. It seemed that the gods to whom I was swearing allegiance were also real, and capable of terrible vengeance if I betrayed them. I invoked Venus as I was bid.

*'And may I never hope for forgiveness,'* said the Antlered One.

I repeated that too. It felt as though it had a terrible significance. Then the crowd said *So be it*, and the Antlered One announced that I was now a Daughter of the Wood, and told me to be faithful and rejoice.

Then it was over; or was it? The oath had left a taste in my mouth, a scent in my nostrils, a heaviness in my head. It had bound me against my will. I was no longer a witness to the proceedings of this night; I was part of them. The Antlered One had stepped down from the dais and was investing me with the goat mask. It settled over my ears, pressing on the top of my head, resting on my shoulders, making it hard to see, though there was ample provision for breathing.

'You'll get used to it,' someone said. The Antlered One said to me: 'It is done. Be part of us now, and be glad.' Then he turned away and went off towards the hut. My captors let go of me, but other people were taking my hands. Someone was playing a pipe, someone else had begun a rhythmic tapping on a drum. We were going to perform that dance round the bonfire.

We did, and just as before, I found myself entering into the business, picking up the steps, being carried into the dance by the drumbeat and the haunting voice of the pipe. There was a moment, as we circled, when I heard a despairing cry, I thought from within the hut and once more I pitied Jennet, but then the dance took me again. I was no longer Ursula Stannard, lady of Hawkswood, agent for Walsingham, sister of Queen Elizabeth; I was Ursula Stannard, Daughter of the Wood, worshipper of the God of the Greenwood, and of the Goddess Venus, dancing in their honour in the depths of the forest and the deep of the night.

Then, suddenly, I was Ursula Stannard again, out of breath, even though the dance was actually quite slow, and with my feet hurting inside my boots. The dance was over and I was glad to stop, to sit on the ground, to take off my mask and pull my hood forward, and partake of the feast.

I was eating roast goat's meat from a platter of bread, sipping wine and actually making quite ordinary conversation with the woman on my right, who seemed to be concerned by my breathlessness and was telling me that I could of dropped out, like, folk do if they're puffed; no sense killing yourself, a statement with which I heartily agreed, when the Antlered One reappeared, cloaked and masked and leading a tearful Jennet, also wrapped in her cloak but bareheaded, until someone put a goat mask back on her. She was led on to the dais and made to sit at the Antlered One's feet, as he resumed his chair. This time, they did not talk or laugh. He did not eat or drink but sat upright and immobile, hands on knees, masked face seemingly watchful.

The voice of the woman beside me faded away. Few people

were talking now, I noticed, and there was a tightening tension in the air, as though this gathering were somehow bracing itself. As though, I thought suddenly, they were afraid.

Something was going to happen and even they didn't know what it would be. And now, the Antlered One was rising from his seat and I saw that he was carrying a hunting horn. He stepped to the front of the dais and sounded it.

Everyone turned towards him. He lowered the horn and began to speak. 'The time has come. My dear, dear friends, the time has come for the Great Sacrifice. The last throw of the dice; the last plea for aid from the gods, who have so far failed to intervene to save my – our – most gracious lady from a dreadful fate. And so I, her most devoted servant, am brought to this dreadful pass. I have heard the word of God speaking in my head; I know I must obey . . .'

He rambled on further, something about the example set in the Old Testament and the virtue of obedience. I was bewildered, for what he was saying made no sense to me. What was all this about the Old Testament? He had said *the word of God*. Which god? It sounded remarkably like the God of the Christian faith but here we were supposed to be worshipping Herne and Venus . . .

The Antlered One had finished his speech. Now he was thundering an order. 'Rise and come hither, Benjamin son of Daniel!'

Benjamin rose and made his way, hesitantly, I thought, as far as one could read anything into the movements of a boy in a goat mask and an ankle-length cloak. The Antlered One said: 'The Christian God failed me long ago. Yet here in this clearing, I have heard His voice. He and Herne and Venus are all one, aspects of each other, a Trinity in themselves.'

He stepped down from the dais just as Benjamin arrived there, pulled the boy's mask off and whisked his cloak away. Benjamin, dressed in shirt, jacket and breeches, stood before him. I thought he looked frightened.

'It must be done,' declared the Antlered One, now with a quaver in his powerful voice. 'I have prayed that this cup should pass away from me, but prayed in vain . . .'

From somewhere close to me, a voice muttered: 'Here, that's

not right. That's blasphemy, that is, he's quoting from the Bible!' and a couple of other voices grumbled in agreement and suddenly, Benjamin's voice cried out: 'What are you doing? No! No!' and to my horror I saw that the Antlered One had seized him by his queue of long hair, and was bending him backwards over the edge of the dais, and that in the Antlered One's spare hand, that wicked knife was once more glinting red in the firelight.

The tension in the air now was like the breathlessness before a big thunderstorm breaks. Benjamin cried out again: 'No, *no, God help me . . . no! NO!*' and there was no time to stop and think about my own danger; I was about to see a young boy murdered in front of my eyes and I couldn't let it happen.

I leapt to my feet and started forward, shouting: 'Stop! *Stop!*' and then a voice which I recognized, amazingly, to be that of Jacky Dunning, shouted: 'Here, we're not having that there; you with the stag's horns, you can't go sacrificing yuman beings! Who do you think you are?' and there was Jacky beside me, shoving people aside, kicking dishes and winecups out of the way. Others were joining in, shouting and scrambling to their feet as well. The whole crowd was in confusion.

Jacky and I reached Benjamin and I seized the Antlered One's upraised arm, and then, as if in answer to Jacky's *who do you think you are?* the Antlered One, one-handed, tore his mask off, and there with the torchlight and the firelight playing over his narrow features was Daniel Atbrigge, his face distorted as though he were crying, and yes, the torchlight was picking out tears on his thin cheeks. Ben shrieked: '*Father, Father!*' Jacky bawled: 'You stole my granny's goat to make a feast of it last Lammas! My dad told me! Broke her heart that did, finished her off, poor old soul, and now you want to go murdering *your own son*!'

Daniel tore his arm from me and kicked out at Jacky, throwing him backwards. He raised his face to the sky and cried out: '*I don't want this but the word of God must be obeyed! I heard His voice!*' and once more raised the dagger above Benjamin's heart.

Then, from behind us, a cloaked shape swept forward, a muscular and extremely hairy arm stretched up to seize Daniel's wrist, and a voice which I knew at once belonged to Felix Armer, bellowed: 'What are you about, you bloody fool? Killing your own son! A pox on you and your silly voice of God!'

Daniel was screaming something, a meaningless babble, and then a few clear sentences in the midst of it: '*God wouldn't answer my prayers! She'll go to the block, my beloved beautiful lady, that I swore to serve with soul and body, my Queen Mary, true queen of us all!*'

Here in the Wood, an attempt had indeed been made to save Mary of Scotland's neck. But it was not the conspiracy that we had feared. It was only an attempt by an insane man to invoke the help of deities that did not exist.

For insane he certainly was. His face was twisted and there was spittle round his mouth. He was struggling against Felix but uselessly, for Felix was extremely strong and others had rushed to his aid. The weird atmosphere in the clearing had vanished, as though a bucket of water had been emptied over a campfire. Jacky's voice, normal as earth or water, had awakened common sense in everyone. The real world was back.

By the time we heard the hoofbeats of Sir Henry Compton's rescue party, summoned by Mildred and thundering towards us through the track from the village, Daniel had been thrown down and tied with bonds consisting of various girdles and belts. His blade had been torn from him and flung aside like mine (I found mine before I left the clearing). In the midst of it all, someone had found a jug with some wine still in it and was giving a comforting drink to Jennet, who had jumped up, torn her mask off and seized the opportunity to stoop over her immobilized consort and spit in his eye before sinking on to the edge of the dais in floods of tears.

It was over, and I had taken little part in it. What had happened, would have happened without me. I hadn't saved Benjamin, for the villagers would have done it anyway. I hadn't saved Jennet, who would need more comforting than an arm round her shoulders and a cup of wine. Nor was it I who made Mildred a widow. For when Sir Henry's men came to take Daniel, he resisted, cursing incoherently, burst the insubstantial girdle with which his wrists were tied, broke free enough to snatch up his knife from the ground nearby, and drove it into his body, once, twice, three times, piercing his belly and his heart, until he collapsed, and was dead within one minute.

# TWENTY-TWO
## Anathema

It was not the end of the affair. Confusion continued for many days thereafter. Sir Henry took me, along with Benjamin, back to Minstead, where we found Mildred and Hannah anxiously awaiting us. We comforted Benjamin as best we could. He had been betrayed by his own father and couldn't stop saying so, over and over. Brockley took charge of him eventually and managed to calm him somewhat.

We all needed some sleep but later that same day, the first of November, we returned to Chenston, using my carriage for Mildred and Hannah, and it was then that a surprisingly controlled Mildred commanded that Daniel's body, which had been deposited on the floor in his church, should be laid out properly and then left in the church in a dignified fashion, until it should be buried. Restoration of order had begun.

The village, of course, was in turmoil, since Sir Henry's men had been questioning people, especially Felix Armer and the Dunning family. It was a muddled kind of turmoil, however, because for one thing, no actual crime had been committed, except possibly blasphemy and the principal blasphemer had killed himself.

Armer, true to his calling, offered the questioners liquid refreshment on the house, for fear, he told me later, his face solemnly straight but his dark eyes dancing, that so much asking of questions had made their throats dry. The Dunnings, confronted by the questioners, were surly and resentful, complaining that they had been up all night and what did anyone need to ask Jacky questions for? Tried to stop a crime being committed, hadn't he? Was that some sort of misdemeanour?

'I don't know exactly what I'm doing here,' Sir Henry said to me as, towards evening on that day, we sat wearily in

Daniel's front parlour. Bella and Joan, neither of whom, I was glad to hear, had attended the forest revels, were in the kitchen, assembling a meal for us while exchanging appalled remarks, and, I suspected, enjoying themselves thoroughly.

'There doesn't seem much to *be* done,' Sir Henry said. 'My fellows have found out most of what we want to know, especially from that innkeeper, Armer. Seems that what was once a fairly harmless once a year revel in the forest to mark midsummer has been getting more frequent and more serious since Atbrigge came here. Armer was the original fellow with the antlers but when Atbrigge took over the vicarage, Armer told him about the Midsummer feast. Seems he admitted to Atbrigge that he was the antlered leader. Atbrigge joined in for the next feast and then wanted to take over. Armer objected but they played a game of darts to decide the matter.'

'They did *what*?' I said. Brockley let out a bark of laughter. and even poor Ben briefly smiled.

'Played darts,' said Sir Henry. 'Atbrigge won. First thing he did, was put the word round that there was to be an extra gathering at Lammas. Made Armer tell folk; made him swear not to reveal who'd given him his orders. Threatened to get him put out of his inn if he broke his word. The next year, Walpurgis was added to the list of forest festivals, and this year, Halloween as well. Atbrigge loved power, I think. Loved getting his parishioners all excited, welded into a body that he could sway. That's how Armer puts it, how it seems to him, and I'd say he's right. And it all grew and got worse because of Mary Stuart. I know Atbrigge's background. He was Catholic to start with. One of his first posts was as a curate to Mary's chaplain when she was at Chatsworth – one of the properties of the Earl of Shrewsbury, who was her custodian at the time. I fancy that was where Atbrigge became so enamoured of her. He had to leave when her household was reduced at some point but he must have been still obsessed with her. He apparently converted to the Anglican Church after that and became a respectable vicar. Or so everyone thought. In fact, he was still Catholic in secret.'

Mildred said: 'It's all in his diary. Not in the earlier pages

– it must have grown on him. Then, all of a sudden, there are pages of wild devotion to Mary, curses against Queen Elizabeth – he calls her the Usurper – and ravings against his God – his Catholic God, I suppose – because he has prayed and prayed for Mary's release, for her restoration to the Scottish throne and her establishment on the English one as well, all with no result. He describes how he found the secret chapel when he moved in. His predecessor probably hadn't known about it. No one knows who had it built to begin with or why. At first he used it for saying Mass in secret but then – it's in the diary – he became angry because his God had failed him and that's when he smashed the chapel up. Sometimes, he'd go back and look at what he'd done and shake his fist and curse the God who wouldn't heed his petitions. By then he was already turning to pagan gods. And then come complaints that his pagan gods have failed him too; and then there are some muddled bits about the Old Testament, and how the Puritans are right to pay attention to that – it's all mixed up and hard to follow – and finally he started writing that perhaps he must placate the pagan gods by sacrificing his son, because his son is the greatest love of his life. He likens himself to Abraham who came so near to murdering his son Isaac. Ben, I'm sorry!' Ben had gone white.

'You're safe now,' Brockley said to Ben. 'And your father was ill in his mind. It wasn't his fault.'

'It might have been me,' said Mildred, who had also gone rather pale. 'He might have chosen to sacrifice *me*! And I was his wife and I loved him, as you did, Ben. We both loved him and I had no idea, not until I read . . .'

She could say no more. Hannah, sitting beside her, put an arm round her, timidly at first and then lovingly. I said: 'Sir Henry, I wish you had told me about Atbrigge's background. It might have led me to the truth much sooner.'

'I didn't take your mission seriously,' said Sir Henry contritely. And then, with some vigour: 'And you didn't ask!'

I had just not been able to see Daniel as the Antlered One. So I didn't ask. I didn't investigate his past. Until it was nearly too late.

* * *

Other things emerged, or took place. One of them concerned Jennet Pickford, who feared that Ralph Argent, her silversmith from Lyndhurst, would regard her as damaged goods and break their betrothal.

'I told her not to worry,' Joan said to me. 'Other girls it's happened to have got wed all right. There's tricks to these things, old as the oldest oaks in the forest. Girls just prick theirselves with a pin, quiet and stealthy like, while it's going on and there's the drops of blood and no questions asked. Only Jennet's as honest as good bread and wouldn't have it; said she'd got to tell Ralph the truth, and he . . . she's well rid of him – two yards of ice-cold virtue, that's what he is. Ooh noo' – here Joan spoke through pursed lips and her voice took on a note of fastidious primness – 'Ay can't be doing with a tarnished bride. Ay'm much too pure in may soul to offer charity to a woman who has lost her honour. Ooh noo . . .! Though she may be in the right of it,' said Joan thoughtfully. 'Best she was open, maybe, because now she's rid of a very bad bargain.'

It was Jennet who told me about the tokens, the little wooden discs with the white blob in the middle. It was the sign that was given secretly to the chosen girl, who must take her seat at a certain place when the so-called revels began. Those who escorted her when the moment came would sit down on either side of her.

'The tokens just appear,' Jennet told me, in a hushed voice as though, even now, Daniel might hear her and invoke the wrath of the gods against her. 'She'll find it in her purse, on her dressing table; slipped into a glove or a pocket. I found mine inside my hat.'

'And as vicar, Atbrigge could visit anywhere he liked. If anyone could find opportunities for that sort of thing, he could,' I agreed.

The culmination of it all was a visitation by his lordship Thomas Cooper, Bishop of Winchester, to whom the disgraceful behaviour of his Chenston flock had been reported. He arrived on a splendid horse, in full panoply of robes, subordinate clergy, servants and outrage.

'A bishop in his anathema, gules,' Sir Henry said to me, as

though blazoning a coat of arms. 'Certainly gules. When he went into that pulpit he was scarlet with fury.'

I had come to like Sir Henry very much. Even if he did disapprove of women acting as secret agents, he had a delightful sense of humour and a good heart. He had promised to assist me if I asked it and he had kept his word. He had brought my reinforcements at the fastest pace he could and chivalrous knight that he was, he wished that he had rescued Ben himself. He was actually disappointed because Jacky Dunning and I had got in first.

Mildred was also inclined to regret our intervention because she too wished that Sir Henry had been the rescuer. After reading in his diary of Daniel's terrible intentions, she had taken Hannah and gone on foot, in haste, all the way to Minstead in the dark, to summon help from Sir Henry. A frantic mission which, as she said to me, was all in vain.

'No, it wasn't,' Brockley told her. Brockley always knew the right thing to say. 'It was difficult and brave and brought someone with authority to that clearing, to take charge of the mess and tell everyone what to do. We're all beholden to you.'

As for the bishop: from Daniel's deserted pulpit in the church of St Michael's he thundered at the folk of Chenston that they were no better than heathen; threatened them with hellfire for dallying with horned devils and pagan gods, and then, having got them all into a quivering and contrite state of mind, softened his tone and said that they could reverence no holy lady but the Virgin Mary, and place their faith only in the Holy Trinity of the Christian faith. Then, with a great air of forbearance, he granted forgiveness to them all and after that, told them that they would be fined heavily for their inconstancy to the established faith of England.

But on the following Sunday he took the pulpit again and, with the help of a fellow cleric, allowed the chastened parishioners of Chenston to take communion and the business was ended. We had all gone back to Minstead on the evening of November the first, and had been staying there, as had the bishop. On the day of that resounding final sermon, Sir Henry and I accompanied his lordship to Chenston and were there to hear it. Ben and Mildred preferred to stay behind.

Because he was mad and therefore not responsible for his actions, the bishop granted him Christian burial. His grave was unmarked, however, covered with a mound that would soon be taken over by the grass. Then it would be as though he had never lived. I don't know how much Mildred mourned when she was alone. In company she was calm, dignified as I had never imagined she could be.

It was time to go home but before we did so, I had one last call to make. I slipped out early one morning, dressed in an old gown with no farthingale, got Joseph to saddle Jaunty for me, and rode to Edham.

There I left my horse and went on foot to the clearing. Even without a farthingale, my skirts weren't narrow enough for that difficult path. There were too many low branches with scratchy twigs, clawing at me. But I reached the clearing and stood beside the remains of the bonfire, and let myself sense the air.

Yes, I had been right. The forest, Herne's Greenwood, pressing close round the edge of the clearing, was a living thing, a world of its own. It didn't want or need human intrusion. I felt it all about me. Perhaps Daniel Atbrigge had felt it too. Perhaps Herne – or Pan or Cernunnos – did have some reality, had got him into its power, issuing the commands that he had so hideously tried to obey. I would never come here again.

I made my way quickly back along the narrow path to where Jaunty awaited me.

Tomorrow we would start for home.

The party that left Minstead for Hawkswood was different from the party that had originally arrived. Mildred was there, of course, for she could not stay in the vicarage in any case; a new incumbent was already appointed and would arrive in another week. She could do nothing but return to me, though this time she travelled in the carriage, with Grey Cob on a lead behind. It was a wonder that in the circumstances, she hadn't lost her baby. On no account, I said, must she mount a horse again until the child was born.

But it wasn't only Mildred I needed to help. I took Ben

back to Hawkswood as well. He had no kinfolk that he could go to and he needed the company of people that he knew. Again and again, he repeated that his father, *his own father* had betrayed him; was willing to murder him in *cold blood* . . . he said it over and over. He would be best away from Chenston, I thought, and Sir Henry agreed. We asked Ben if he would like to come with me and he said yes. Ben, therefore, was in the party, riding his white pony.

A third new member was Jennet, who had asked to come. Hannah had suggested it. Hannah knew that now that she was Mildred's personal maid, I would need another maid to work in my house. If Jennet wanted to get away from Chenston and its memories and its gossip, she would be welcome, I said. She therefore joined Hannah and Mildred in my carriage. It was quite a squash, with all the baggage as well.

All was in order at Hawkswood. We settled down together, as best we could. Jennet had been wretchedly shaken by her experience in the Wood, but I thought she would recover in time. I had once been raped myself; I knew what to say to her. Ben worried me more. Except for the frequent repetition of his bitter litany that his father, *his own father* had betrayed him; was willing to murder him in *cold blood* . . . he had hardly spoken on the journey home and at Hawkswood would have sat all day in one of the parlours, staring out of the window, if I had let him.

More than once, I gently reminded him that his father hadn't truly wished to harm him, that Daniel had been ill in his mind, but Ben's reply was always the same and was discouraging. 'I know, but I can't *feel* it. That knife! The firelight made it look as though it was already running with my blood.'

It was like that until Brockley, in company with my son's elderly and very competent tutor Peter Dickson, took to insisting that Ben should share Harry's studies and ride out with him to exercise Whitey and Harry's cob Mealy. 'Harry's the best medicine for him,' Dickson said to me. 'He's another boy, even if he's a year or two older. And there's nothing like Latin and Greek for distracting the mind from bad memories.' Brockley said: 'Riding in the open air's good physic too. And our tame woods will cure him of being afraid of forests, which he is, and little wonder.'

I hoped they were right. Meanwhile, Etheldreda had cared very well for all the poultry and her sow had farrowed. We had sucking pig and some plump birds for our Christmas dinner. We kept Christmas quietly but pleasantly, with games and songs, in which Ben joined, if somewhat reluctantly. Beforehand, I had a few quiet words with the Hawkswood vicar Dr Joynings, and his sermon on Christmas morning was on the theme of overcoming adversity as Joseph and Mary had to do when they could find no room at the inn and had to make the best of a stable.

In the New Year I was called to court again, to spend a little time with my sister the queen.

For whom I had still to perform one service.

# TWENTY-THREE

## Death of a Queen

I hoped, as I set out for the court, that in my absence, Mildred wouldn't fall in love with another unsuitable man. In due course, I thought, I must try to find a new husband for her, but this time, a law-abiding and reliable one that she could learn to love, quietly. I didn't want her toppling over the cliff edge of passion again.

I re-joined the court in the middle of January. It was at Whitehall. The Brockleys were with me, of course. Brockley had had one more bout of fever, over the New Year, but had recovered quickly. The malady probably was burning itself out by now. In any case, when I received a dramatic command to travel to Northamptonshire, he and Dale were not needed.

It was before dawn on the sixth of February that I was awakened to find my room illuminated by a four-branched candlestick in the hand of a servant, and Sir Francis Walsingham leaning over me, looking in the wavering light so like a spectre that I sat up with a yelp of fright.

'Hush,' said the Secretary of State. 'You must rise at once. Your woman next door is ready to dress you and has already assembled your baggage. Quickly, now. Up you get.'

'But what . . . where . . .?'

'The queen has at last signed the warrant for Mary Stuart's execution. She hasn't ordered it to be used but her secretary William Davison had the good sense to bring it straight to the Council and the Great Seal has been affixed. I have despatched a courier to Fotheringhay where Mary is at present held and the deed will be done at first light the day after tomorrow. The queen wished you, when the time came as she knew it must, to be a witness for her. She said – these are her words – *I shall hear the details from others but they will all be men. The Earls of Shrewsbury and Kent have been appointed as witnesses, as has Mary's present keeper, Sir Amyas Paulet. There will be guards, and senior officers from the households of the earls and Sir Amyas, too. But the only women will be two of her own and they will not wish to be witnesses for me. I want to use the eyes of another woman and of a woman close to me.* She has told you that she desires you to be that woman, I believe.'

'I know, but . . . I hoped she might change her mind.' But I was scrambling out of bed, all the same, reaching for my dressing robe. 'Mary Stuart knows me, she will recognize me, wonder why I am there; perhaps seeing me may break her resolve at the last. I think she will try to be brave; she is of that nature, but . . .'

'You can be veiled,' said Walsingham. 'As her women will be. A veil has been supplied and you will find it in your baggage. Your woman Dale says you own a black gown and she has packed it for you. You can stand behind Sir Amyas and look past him; Mary will probably not know that any woman other than two of her own attendants is present.'

With that grim humour of his, Walsingham added: 'She will hardly be taking an inventory of the witnesses. You must be there. It is her majesty's wish. I have explained her reasons.'

'I know. She told them to me as well, the last time I was here.'

'Then make haste. I am sorry this has come on you so suddenly but it has to be done this way. After the Babington plot, Mary's execution was a certainty but the queen has hesitated and refused to take the final and necessary step. But while Mary lives, another Babington plot may arise. There may be others, apart from that crazy Daniel Atbrigge, who apparently confused her with the Virgin Mary and Venus at one and the same time. When it's over, you will make your report to Elizabeth. She may be angry but not with you. I shall make it clear that I ordered you to Fotheringhay, to carry out her own wishes. You won't need the Brockleys; I have arranged an escort for you – it's waiting downstairs. Dale couldn't manage the ride, anyway. Your horse is saddled. You can use her majesty's remount service. You have over ninety miles to cover and I don't expect you to ride as the courier must, not stopping for food or sleep. You have today and tomorrow but it will still be a hard ride. You must start now.'

It was a hard ride, long and cold. We passed one night in an inn, where, fortunately, the supper and breakfast were good and my bed was comfortable. The second day was the worst, for it began to rain and the track became muddy. It was late afternoon before we got to Fotheringhay and I was mud-splashed, weary and chilled. However, my welcome was gracious. I was shown to a bedchamber where there was a fire, and a young maidservant was there to receive me and help me into fresh clothes. Later, I was shown downstairs and into a small candlelit supper room where I found myself alone with Sir Amyas Paulet.

'I want to tell you what's to happen tomorrow,' he informed me. 'You must be placed where there's no one to notice if you are upset, Mistress Stannard.' Paulet had a reputation for integrity but he was also a cold man. Mary's guardians needed to be, of course. Paulet was one of the few men on whom Mary's famous charm had no effect whatsoever. He clearly saw any possible squeamishness on my part merely as an extra inconvenience to be catered for and he offered no sympathy. 'You'd best be prepared,' he said and went on to explain the details of the unpleasant ceremony I had come to witness.

'It's no pleasure to anyone,' he said when he had finished. 'But it is the lawful way to dispose of her. Remember that.'

I also remembered that according to rumour, Paulet had refused to dispose of Mary privily, because privy murder would dishonour his name. I hated to think that Elizabeth had ever suggested such a thing but in a way I understood it. She wanted Mary gone but didn't want to be the one who actually commanded her death. Honest Sir Amyas refused to be her instrument and of course he had done right. If only he hadn't also deposited the responsibility for Mary's death so firmly on my sister's unwilling shoulders! I pitied Elizabeth. I also pitied Mary. I tried not to think of what I must see tomorrow but I couldn't help it. I was tired out and aching all over from those long hours in the saddle but I did not sleep. I kept thinking of Mary somewhere in this same castle, living through her last night on earth, and wondering how she was passing it. Not in sleep, I thought, any more than I was.

Dressed in black and veiled as though in mourning, I stood in the great hall of Fotheringhay Castle. A square platform had been built there, and draped in black cloth. On it was the block, with a cushion for Mary to kneel on. She was to die in comfort, it seemed. I wondered if it would make any difference to her.

There were soldiers at each corner of the platform, as though someone feared that a rescue would be attempted, and the witnesses stood all around, a wall of onlookers. I was placed partly behind Sir Amyas, whose build was substantial. I could peer past him, not that I could see too well anyway, because of the veil.

We waited in a dreadful hush. The air sang with tension. It made me think of the gatherings in the Wood, especially the last one, when the tension there was so great that it was easy to imagine that it could be plucked like a lutestring and would emit a sound. I wondered distractedly what sort of sound it would be. It might toll like a church bell or maybe ring on a note so high that it would pierce one's eardrums. I think I was half-dreaming, for I was very weary, after that long journey and my sleepless night.

Then they came, Mary, the victim, the sacrifice, cloaked (so very like the folk of the Wood), supported by two women, veiled like me, and guarded by armed men. Did anyone really believe that at this final moment, a rescue might be mounted? Or did they suppose that she would try to run away?

Mary walked towards the platform and then stopped, facing it. Her women took her cloak off. Beneath it, she was dressed in red. I heard some gasps and Paulet drew a hissing breath in through his teeth and muttered: 'Red! The traditional colour of martyrdom. Damn the woman; she thinks she's a Catholic martyr!'

'Hush,' said the man next to him, whom I had recognized as George Talbot, Earl of Shrewsbury.

'She was up to her eyeballs in the Babington plot. She'd have had the queen assassinated if she could!' Paulet said it in a growl, a quiet one but it still reached several people near him and there were assenting murmurs. 'She's been Catholic all the twenty years or so she's been in England and no one interfered with that and she wasn't damn well tried for it! She was tried for plotting to grab our good queen's throne and taking our good queen's life. Catholic martyr indeed! Hypocrisy!'

'*Hush!*' repeated Talbot urgently. Paulet desisted.

I was feeling dreadful. I was afraid I might faint but I must not. I moved my weight stealthily back and forth between heels and toes and the world stopped swimming. Mary hadn't turned faint. With astonishing courage, she was making a little joke about disrobing in public. A Protestant cleric was offering his services and she declined them, gracefully. I was grateful for her bravery. If she had been dragged here, weeping and struggling, I didn't think I could have borne it. I would have shut my eyes and blocked my ears, backed away, got somehow out of the hall, crouched in a corner to sob.

As it was, Mary, unaided, was mounting the steps up to the platform and the executioner had come on to it from the opposite side. He was kneeling before her and asking her forgiveness. He was also holding out his hand for the traditional payment of money or jewellery, an inducement to make the business swift and painless.

Mary, in a very queenly manner, was granting him forgiveness and handing over her jewellery, taking rings from her fingers and unclasping a gold necklace, dropping them into that outstretched palm. Was forgiving and paying her butcher; I thought and wondered how I would conduct myself if I were in her shoes. How could she be so calm, how could anyone be so dignified when their life was to end within minutes? Would she break at the last? I prayed not. I crossed my fingers. In the past I had more than once spent a brief time as one of Mary's ladies. I had played cards with her; sat side by side with her, doing embroidery, discussing patterns and stitches and the choice of colours. Simple things, devoid of drama. They didn't go with this. How could this be real?

But it was, and I must watch. The queen had ordered it. My sister Elizabeth needed to know for sure that her cousin had not, at the last, disgraced the royal status that they shared. With shaking hands, I lifted my veil aside so that I could see.

Mary knelt down on the cushion. Her two women came forward and bound her eyes with something white, with gold embroidery on it. They withdrew. One of them was using her veil to staunch tears. Mary laid her head on the block. The headsman, who looked quite young, seemed to brace himself, leaning on his axe, and I had an odd impression that he was more nervous than she was. Beheading a queen must be a daunting task. She stretched out her arms and cried out: '*In manuas tuas, Domine, commendo spiritum meum!*' I understood Latin. *Into thy hands, O Lord, I commend my spirit.*

The swift end her gift of jewellery should have bought was not forthcoming. Probably the headsman really was nervous. It took him three blows to finish his task. I think she gasped out words of some sort after the first blow, which cut a deep wound in the side of her head. The second didn't quite sever her head but it must have ended her life. The third completed the business. The axeman reached down, tried to pick up the head and then dropped it. He had grasped it by her auburn hair and the hair was a wig. Beneath it, she seemed to have hardly any hair of her own.

He tried again, managed to grip the head properly this time and held it up, dripping blood. He said something about so perish all the queen's enemies. I couldn't hear him very well. I was feeling dizzy again. Black spots danced before my eyes. I rocked heel and toe, heel and toe, as hard as I could and my senses cleared a little, in time for me to hear a whimpering sound and see, of all things, a little black and white terrier, his coat splashed with blood, emerge from under the skirts of the inert body that now lay collapsed behind the block.

I knew that terrier. His name was Timmy. I had once had to pursue him through the passages of Sheffield Castle and retrieve him from the castle kitchen where, for a dog so small, he was causing a remarkable amount of trouble.

Dogs have keen senses. He must have felt the horror in the air as Mary's women made her ready for the block. Dog-like, he had crept close to the human being who was his protector and was also the being he in turn wished to protect. I saw him creep, cowering as frightened dogs do, to the front of the block, where the axeman had put the head down again. He lay down beside it.

I wanted to cry for Timmy, for his grief and his fear and his loyalty to the human creature he had loved. But Mary's two women, both of them now in tears behind their veils, came running, picked him up and took him away. I heard him whimpering again as they carried him out.

Paulet turned to me, looked at my no doubt ashen face and said: 'God's teeth, you can't faint here! Get to your chamber and do it there. Here, lean on me.' He steadied me out through a small door behind me, tapped on another door, handed me to the page who opened it and snapped out a few instructions. The page, a sensible-looking lad of about sixteen, took my arm and steered me to my room and I kept my head up, trying to behave, following Mary's example. She was dead. I ought to be glad. I had been so very tired of her intrusions into my life and she had been such a danger to my beloved sister.

I wasn't glad at all. I couldn't be.

The maid I had been given was waiting in my room. She was a kind and practical country girl, who took me from the page and guided me to the bed. Once there, I did faint, coming round a few moments later to find her mopping my face with cold water.

'What you need, madam, is a good long sleep. Rode all the way from London in a hurry didn't 'ee? And soaking wet you was when you got here. Now let me get that black gown off and then you lie back and I'll put the coverlet over 'ee and you drift away into dreamland.'

I slept all that day, waking only for supper, which was brought to me in my room, and then sleeping again. In the morning, the same sensible-looking page came to tell me that my escort was ready. I must take a quick breakfast and be away before eight of the clock.

I longed for Hawkswood but I must report what I had seen

to Queen Elizabeth. And possibly face her wrath, whatever Walsingham said.

However, he had been right. The queen was not angry with me. She seemed pleased that her order to me had been obeyed. She heard my report in silence, thanked me, and dismissed me. I learned later that she expended her wrath on the unfortunate William Davison, who had been sent to the Tower. She repented of that eventually and released him but the poor man must have been very frightened, wondering if he were going to share Mary's fate.

Mary had friends, of course. She had one very powerful one. To dispose of Mary Stuart was to infuriate Philip of Spain.